Other Books by Rochelle Alers

Happily Ever After
Hideaway
In the Holiday Cheer Anthology—"First Fruits"
Home Sweet Home
In the Love Letters Anthology—"Hearts of Gold"
Hidden Agenda
Vows
Heaven Sent

HEAVEN SENT

Book Four in the *HIDEAWAY* Series

Rochelle Alers

Pinnacle Books
Kensington Publishing Corp.

http://www.arabesquebooks.com

WITH APPRECIATION TO:

Ayishah Dawn-Marie Dennis—for Costa Rica,
Kimberly Johnson—for your nursing expertise,
The Janes: Jane Peart and Jane Toombs—for your
encouragement.

THE HIDEAWAY LEGACY

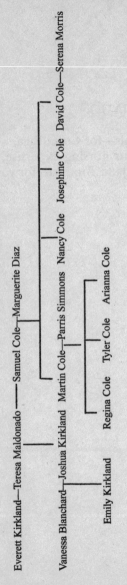

Everett Kirkland—Teresa Maldonado   Samuel Cole——Marguerite Diaz

Vanessa Blanchard—Joshua Kirkland   Martin Cole—Parris Simmons   Nancy Cole   Josephine Cole   David Cole—Serena Morris

Emily Kirkland

Regina Cole   Tyler Cole   Arianna Cole

Alejandro Delgado—Eve Blackwell—Matthew Sterling

Christopher Delgado   Sara Sterling

For this son of mine was dead, but now he is alive; he was lost, but now has been found. And so the feasting began.   Luke 15:24

One

David Claridge Cole felt the jet losing altitude, but he did not stir. He sat, eyes closed, his chest rising and falling heavily from the change of pressure within the descending aircraft. The set of his strong jaw and the vertical lines between his eyes marred the normally attractive face of the musician-turned-businessman. He wanted to be anywhere but on a plane flying to Costa Rica in the middle of June.

A slow, crooked smile replaced his frown as he recalled the prior evening's festivities. It had been a long time, too long, since he had enjoyed a night filled with music, sumptuous food, and celebrating that lasted until pinpoints of light from the rising sun pierced the cover of the nighttime sky.

He had been the best man in a wedding party, and the reveling following the ceremony had reminded him of how much he missed a life-style that had been a never-ending party. As the percussionist for the popular jazz band Night Mood, he lived nights and days measured by recording sessions, live performances, and promotional parties and tours. He'd been on a dizzying merry-go-round that he never wanted to get off.

But it all stopped when his older brother Martin resigned as CEO of ColeDiz International Ltd. to embark on a political career. He had been expected to take over the responsibility of the day-to-day operation of the family-owned export company. He'd even surprised himself, once he learned all of the laws and regulations regarding export tariffs as well as environmental sanctions and controls.

He'd assumed control of ColeDiz at twenty-seven and now, at thirty-six, he wanted out. Running ColeDiz for nine years had offered him the experience he needed for a future undertaking. It wasn't that he minded being a businessman. However, he didn't want to have to concern himself with the fluctuating price of bananas or coffee. What he wanted to do was focus his energies on discovering new musical talent. The idea of setting up his own recording company had come to him more than a year ago, and the notion grew stronger each time he boarded the corporate jet for a business trip.

His last meeting with Interior Minister Raul Cordero-Vega had not gone well. What should have been a civil meeting ended with a hostile verbal confrontation. David hadn't waited for the corporate jet to fly him back to Florida, but had taken a commercial flight instead. Vega had threatened to increase the tariffs on bananas for the second time in less than a decade, because he claimed the plastic casings used to protect the fruit during harvesting were found in the digestive tracts of turtles washed up along the Costa Rican coastline. Environmentalists were pressuring the government to fine or expel the foreign-owned companies, and Vega's solution was to double the already enormously high tariffs.

Martin Cole's last act as CEO had been to transfer many of the ColeDiz ventures to Belize, while leaving the conglomerate's most productive banana plantation

near Puerto Limón. And after conferring with Martin
and his father Samuel, David was given the go-ahead to
negotiate the sale of their one remaining Costa Rican
business enterprise.

He opened his eyes, his smile widening. This was to
be his last trip to the Central American country. Under
another set of circumstances he would have enjoyed the
lush nation filled with more than fifty active volcanoes,
because the region was beautiful and so were its people.
They were a warm, polite, and friendly exotic mix of
native Indians, Spanish, and people of African descent.

Estimating it would take him less than two weeks to
conclude his business dealings with Vega, he felt some
of his resentment waning as the sight of the San José
airport came into view.

Pain, frustration, and fatigue were clearly etched on
the face of Interior Minister Raul Cordero-Vega, aging
the man. Two weeks before, anyone glancing at the tall,
erect, graying man would not have taken him for sixty-
two. Now he appeared to be ten years older. That morning he'd received a telephone call telling him that his
only child, a son, had been arrested and charged with
drug trafficking and the murder of a United States DEA
agent. This bit of news had torn his world asunder.

Gabriel Diego Vega was locked away in a U.S. prison
and denied bail because the prosecutor feared he would
leave the States and not return for his trial. Not even
the high-priced lawyer Raul had retained to handle his
son's case could get the judge to change his decision,
though he pleaded that Gabriel would willingly surrender his Costa Rican passport.

So much for American justice, Raul seethed silently. A
surge of rage darkened his brown face at the same time
his hands tightened into fists. While his son languished

in the bowels of an American prison, other known criminals ran rampant through the streets thumbing their noses at U.S. justice. Men who were known to openly engage in illegal activities felt the warmth of the morning sun and enjoyed the smell of fresh air while Gabriel lay in a small concrete jail cell on a narrow cot inhaling the stench from his open commode.

"Not my son!" he whispered to the empty room. Not the child he'd waited thirty-six years to father.

A sharp knock on the door disturbed his turbulent thoughts. "Come in!" There was no mistaking the harshness in the command. The door opened slowly and his eyes widened in surprise. She had disobeyed him. He'd told her not to come to Costa Rica. She was to have remained in the States—with Gabriel. She was all his son had there.

Large, clear-brown eyes took in the thunderous expression on the face of the tall, white-haired man. At one time that expression would've sent her running from his celebrated temper, but no longer. She was thirty years old, a grown woman. The tyrant she had once feared was gone forever, and in his place a broken man. Serena could see her stepfather hurting. What he was feeling at that moment, she also felt. Raul had lost a son and she her half-brother.

Holding out her arms, she walked slowly into his study. "Poppa." Her normally husky voice shook with raw emotion. "I had to come."

Raul crossed the room and pulled her gently to his chest. Burying his face in her wealth of unruly curls, he held her close, feeling the trembling in her tiny body. "I told you to stay, *Chica*. I told you to stay because Gabriel needs you."

Pulling back slightly, Serena blinked back the tears flooding her large round eyes. "Gabe wouldn't see me."

Raul frowned. "What do you mean?"

"He refuses to see me."

His frown deepened. "Why?"

Serena shook her head, a riot of reddish-brown curls moving as if they'd had taken on a life of their own. "I don't know. I spoke to his attorney, and he says that Gabe doesn't want to talk to anyone except those who are his legal counsel." She sniffled, bringing a tissue to her pert nose. "I'm his sister, and he won't see or talk to me."

Embracing her again, Raul brought her head to his chest. "Whatever you do, don't breathe a word of this to your mother."

"How is she holding up?"

"Not well. She won't leave her room."

Extracting herself, Serena paced the length of the carpeting lining the expansive room. "I don't understand any of it, Poppa. Gabe called me and said he was going down to the Keys—"

"What keys?" Raul interrupted.

Remembering that her stepfather was not an American, and that he was not familiar with the terminology, she smiled for the first time in two weeks.

"The Florida Keys. He told me that he and a friend were going on a sailing expedition down to the Caribbean. They had planned to pick up a few more people in the Bahamas before returning to the States. On their return trip they were intercepted by the United States Coast Guard. What followed is a jumble of confusion, and U.S. officials claim that the boat they were on was filled with drugs, and that Gabe and his fellow passengers are smugglers."

"That's a lie!" Raul shouted.

She stopped pacing. "We both know that! If that boat was carrying drugs, then Gabe knew nothing about it. He had to have been set up."

"And I know who set him up."

Serena arched a delicate eyebrow. "Who, Poppa?"

Raul gave her a long, penetrating look before his heavy eyelids lowered, concealing the hatred and distrust burning within them. *"Los Estados Unidos."*

Her jaw dropped as she stared back at her stepfather. "Why the United States?"

"Because I won't permit them to rape my country. Because I make them pay for the destruction they leave behind when they take what they want from Costa Rica. These Americans grow rich and stuff their already swollen bellies . . ."

"Do you actually believe the United States would blackmail Gabe because of you?"

He nodded, unable to disclose the political machinations going on between Costa Rica and other foreign powers about business ventures. Foreign companies were responsible for the slow but methodic destruction of the rain forest and its indigenous wildlife. If left unchecked, the foreigners would make the land uninhabitable, make it impossible for Costa Ricans to survive in their own country. Their nation would fare no better than the people and the vanishing wildlife of the Brazilian Amazon.

"I don't believe that," Serena countered angrily.

"That's because you are an American, *Chica*. I expect you to defend your country."

Swallowing, she chose her words carefully. "We'll talk about this later. I must see my mother."

She loved her stepfather because he was the only father she'd ever known. However, Serena could never understand his virulent dislike of Americans. She found this hard to fathom because he'd married her mother, who had never given up her American citizenship.

He inclined his near-white head. "Yes. We'll talk later." He waited and he wasn't disappointed when she walked over to him and rose on tiptoe to kiss his cheek.

Cupping the back of her head, he pressed his lips to her forehead. *"Te amo, Chica."*

"And I love you, too, Poppa," she whispered, then turned and made her way out of the room.

Raul waited as the door opened and closed behind his stepdaughter's retreating figure. He was still staring at the door when it openly slightly and his driver stepped into the room.

"What is it?" he snapped. Rodrigo knew better than to enter his study without knocking.

"Señor Cole has arrived in San José and is waiting for you."

Raul's scowl deepened quickly. David Cole had returned to Costa Rica. The last time he and the brash young man met they'd traded words—words that had left a bitter taste in his mouth. Words he never would've permitted another man to utter in his presence. Words that David Cole would find himself swallowing and choking on.

"Tell Señor Cole that I cannot leave Puerto Limón at this time. If he refuses to come, then bring him here—either standing or reclining. The choice will be his. That will be all, Rodrigo."

"Sí, Señor Vega."

Raul waited for the door to close, a feral smile curling his upper lip. The United States government held his son prisoner, and now he wanted Samuel Cole to feel the same pain when he imprisoned *his* last born.

"An eye for an eye, and a son for a son."

His threat, though spoken softly, carried throughout the space and lingered like a musical note before fading into a hushed silence.

Two

Serena Morris took a back staircase up to her mother's bedroom. Heaviness weighed on her narrow shoulders like a leaded blanket. She had felt so helpless once she realized there was nothing she could do to change her brother's mind. Her letters were returned and her calls went unanswered. It was as if Gabriel Vega had divorced his family.

His eyes—she would never forget the vacant, haunted look in his dark eyes when their gazes met across the space in the Florida courtroom. His glance was furtive before he turned his head and stared ahead while pleading innocent to the formal charges of drug trafficking and murder. When he was led out of the courtroom he refused to meet her gaze again.

She and Gabe were only four years apart, yet she'd always felt much older. When her mother had come home from the hospital with the baby, she held her arms out and said firmly, "Mine."

Juanita Morris-Vega had glanced at her beaming husband, then placed the sleeping, three-day-old infant boy in his half-sister's outstretched arms. The little girl and boy, who uncannily shared the same birthday, bonded instantly, and over the years had become inseparable.

Making her way down the cool, wide hallway, Serena

realized she had almost forgotten how beautiful the house in Limón was. A white, two-story, stucco structure built on a hill overlooking the lush rain forest, it claimed expansive hallways, arched entrances, highly waxed mahogany floors, and whitewashed walls. It was a home designed in the manner of a spacious Spanish *hacienda*. She had once called the house home, but now her one-bedroom apartment in a teeming New York City neighborhood was home.

Her stepfather had named the house *La Montaña*. Her mother much preferred their smaller residence in San José because of the capital city's cooler temperatures. Serena never tired of coming to *La Montaña*. She was never bothered by the heat.

Knocking lightly on the solid mahogany door, she pushed it open. The lengthening morning shadows shrouded the petite figure of Juanita Vega reclining on a massive, antique four-poster bed. Moving closer, Serena watched for movement which would indicate that her mother was awake.

"Mother?" she whispered.

Juanita sat up and stared at her daughter as if she were an apparition. "Serena!" There was no mistaking the elation in her voice.

Seconds later Serena found herself in her mother's embrace, inhaling the familiar fragrance of Joy. Her mother had worn the perfume since the first time Raul had given it to her, after the birth of Gabriel.

"I knew you would come. I prayed you'd come," Juanita said softly.

"I couldn't stay away, Mother. You need me and I need you."

Juanita pulled back and stared at a face so much like her own. Her daughter claimed a perfectly round face with large eyes that barely slanted upward at the corners. Her hair and eyes were an exact match: a warm brown with gold highlights. As she smiled, her gaze inched over Serena's short, pert nose and full, pouting mouth.

It was hard to believe that her oldest child was thirty years old, because everything about her appearance was so delicately and delightfully young. Perhaps if she secured her crinkling hair in a severe chignon it would detract from her youthful appearance, but she doubted it. Her daughter had inherited her dominant genes. At fifty-eight, Juanita could easily pass for a woman in her early forties.

Serena stared back at her mother, noting the evidence of strain on her delicate face. Her eyes were swollen from what she knew had been constant weeping, and her cheekbones were more pronounced, indicating that she had lost weight she could not afford to lose. Juanita Vega was an inch shorter than her own five-foot-four inches, and weighed no more than one hundred ten pounds. She estimated that the older woman's weight now hovered closer to one hundred.

"You've lost weight, Mother." A disapproving frown accompanied the accusation.

Juanita closed her eyes. "I can't eat or sleep. The thought that my son is accused of being a murderer haunts me day and night. I can believe anything except that he murdered someone."

"Gabe must not have known about the drugs being on that boat, and the story about him shooting that DEA agent with his own gun is preposterous. Law enforcement people are trained to apprehend and subdue a suspect, not let themselves be overpowered so that their own lives are at risk."

"That doesn't change the charge of murder," Juanita argued, her eyes filling with tears.

"No, it doesn't," Serena acknowledged, "but something tells me that Gabe will not be found guilty of any of the charges."

"Right now I'm not as confident as you are." She dabbed her eyes with an embroidered linen handkerchief. "What I can't understand is what he was doing hanging around with the son of a drug lord."

"You know he and Guillermo Barranda are friends. Ex-college roommates."

Running a fragile hand over her face, Juanita shook her head. "Of all of the people to form a friendship with, he had to find the spawn of the most ruthless man in the Western Hemisphere. I should've listened to Raul—"

"Don't say it, Mother," Serena interrupted. "It's too late to say what you should've said or done. Gabe wanted to go to an American college, and he did. And if he hadn't, who's to say that he wouldn't have met Guillermo Barranda at another time or another place? Poppa made certain that he has the best defense attorney in the state of Florida, and it's only a matter of time before Gabe will come back home." She prayed silently that she was right.

Smiling, she pressed a kiss to her mother's forehead. "I'm here now, and it's my turn to take care of you."

Stiffening in Serena's embrace, Juanita held her breath before letting it out slowly. "How long do you intend to stay?"

"I've taken a three month leave of absence."

Juanita pulled back and stared at her daughter, knowing that Serena had waged a long and bitter battle for a promotion as nursing supervisor at a prestigious New York City hospital. Now, a week after obtaining the job title, she had taken a leave of absence.

Holding up her hand Serena said softly, "Don't say anything. I know what I'm doing. *Mi familia* comes before my career."

La familia. It was something Juanita had come to cherish as she had matured. Her husband and her children were her only earthly treasures.

The roles reversed themselves as Serena sat on the bed with Juanita, holding her gently to her heart and easing the pain her mother had carried for the past two weeks.

David Cole lay across the large bed in his hotel room, waiting for the telephone call which would inform him that Raul Vega would meet with him. Their prearranged meeting for four o'clock that afternoon had been canceled, and the delay had not improved his disposition.

Two weeks—fourteen—days was all he'd allowed himself to negotiate and close on the sale of the banana plantation.

Resting his head on folded arms, he closed his eyes. Only now that he lay on the bed did he realize how exhausted he was. Eating rich foods, drinking alcoholic concoctions, and dancing until dawn had taken its toll. His head was throbbing and his mouth was unnaturally dry.

There were times when he'd engaged in two to three day binges of nonstop performing, drinking, and dancing, collapsing only when his debilitated body refused to remain in an upright position.

Now that he was experiencing the lingering effects of the prior night's carnival-like reveling he wondered if he really did miss his former life-style. A slow, crooked smile creased his sun-browned face as deep dimples winked boyishly in each of his lean cheeks. "I do," he whispered to the silent space. And he did.

He'd barely drifted off to sleep before the telephone on the bedside table rang loudly.

Picking up before the second ring, David spoke into the receiver. "Cole."

"Señor Cole, I've been instructed to take you to Señor Vega. He has offered you the hospitality of his home for your stay in Costa Rica."

As he registered the unfamiliar male voice a slight frown creased David's forehead. "Tell Señor Vega that I thank him for his generosity, but I prefer the hospitality of my own hotel suite." He did not want to give Vega the advantage of home court. As it was, *he* was a foreigner in the man's country.

"But, Señor Cole, he insists."

"And I insist on remaining at my hotel."

"I'll tell Señor Vega."

"You do just that," David countered angrily before hanging up.

Swinging his trousered legs over the side of the bed, he stood up. Going back to sleep was impossible after the phone call. Raul Cordero-Vega had become his nemesis. He was willing to sell the banana plantation— at a sizable loss if necessary—and still Vega continued to harass him. The Interior Minister would never see or treat him as an equal. David did not care anymore. Vega would come to him, on his terms, or he would let the bananas fall off the trees and rot where they lay.

Unbuttoning his shirt, he pulled it off and flung it on a chair in the opulently decorated bedroom. Minutes later his trousers and underwear followed. He would shower, change clothes, then order something to eat from room service.

Making his way into the bathroom, he turned on and adjusted the water temperature in the shower stall until it was a refreshing lukewarm. Standing under the spray of the water was invigorating. It rained down on his liberally gray-streaked black hair, plastering the short strands to his scalp. Turning his face up to the force of water coming from the showerhead, he closed his eyes. He waited a full minute, opened his eyes, then adjusted the water temperature, letting it run cold until icy, stinging fingers massaged his body.

He felt the chill, then a surge of warmth, but when he turned to his right it was too late. The figure of a man stood at his side, arm raised above his head.

David moved quickly, but not quickly enough. A huge fist cradling a small object came down alongside his temple. He felt blinding heat explode over his left eye before everything faded as he slumped lifelessly to the floor of the shower stall, his right leg twisted awkwardly under his body.

The man, who stood more than half a foot taller than David Cole's six-foot-two and outweighed him by more than sixty pounds, leaned over and turned off the water. Bending down, he lifted David effortlessly from the floor of the shower stall as if he weighed no more than a small child. Returning to the bedroom, he laid the inert body on the bed, wrapped him in a sheet, then zipped him into a ventilated body bag.

Two other men gathered everything belonging to David Cole. Within minutes the lifeless man, his luggage, and his captors rode a freight elevator to the basement and made their way out of the hotel to an awaiting van. The encroaching darkness shadowed their movements, and if anyone saw them they would be identified as hotel staff, because their coveralls bore the name and insignia of the Hotel L'Ambiance.

David Claridge Cole was on his way to Puerto Limón—reclining.

Three

Puerto Limón, Costa Rica

Rodrigo knocked on the door to his boss's study, his heart pounding loudly in his ears. The abduction had not gone well. Señor Cole was now in Limón, but he doubted whether Raul Cordero-Vega would be pleased with the man's condition.

"*Sí,*" Raul barked behind the door.

Rodrigo pushed it open and stepped into the room. Raul sat in the dark, his back to the door. The only light coming into the large room was from a full moon.

"There is a problem, Señor."

"What kind of a problem?" Raul asked, not turning around.

"He has arrived."

"Where is he?"

"He's—he's in the van, Señor."

"In the van where?"

"Along the road leading to *La Montaña*. We had a flat tire."

"Did you walk here, Rodrigo?" Raul's voice was dangerously quiet.

"*Sí,* Señor Vega."

"Señor Cole is younger and stronger than you are,

Rodrigo. There should not be a problem for him to make it up the road."

"*Pero—*"

"But what?" Raul still did not stir from his sitting position.

"He has been injured."

Raul stiffened, but did not stand. "Injured how?"

"A head wound, Señor Vega."

"How serious?"

"He needs a doctor."

The chair clattered noisily to the floor as Raul sprang to his feet. "Fools and idiots! I'm surrounded by complete idiots! I don't care how you do it, but get him up to the house, then go get the doctor! And let me remind you that if he dies—"

"*Sí,* Señor Vega," Rodrigo said quickly as he closed the door softly, shutting out the sound of his boss's ranting.

Raul walked over to the sliding French doors leading out to the gallery, and stared into the silvery moonlight. Rodrigo and the men he had hired to abduct David Cole had bungled it. Shaking his head slowly, he prayed that the American wasn't seriously injured. He needed a live body to trade for a live body. David Cole would be of no use to him dead.

Forty-five minutes had elapsed when Rodrigo knocked on the door and informed Raul that David Cole was at *La Montaña.*

"He is in the bedroom at the back of the house," Rodrigo said softly. "The doctor is on his way."

"Have someone get rid of the van and pay the men so much money that they'll forget their own mother's names if they are questioned by anyone," Raul ordered.

Rodrigo nodded, backed out of the room, and closed the door. He had managed to redeem himself.

Raul crossed the room and opened the door. His footsteps were muffled by the carpeted runner along the length of the wide hallway as he took the back staircase to the room which was to become David Cole's prison cell. A cell much better than the one where Gabriel now resided.

He did not realize how rapidly his heart was pumping when he stepped into the bedroom and stared at the motionless body of the arrogant young man who had openly insulted him during their last encounter.

Soft, golden light shone on David's handsome face, but it wasn't until he stood over the prone figure that Raul saw the damage to the left side of his face. His eye was swollen shut and the blood pooling in his ear had drained out onto the pillow cradling his head.

Swallowing back the bile rising in his throat, Raul turned quickly and left the room. Minutes later, he knocked on the door of his stepdaughter's bedroom. He had ordered her not to return to Costa Rica, but was thankful that she had disobeyed him.

"*Chica*, I need you." His voice came out in a harsh whisper. He didn't want to wake up his wife, who was now resting comfortably in a room at the opposite end of the hallway.

Serena laid aside the book she'd been reading and scrambled from her bed when she heard her father's voice, pushing her arms into the sleeves of a silken robe. Not bothering to put on her slippers, she opened the door and found him pacing back and forth.

"What's the matter, Poppa?"

Raul grabbed her hand. "Someone is injured and he needs immediate medical assistance."

As they raced along the hallway, Serena's pulse quickened. "Where is his injury?"

"His head."

Raul watched Serena move into the bedroom where David lay motionless on a large four-poster bed. Turning a switch on a lamp, she flooded the space with more light.

Holding the lamp aloft, she stared at the face of the man sprawled on the bed. She didn't notice the sensual perfection of his generous mouth, the arching curve of jet-black eyebrows, and the stubborn set of a strong chin. But she did see that his nose seemed too long and too delicate for his arresting face. Thick black lashes lay on his high cheekbones like brushes of silk, while the hair covering his scalp reminded her of the shimmering feathers on the wings of a large gray and black bird. And just for a brief moment she wondered what color his eyes were. Would they be as dark as his hair, or would they be a compelling lighter contrast to his sun-browned, olive skin?

She sat down on the side of the bed and picked up his hand, measuring his pulse. It fluttered weakly under her fingertips. He was still alive! Placing a hand on his forehead, she pulled it away quickly. His flesh was hot and dry.

"Hold the lamp, Poppa, while I take a better look."

Raul moved closer and took the lamp from her. He averted his gaze as Serena's fingers moved gently over David's head and cheek.

"He needs a doctor," she concluded. "He's going to need sutures to close the wound along his temple. He also must have antibiotics to combat any infections that may have set in. His fever is probably somewhere near one-o-three."

Raul's hand wavered slightly. "I've already sent for one. Is he going to make it?"

Serena's gaze met his. "I'm not sure."

"You're a nurse. You should know."

Her gaze narrowed. "I'm a health care professional, not a miracle worker. And my professional opinion is that if the bleeding doesn't stop, or if his body temperature continues to rise, then yes, he will die."

"He can't," Raul whispered.

"I'll stay with him and do what I can until the doctor arrives."

Raul placed the lamp on the side table and raced out of the room. He needed to make certain Rodrigo had sent for the doctor. He had been called many things, but he was not a murderer. As much as he despised David Cole, he never would have deliberately taken his life. Besides, he needed the man alive.

Serena unwrapped the sheet covering David's body, searching for other wounds. The golden light illuminated a perfectly formed male body that appeared to be at the peak of superior conditioning. There wasn't an ounce of excess flesh or fat on his frame. He was lean and muscular at the same time. There was no doubt that he worked out regularly.

Her professional gaze moved slowly over the matted hair on his chest, his flat belly, and down to his long, muscular legs. Her fingers went to his right ankle. It was swollen twice its normal size, and she hoped it was only severely sprained, not broken.

A flurry of questions swirled in her mind as she retreated to an adjoining bathroom and filled a large ceramic pitcher with cool water. Cradling the pitcher in a matching bowl, she carried them back to the bedroom. She returned to the bathroom a second time and came back with a facecloth and towel. She needed to cleanse the wound and attempt to check the bleeding.

Sitting on the side of the bed, Serena emptied half the pitcher of water into the bowl. Methodically, she wet the cloth, wrang it out, then laid it gently along the cheek of the man lying so still, so motionless, on the bed in her parents' guest bedroom.

She repeated the motion at least a dozen times before most of the blood was washed away. Her eyebrows shifted when she finally surveyed the extent of the wound. Her diagnosis was correct: he would require sutures. The open laceration began at the sphenoid bone and ended mid-cheek; she doubted whether it would heal without leaving a noticeable scar.

David stirred restlessly as he tried surfacing from the heavy darkness holding him prisoner. His tongue felt as if it were too large for his mouth, and the pain in his head tightened like a vise. Had someone put something in his drink?

Opening his mouth several times he tried forming the words, but nothing came out. Was he mute? After several attempts he managed, *"Tengo dolor."*

Serena placed a cool hand on his hot forehead. Even though he wasn't fully conscious he'd spoken Spanish, and she assumed it was his native tongue.

"I know you're in pain," she replied in the same language. "You've hurt your head." Resting the cool cloth over his left eye, she pulled his head to her breasts, cradling him gently.

David mumbled incoherently before he retreated to a place where there was no pain. He felt himself floating, high above the ground. He floated above treetops, sailing along the wind currents with large, powerful birds.

A sweet, haunting fragrance wafted in his nostrils, and he wondered how was he able to smell flowers so close to heaven. He soared higher and higher, then fell headlong toward the earth in a dizzying tailspin. He opened his mouth to scream. However, nothing came out. The ground rose up quickly to meet him, but instead of crashing he was lifted up again.

This time he felt a pair of comforting arms holding him gently and the voice of an angel telling him that he was going to be all right. She was going to take care of him. Something unknown whispered that he had died and gone to heaven.

Serena realized the man in her arms had quieted, retreating to a world of darkness and forgetfulness once again. She eased his head onto another pillow, noting that the flow of blood had slowed. Covering his body with a sheet, she turned and left the room. She needed to change her clothes before the doctor arrived.

It wasn't until she was in her bedroom that she wondered about the man, wanting to know who he was, what had happened to him so that he'd sustained such a serious injury, and what he was he doing at *La Montaña*.

She quickly exchanged her bathrobe and nightgown for a pair of jeans and an oversized T-shirt. At the last minute she brushed and secured her curly hair off her face with an elastic headband, displaying her round face to its most attractive advantage.

It had taken her less than ten minutes to change her clothes, but in that time the doctor had arrived and begun an extensive examination of the injuries of the man in the bed at Interior Minister Raul Cordero-Vega's country residence.

Standing in a far corner of the bedroom next to her father, Serena stared at the incredibly young looking doctor as he checked his patient's vital signs.

"Who is he, Poppa?" she asked Raul quietly.

"Dr. Rivera."

"Not the doctor."

Raul hesitated. He had to tell Serena the truth—or

most of it. She would find out eventually. "His name is David Cole. He's an American businessman."

"What is he doing in Costa Rica?"

"He came to meet with me."

Serena shifted a delicately arched eyebrow. "What happened to him?"

"Rodrigo found him in an abandoned van several kilometers from the house. He recognized him and brought him here."

Her next question died on her lips as the doctor stood up and motioned for Raul.

"Señor Vega. I'd like to talk to you." He put up a hand as Serena followed closely behind her father. "Please, Señorita, do not come any closer."

"It's all right, Dr. Rivera. My daughter is a nurse," Raul explained.

Leandro Rivera's eyes widened as he took in the petite figure beside one of Costa Rica's most revered government officials. He knew Vega had a son, but he hadn't known of a daughter.

He smiled easily. "Will you assist me, Señorita Vega?"

"It's Morris, not Vega," she corrected quickly. "And yes, I will assist you."

Raul missed the obvious interest in Leandro Rivera's gaze as the young doctor stared openly at Serena. "How is he, Doctor?"

Leandro jerked his attention back to Raul. "He's suffered a severe concussion. There's been some trauma to the orbit opening and sphenoid bone. His right ankle is also severely bruised. I won't know if there's a break unless it is X-rayed. But it's his head injury that concerns me."

"My daughter said that he's going to need to be sutured."

Leandro nodded. "She's correct. The laceration is too deep to close on its own."

"What are his chances for surviving?"

"I wish I could be more optimistic, Señor Vega, but we'll have to wait."

"How long?" Raul snapped in frustration.

"We'll have to wait to see whether he regains consciousness, and if the medication I give him will counteract the infections in his body. Even if we can break his fever, there still is the risk that he may have sustained some brain damage."

Serena placed a hand on her father's shoulder. "Poppa, Dr. Rivera and I will take over now. Please go and wait in your study for us to do what we have to do here."

Raul stared at Serena, a gamut of emotions crossing his face. It was the second time that night that she'd ordered him about. The tiny girl he had taken into his household and claimed as his own daughter had grown up into a beautiful woman who was still a stranger to him. And it was only now that he realized that he had never taken the time to get to know who Serena Morris actually was. He had called her daughter, yet had never legally adopted her. She continued to carry the name of a man who had not lived long enough to see her birth; a man whose face she only knew through old photographs, while he had bounced her on his knee, sung native Costa Rican songs to her, and nicknamed her *Chica*.

He loved her, but he hadn't given her the attention he had given his son. Gabriel was the fruit of his loins, but Serena was the delight of his heart. She was the joy in his life, because she looked so much like the woman he had fallen in love with at first sight.

He might have temporarily lost his son, but he still had a daughter. A daughter who would come to know the full extent of his love before she returned home to the United States.

"I will wait," he said quietly, then turned and left the room, closing the door behind him.

Dr. Leandro Rivera removed his lightweight linen jacket and rolled back the cuffs of his shirt, his gaze fixed on Serena Morris. He picked up a package of sterile, latex gloves and handed them to her before reaching into his large, black bag for another pair.

"Let's get to work, Señorita Morris."

She smiled at him, delighting him with the soft crinkling of skin around her large, round eyes. "Please call me Serena."

He returned her smile. "Only if you'll call me Leandro."

There was the familiar resounding snap of latex as they pushed their hands and fitted their fingers into the gloves. And, as if they had worked together many times in the past, the doctor and nurse shifted the patient until the light coming from the bedside lamp highlighted the left side of his face.

Serena climbed up on the bed, holding David Cole's head firmly as Leandro prepared to repair his injured face.

Four

Serena silently admired Dr. Leandro Rivera's skill as he deftly closed the deep wound. He covered his handiwork with Steri-Strips and large gauze dressing that covered the entire left side of David Cole's face. Their patient had not stirred throughout the emergency medical procedure, enabling them to work quickly and efficiently. It had been accomplished without a local anaesthetic.

Leandro withdrew several syringes from his bag and handed them to Serena. "I'm going to leave a few vials of antibiotics with you to administer every six hours."

"I'm going to need a stethoscope and a sphygmomanometer," she informed him.

He gave her a questioning look, then glanced at the syringes in her hand. "Your father said that you're a nurse."

She smiled at the tall, good-looking doctor whose delicate features were better suited to a woman. Gleaming black hair covered his well-shaped head, and only a deep wave across the crown kept it from being labeled straight. His slanting, dark eyes and rich, golden complexion boasted a blending of Chinese and of the Ticos, who were identified as direct descendants of Spanish settlers.

"I am a nurse, but not here. I received my formal training in the United States," she explained.

"You are not a Tica?" Leandro questioned, using the self-appointed nickname Costa Ricans called themselves.

"No. I am American. I was born in the States, but I was raised here when my mother married my stepfather."

So, that explained why he hadn't heard that Minister Vega claimed a daughter, Leandro mused. "Do you live in the United States?" he questioned as he prepared a syringe filled with a potent antibiotic.

"I've lived there for the past twelve years."

Concentrating on swabbing an area high on David's bare hip, he continued his questioning. "Do you think you'd ever come back here to live?"

"I don't know," she replied as honestly as she could.

There was a time when she thought about returning to Costa Rica—after her marriage ended less than a year after it began—but she didn't. She hadn't wanted to begin the practice of running away. In the end she'd remained in New York City, where she saw her ex-husband every day until he left the hospital to set up a practice with another doctor.

Leandro injected David with an antibiotic. Turning back to Serena, he flashed a wide grin. "I set up my practice three months ago, and I could use an experienced nurse to assist me."

"I'll keep that in mind."

She did not say that she would never get involved with, work with, or marry another doctor. Being the wife of Dr. Xavier Osbourne for eight months had changed her forever.

"I'll leave my stethoscope and sphygmomanometer for you to monitor his blood pressure, and a digital thermometer. I'll also leave my telephone number. Contact me if his condition worsens before I return tomorrow morning. If he comes to he probably won't feel like eating, but try to get some liquids into him."

Serena nodded. "I'll take good care of him."

Leandro smiled again. "I'm sure you will. You and David Cole are fellow Americans, and I wouldn't want his family to think that he received less than adequate medical treatment while in Costa Rica."

"Why would they think that?"

He stared at her, complete surprise on his face. "You don't know who David Cole is?"

She shook her head, and auburn-tinged curls danced softly around her neck. "No, I don't."

"Then I suggest that you ask your father about him."

She was left to ponder his cryptic statement as he prepared to take his leave. After placing the medical supplies and equipment in a drawer in a highboy, she returned to her bedroom to retrieve her watch. It was nearly midnight, and in another six hours she would have to give her patient another injection.

Serena walked out of her bedroom at the same time her father made his way toward David Cole's. "Poppa." He stopped and turned to face her. "I need to talk to you."

Raul waited for Serena's approach, noting the frown marring her forehead. It was a look he was familiar with. Juanita affected the same expression whenever she was annoyed with something or someone.

"Yes, *Chica.*"

"Just who is David Cole and what is he doing here?"

Raul's mouth tightened noticeably under his trim white mustache. "I thought I answered those questions."

"You only answered part of them. Who are the Coles?" she demanded.

He thought of not answering her, but realized that

she would eventually discover that he intended to hold David hostage until Gabriel was released from his U.S. prison.

"The Coles are one of the wealthiest black families in the United States. Their money comes from the exportation of tropical produce and the sale and rental of private villas and vacation resorts throughout Central America and the Caribbean. I was to meet with David to finalize the sale of his family's last Costa Rican holding."

"How was he injured?"

"I don't know," he replied honestly. "You have to ask him when he regains consciousness."

If he regains consciousness, she mused. The fact that he had not awakened when the doctor stitched his face alarmed her, and she wondered if David Cole wouldn't fare better in a hospital, where sophisticated machines could monitor his brain's activity. She made a mental note to speak to Leandro about moving his patient.

"I'm going to sit up with him until Dr. Rivera returns," Serena offered.

Raul laid an outstretched hand on the side of her face. "Aren't you tired from your flight, *Chica?*"

"A little," she confirmed, "but I'm used to functioning on little or no sleep." And she was. She couldn't remember the last time that she had managed to get eight uninterrupted hours of sleep. She worked at a large, urban hospital where cutbacks had caused nurses working double shifts to become the norm rather than the exception.

Raul managed a tired smile. The strain of the past two weeks and now the fact that David Cole appeared more dead than alive had depleted the last of his waning spirit. All he wanted to do was go to sleep and awake to find his son standing at his side and the knowledge that the Coles had completely divested themselves of everything Costa Rican.

"I'm going to sleep in my study. I don't want to disturb your mother." He dropped his hand and motioned with his head toward the bed. "I want you to call me if his condition worsens. As long as he resides under my roof I feel responsible for him."

"Are you going to contact his family?"

"Yes," he replied honestly. He didn't think the Coles would be too pleased to hear his demands. "Good night, *Chica.*"

"Good night, Poppa."

Serena pulled an armchair and matching ottoman close to the bed. Turning off the lamp, she settled down in the chair and raised her bare feet to the ottoman. The fingers of her right hand curled around David Cole's inert left one, and within minutes she joined him in sleep. There was only the whisper of her soft breathing keeping perfect rhythm with that of her patient.

David stirred restlessly, his eyelids fluttering uncontrollably. The insufferable heat along with the oppressive weight had returned. He couldn't move; he couldn't see or speak. He had not gone to heaven, but Hell!

What had he done to fall from Grace, to spend an eternity in Hell? Had he been too arrogant, too vain? Who had he turned away when they needed his help? What sins had he committed that would not be forgiven?

His head thrashed back and forth on the pillow as pain assaulted the left side of his face. His uninjured eye opened after several attempts, and he encountered a wall of solid blackness. He was in a deep hole in the bowels of the earth, with an unseen raging fire that continually scorched his mind and body.

He heard a long, suffering moan of pain, not realizing that the voice was his own. "Help him, help him," he pleaded over and over. He wanted someone to help the tormented man so he would stop the heartbreaking moaning.

Serena came awake immediately. Moving from the chair to the bed, she sat down next to David and laid her hand on his forehead. The heat under her fingers disturbed her. His fever had not abated. She reached over and turned on the lamp, a soft glow coming from the three-way bulb. Glancing at her watch, she saw that it was only four-ten, and she had to wait another two hours before she administered another dose of the antibiotic.

David's thrashing had twisted the sheet around his waist, exposing his chest and legs. The tightly wrapped bandage on his right foot gleamed like a beacon against his dark, muscular, hairy leg.

He continued his pleading for someone to help the man in pain as Serena inserted the thermometer in his right ear. Within seconds she read the findings. His body's temperature was 102.8.

"I'm going to help you," she replied softly, realizing that he had spoken English instead of Spanish.

David heard the soothing feminine voice, his brow furrowing in confusion. The voice sounded like that of his oldest brother's wife. Why wasn't Parris Cole with her husband and children? What was she doing in Hell with him?

"Parris . . ." His voice faded as he floated back to a place where he no longer heard the man's moaning or his sister-in-law talking to him.

Serena filled the large crock pitcher with cold water from the bathroom and emptied it into the matching bowl. Methodically, she dipped a cloth in the water and bathed David's fevered body with the cooling liquid.

She laid the cloth over the right side of his face, waiting until the moisture was absorbed by the heat of his burning flesh. Repeating the motion, she bathed his throat, chest, and torso.

Her touch was professional, although as a woman she could not help but admire the perfection of his conditioned male body. Her fingertips traced the defined muscles over his flat belly and along his thighs and legs. His uninjured foot was narrow and arched, yet large enough to support his impressive bulk. The fact that his hands and feet were professionally groomed was testimony that David Cole was fastidious about his appearance. He had every right to be, she thought, because he truly was a magnificent male. What intrigued her were the calluses on the palms of his hands and fingers. Businessmen usually did not claim callused hands, and she wondered if he perhaps were skilled in the martial arts.

She had noticed that there was no telltale band of lighter flesh around the third finger of his left hand, indicating he hadn't worn a ring on that finger. Something unknown told her, too, that David Cole was not married, and probably would never marry.

Finishing her ministrations, she covered his body once again with the sheet. This time, instead of sitting on the chair she lay down beside him. Turning on her side, she curved an arm over his flat middle and slept until the silvery light of the full moon was overshadowed by the brighter rays of the rising sun.

Five

June 15

David woke up, the haze lifting and his mind clear for the first time in twelve hours. He opened and closed his right eye several times before he was able to focus on the face looming above his. He saw hair—lots of reddish-brown, Chaka Khan type curls.

"Ouch," he gasped, feeling a sharp prick in his buttocks.

"It's over," Serena said, smiling at her patient. "How are you feeling?"

"Like someone kicked my head in." His voice was ragged and sounded unfamiliar to his ears.

Her smile vanished when she wondered if someone had indeed assaulted him. Answers to questions that nagged at her about David Cole would have to wait, because the injuries he had sustained were more critical than any question she had.

She took his temperature, aware that his uninjured eye followed her every move. She had an answer to one of her questions—his eyes were dark—very dark.

"I think you're going to make it, Señor Cole. Your temperature is down a full degree." Sponging his body with the cool water had helped lower his fever.

Leaning over, she curved an arm under his head,

lifting it gently while she held a glass with a straw to his parched lips. "It's water," she informed him when he compressed his mouth in a tight line. "You have to take some liquids or else you're going to become dehydrated."

David felt a wave of dizziness and thought he was going to throw up. "I can't," he mumbled, pushing her hand away.

The glass fell to the bed, the water wetting the sheet and pasting it to his groin. The wet fabric clearly outlined the shape of his maleness, and Serena felt a wave of heat steal into her cheeks. She had bathed every inch of his body, seeing him as a male patient; but observing him in the full daylight, awake, she realized she now saw him as a *man*. A very handsome man.

She released his head, a frown forming between her eyes. "I'm going to get another glass of water and you're going to drink it, or else I'll have the doctor hook up an IV for you. The choice is yours."

David's respiration quickened as his head rolled back and forth on the pillow. "I don't like needles," he moaned.

Leaning over his prone figure, she patted his stubbly cheek. "I suppose that means you'll drink from the glass."

"*Sí,*" he answered in Spanish even though she had spoken to him in English.

Serena worked quickly as she refilled the glass, realizing that he was slipping back to a state where he shut out his pain and everything going on around him. She managed to get David to swallow a half dozen sips of water before he retreated to a place of painless comfort.

There was no doubt that Spanish was his first language and English second. She spoke English the first two years of her life. She'd learned Spanish after she and her mother had moved from Columbus, Ohio, to San José, Costa Rica.

He slept soundly as she changed the bedding, rolling him over on his side as she stripped the bed, and put on a set of clean linen. She was breathing heavily when she finished. As a nursing student she had been trained to change a bed without removing the patient, but shifting David Cole was like moving a boulder uphill with a pencil. He was lean, but she estimated his weight to be close to two hundred pounds.

Retreating to her own bathroom to shower and change her clothes, she heard doors on the lower level opening and closing. It was six o'clock and the household was beginning to stir.

She adjusted the water in the shower stall until it was lukewarm, reveling in the sensation of the rejuvenating waters flowing over her body. The healing moisture washed away her fatigue and tension.

Serena lingered in the shower beyond her normally allotted time. If she had been back in the States, she would have showered in three minutes after a strenuous jogging workout in New York City's Central Park before heading off to work.

Shampooing her hair twice, she applied a conditioner/detangler, then lathered her body with a scented bath gel and rinsed her hair and body. The seductive aroma of flowers and musk lingered on her sleek, moist form.

She turned off the water and stepped out of the shower stall. Reaching for a towel, she folded it expertly around her head, turban-style. A second towel blotted the droplets of water from her body as she bent and stretched, using isometric maneuvers.

The image of her ex-husband came to mind, eliciting a smile. The best thing to have come from being married to Xavier was his emphasis on body conditioning.

A number one draft pick by the National Football League's New York Giants, Xavier was able to combine his two passions: football and medicine. He attended medical school in the off-season, choosing sports medicine as a specialty.

She met Xavier when he was a resident at the hospital. She had been the head nurse in the operating room, and the attraction between them was spontaneous.

They dated for four months, then married. Serena realized their marriage was in trouble before their honeymoon ended. Xavier had managed to camouflage his explosive displays of jealousy while they had dated, but the second day into their honeymoon he verbally abused a man whom he thought had made a pass at her. The only thing that prevented a violent confrontation was that the man did not understand English. What should have been an exciting and romantic interlude in France became a suffocating prison when she refused to leave their hotel room until the day of their scheduled departure.

Xavier tried curbing his unfounded bouts of jealousy, but it all ended for Serena when he confronted her and the hospital orderly who had walked with her to hail a taxi in a blinding, late spring snowstorm, brandishing a scalpel while threatening to cut the man into tiny pieces.

Her marriage ended that night after she checked into a hotel instead of returning to their apartment. A week later, with two New York City police officers in attendance, she moved her personal belongings out of the spacious Fifth Avenue apartment overlooking Central Park, and six weeks later Xavier was served with certain documents. She hadn't asked him for anything from the union except that he agree to an annulment. He did not contest her demands. And she took her maiden name.

Her exercise regimen increased her stamina, and her jogging endurance resulted in her entering the annual New York City Marathon. It had taken three years, but she now could guarantee that she would cross the finish line with the first fifty entrants. She didn't have the Central Park jogging trails in Limón, but there was always the beach. She decided to wait another day before beginning her jogging regimen. The lingering effects of jet lag continued to disrupt her body's circadian rhythms.

Her motions were mechanical as she smoothed a scented moisturizer over her body, walked into the adjoining bedroom, slipped into a pair of floral print panties, and covered them with a loose, flowing, cotton tank dress. Poppy-red mules matched the airy cotton fabric.

There was a light knock on her bedroom door moments before her mother's head emerged. A bright smile softened the noticeable strain on Juanita's face.

"I knew you'd be up, Sweetheart" she said, walking into the room. "No matter how tired you are, you never can sleep beyond sunrise."

Serena returned the smile. "Good morning, Mother. You look wonderful this morning."

"Makeup does wonders," Juanita replied.

Relieved that her mother had left the sanctuary of her bedroom, she curved an arm around Juanita's slim waist and kissed her cheek. Her clear gaze swept over the older woman's neatly coiffed, short hair and her petite body swathed in a crisp, white linen sheath.

"Makeup cannot improve on perfection."

Juanita's smile was radiant. "You're the best daughter a woman could ever have. *When* I have you," she added.

"Mother, please. Don't start in on me. Not now."

Seeing the anguish on Serena's face, she nodded. "You're right—not now."

Over an early breakfast she'd shared with her husband, after he'd awakened her with the encouraging news of their president's intervention regarding Gabriel, they'd discussed their daughter.

Raul voiced concern that Serena had not let go of the pain from her short-lived marriage, recognizing there was an obvious hardness about her that wasn't there before she married Xavier Osbourne. He'd also revealed that David Cole lay under their roof, recuperating from injuries he had sustained somewhere in Costa Rica.

"I want to tell you that your father and I will be leaving within half an hour," Juanita continued in a soft tone.

"Where are you going?"

"We're flying back to San José. President Montalvo wants to talk to Raul about Gabriel. He's set up a meeting with the American ambassador. Hopefully he can work out a deal where Gabriel will be granted bail, and when he returns to Costa Rica he will be placed under house arrest until his trial."

A powerful relief filled Serena with her mother's statement. She wanted to see Gabe, hold him close, and reinforce the bond that had developed the moment she held him in her arms twenty-six years ago. Closing her eyes, she mumbled a silent prayer.

Seeing the gesture, Juanita smiled, and it was her turn to kiss her daughter's cheek. "I'd better go now. Try to make David Cole as comfortable as possible. Even though he and Raul have never gotten along, I like the young man. The problem may be that they are too much alike to recognize their own negative traits."

Serena pondered her mother's assessment of David Cole after she and Raul left *La Montaña* for the short flight to the capital city. If David and her stepfather shared the most obvious negative trait, then it would have to be arrogance.

She looked in on David and found him asleep and

resting comfortably. His skin was noticeably cooler, indicating that the antibiotic had begun working against the infections invading his body. Sighing in relief, she went downstairs to see after her own breakfast.

Six

David woke to the sound of rain tapping against the glass of the French doors. The heat had vanished, along with the oppressive weight, but hunger and thirst had taken their place. The rumblings and contractions gripping his stomach had him wondering when he'd eaten last.

His right hand went to his cheek, fingertips encountering an emerging beard. He jerked his hand away. The stubble on his jaw verified that he hadn't shaved in days. Once he had begun shaving at sixteen, he had never permitted more than a day's growth to cover his cheeks.

Scenes from the wedding flooded his memory. Had he drunk so much that he lay in a drunken stupor for days without getting up to shower and shave?

A frown marred his smooth forehead. He had not gotten drunk. In fact he was very alert and quite sober when he boarded the jet for his flight to San José, Costa Rica! He was not in Florida, but in Costa Rica.

Suddenly he was aware of where he was and what had happened to him. Someone had broken into his hotel room and assaulted him while he was in the shower. Who was it that hit him, and why?

He wasn't given time to ponder the questions. He heard voices—male and female. It was the female's voice that held his rapt attention. He had heard that voice before—but where? It sounded so much like the husky, velvety whisper that belonged to his sister-in-law. He used to tease his oldest brother's wife, telling Parris that she should've been a radio disc jockey because of her hypnotic, X-rated, dulcet tones.

The woman sounded like Parris, but he knew it couldn't be she. This woman spoke Spanish like a native, while Parris had achieved only a perfunctory facility of the language.

Turning his head toward the sound of the voices, David discerned that he had limited use of his vision. Reaching up, he touched the bandage covering the left side of his face. The pressure of his fingers on the area brought on a wave of blinding pain.

The questions tumbled over themselves in his head. Where was he in Costa Rica? How many days and nights had he lost since his arrival? He didn't have to wait for some of the answers.

"*¡Buenos dias!*, Señor Cole. I am Dr. Leandro Rivera. How are you feeling this morning?"

David examined the young doctor for a full minute with his uninjured eye before he replied, "*Quiero algo de comer y beber.*"

Leandro smiled and placed a slender hand on his patient's forehead. The fact that David Cole was hungry and thirsty was a good sign. There was no doubt that he had not suffered any serious head trauma.

"Señorita Morris will make certain you'll get something to eat and drink, but first I want to check your face."

David could not see the Miss Morris the doctor referred to, but he could sense her presence and smell her perfume. It was a sensual, floral-musk scent. Closing his eyes, he tried remembering where he had detected that scent before.

Sitting down on the chair beside the bed, Leandro pushed his hands into a pair of sterile latex gloves, removed the gauze dressing, and peered closely at the stitches holding the flesh together along the left side of his patient's face. There was only a little redness, but no swelling. He had to smile. Given the conditions, he had done an excellent job of repairing David Cole's face. The wound would heal, leaving a barely noticeable scar—a thin scar that could be completely eradicated by a highly skilled plastic surgeon.

The area over the left eye did not look as good. The eye was still frightfully swollen, and the flesh over the lid claimed vivid hues of red, purple, and black.

Leandro replaced the dressing with smaller butterfly bandages, leaving the left eye uncovered. He would caution Serena not to let David see his face until most of the swelling had gone away. The discoloration would take days, if not more than a week, to fade completely.

He checked the right foot, manipulating the toes and registering David's reaction. He winced slightly, but didn't moan or cry out. Leandro had his answer. The ankle was not broken.

"How's my face?" David asked.

"Healing," Leandro said noncommittally.

"I know it's healing," David retorted. "What I want to know is what did you do to it?"

"I put thirty-six stitches in your face to close a gaping laceration."

David stiffened as if the doctor had struck him when he realized his face would be scarred. Closing his eye, he turned his head, the uninjured side of his face pressed to the pillow.

David Claridge Cole knew himself better than anyone, and his haughty self-image was the result of not only bearing the Cole name, but also of his inheriting the genes of his African-American-Cuban ancestors.

He had entered adolescence with full knowledge that girls were attracted first to his face, then his family's wealth. This all continued into his twenties, once he had made a name for himself as a talented jazz musician. The band had garnered worldwide popularity, while he had personally amassed groupies who waited at stage doors for him in every city Night Mood toured.

So many things had changed since he left the band: he'd become CEO for ColeDiz International Ltd., had a custom-designed, ocean-view house built in Boca Raton, Florida, that he hadn't moved into, and he was in the planning stages of starting up his own recording company. What he had not planned for was marrying. He still had too many projects to realize before he settled down with one woman and fathered children.

"Where am I?" he questioned, his voice muffled against the pillow.

Serena looked at Leandro, who nodded. She stepped over to the bed and touched David's bare shoulder. Shifting, he stared up at her, his eye widening noticeably.

He remembered seeing hair—lots of it—and now he knew who the hair belonged to. Dark curls were secured on the top of the young woman's head, a few wayward ones spilling over her high, smooth forehead.

She was a rich, lush shade of brown spice: cinnamon, nutmeg, ginger, and cloves. And the hypnotic fragrance he had detected earlier came from her. It was a seductive musk with an underlying scent of flowers. Her perfectly rounded face claimed high cheekbones, a short, rounded nose, soft chin, a full, overly ripe mouth that was a deep, rich, powdery cocoa shade, and a pair of large, round eyes that were the clearest brown he had ever seen. There was just a hint of gold in their shimmering depths.

"You're in Limón," she said, speaking English. "My father's driver found you in an abandoned van," she continued in Spanish. "He recognized your face and had you brought here." David nodded slowly, grimacing. Serena was aware of the effort it took for him to move his head.

The voice. The deep, husky voice also belonged to her. She was the angel in his dream. She was the one who held him, comforted him, and offered him succor during his pain and suffering. And the pain was back—with a throbbing vengeance.

"How did you come to be in the van?" Leandro questioned.

"Someone broke into my hotel room and hit me while I was in the shower."

"Why do you think they hit you, Señor Cole?" Leandro continued.

"I . . . I don't know," he gasped, breathing heavily. The image of the large man towering above him in the shower came back, along with the memory of the blinding, red hot pain. He wondered why he had been assaulted. By whom and for what reason?

Serena felt the muscles in his shoulder tighten under her hand. Without David saying anything she knew he was in pain.

"Why don't you rest, while I get you something to eat and drink?" Her gaze met Leandro's and she motioned for him to follow her.

They stepped outside the bedroom and she rounded on him. "David Cole may be your patient, but he is in my parents' home. My father has assumed responsibility for him. And that means *he* will monitor any police investigation and *interrogation.*"

Leandro stared at her, complete surprise on his face. His expression mirrored Serena's own shock at her reprimand. Never in her nursing career had she ever come to the defense of a patient. Perhaps it had something to do with the setting, and just maybe it had something to do with the patient, but she was totally out of character. Sharing David Cole's bed had also been out of character for her.

What was it about the man that made her go against everything she had been taught as a health care professional? Over the past twelve years she had earned a B.S., R.N. and a Master's in Public Health, and not once had she ever been cited for any professional violation.

What she had to do was acknowledge the reason behind her behavior: fear. Unconsciously she had substituted David Cole for Gabriel Vega. David, in a foreign land and imprisoned by pain, was in a position so like Gabriel's. The only difference was that once David healed he would be free to return home. Her brother, if found guilty of the charges against him, would more than likely forfeit his young life.

They apologized in unison.

"I'm sorry, Leandro."

"Forgive me, Serena."

Serena gave him a warm smile, her lush mouth softening attractively. "I suppose I'm a little overzealous."

He returned her smile. "You have every right to be. And you're right. Your father is paying me to treat Señor Cole, not interrogate him."

She touched the sleeve of his lightweight jacket. "When will you return?"

"I'll be back tonight."

Serena's clear brown eyes were shadowed by sweeping black lashes. "Perhaps we could share dinner," she offered, hoping to make amends for her scathing rebuke.

Leandro nodded. "I would like that. Is eight too late? I have office hours until six."

"Eight is perfect."

She walked Leandro down the staircase and waited

until he drove away in his Jeep before she returned to the kitchen to see about getting something for David Cole to eat.

The scent of the woman lingered in the room long after she left, and David drew in a deep breath, savoring the lingering smell of her.

A crooked smile softened his parched lips when he recalled the soft press of a feminine body next to his. He'd awakened briefly during the night to find her beside him and tried reaching out for her, but couldn't. He had been too weak.

Women who shared his bed always shared their bodies with him. But this time it was very different. He found it difficult to move his head or even sit up. He was as weak and helpless as a newborn.

Feeling pressure in the lower part of his body, he knew he had to leave the bed or embarrass himself. Moving slowly, he turned over to his left and half-sat and half-lay on the bed. He reached across his body with his right hand and pulled himself into a sitting position, using the headboard for support. Objects in the room swayed before they righted themselves. He sat on the edge of the bed for a full minute before his feet touched the floor. The sheet fell away from his naked body as he stood up. Without warning, the floor came up to meet him, and seconds before he slipped back into a well of blackness he heard a woman screaming his name.

Seven

"David!"

There was no mistaking the hysteria in Serena's voice as she knelt beside him. He lay facedown on the floor, motionless. What she feared most was that he had reopened the gash along his cheek. She managed to roll him over, sighing in relief when she saw that no sign of blood showed through the bandages.

He groaned, then opened his one good eye. Serena's face wavered dizzily before he was able to focus. "I have to go to the bathroom," he explained, his breathing labored.

Slipping an arm under his neck, she cradled his head gently within the crook of her elbow "I'm going to have to help you whenever you want to get out of bed."

David tried shaking his head, but gave up the effort as a ribbon of pain tightened like a vise over his left eye. "No," he whispered.

"Yes," she countered. "You've suffered a concussion, and it's going to be a while before you'll be able to stand up on your own."

Gritting his teeth, he tried pushing himself up off the floor. "Let me go."

Despite his weakened condition, David Cole was still twice as strong as she was, and Serena couldn't hold him when he turned away and pushed himself to his knees.

"David! David," she repeated. This time his name came out softer, almost pleading. "Let me help you."

He halted, staring at her. There was a silent plea in his gaze that implored her to understand his predicament. It was enough that he was injured, helpless, and naked. But it was an entirely different matter that he needed to relieve himself.

Something in his expression communicated itself to her, and Serena nodded slowly. She understood his embarrassment. "I'm a nurse. This is what I do—every day. You're my patient, David Cole, and I'm going to take care of you whether you like it or not, or whether you're embarrassed because you have to do what every living organism must do to survive." Pausing, she noted resignation in his expression. "Now, are you going to cooperate with me?"

Did he have a choice? The pressure in his lower body was so intense that he doubted whether he could make it to the bathroom before he shamed himself.

He hated the weakness, his helplessness. He had always prided himself on having excellent health, only succumbing to exhaustion after a multi-city tour. But exhaustion was a part of his past once he left the band.

Relenting, he said, "Yes." The single word came out in a lingering sigh.

Serena braced a shoulder under his armpit, supporting his greater weight against her hip, and helped him to his feet. He put one foot in front of the other, taking long strides despite the fact that his knees shook uncontrollably.

"Easy there, Sport," she teased. They made it to the adjoining bath, she helping David over to the commode. Sitting down heavily, he sighed in relief.

Stepping back, Serena smiled down at him. "I'll wait outside for you. Call me when you're finished."

"Thanks." The single word conveyed assuagement and appreciation.

She returned to the bedroom, busying herself smoothing out the sheet and straightening the lightweight blanket on the bed. The rain had stopped and she opened the floor-to-ceiling French doors. The sweet, cloying fragrance of tropical flowers and damp earth was redolent in the humid air. A rising fog hung over the nearby rain forest, turning the landscape a wispy, heather gray.

Ten minutes passed and still David hadn't called out to her. Shrugging a bare shoulder, Serena stood at the open French doors staring out at the land surrounding *La Montaña*, recalling the happy times she had spent there.

Her family moved into the large, beautifully designed house twenty years ago, the day she and Gabe turned ten and six, respectively. The move had been planned to coincide with a most lavish birthday celebration, and never had she felt so grown up as she did that day. The housewarming/birthday gala was never duplicated—not even when she was formally presented to Costa Rican society during her fifteenth year. Her mother had gone along with the Spanish custom of presenting her daughter at fifteen instead of the customary American Sweet Sixteen and coming out observances.

Gabe, mesmerized by the grandeur of the house and the number of people filling the expansive living room, never spoke more than ten words all that day. After all of the celebrants left he spent the night sobbing uncontrollably. He wanted his old house and old room back.

Serena realized at an early age that her younger brother detested change. He only wanted what appeared to be safe and familiar. Gabe surprised her and his family when he decided that he didn't want to attend a Costa Rican college. He wanted to follow his sister to the United States.

She was elated when Gabe was admitted to a college in South Florida. They were more than thirteen hundred miles apart, but they got to visit each other more often than if he had remained in Costa Rica.

Their roles were reversed once she decided to end her marriage to Xavier. Gabe flew up to New York from Miami and stayed with her until she settled into her new apartment, and she suspected that he had confronted Xavier about his treatment of his sister. Xavier had alluded to it when they met again at her lawyer's office, but when she asked her brother about the incident he refused to discuss it with her.

From the time that he was born she had taken care of and protected Gabriel Diego Vega. However, at twenty-eight she'd let him protect her for the first time.

Serena found it hard to believe that two years had passed so quickly. It was only two years ago that she had become the wife of Dr. Xavier Osbourne. Determination hardened her delicate jaw. Xavier was her past, and she had taken a solemn oath to never marry again.

All thoughts of her brother fled when she glanced down at her watch. David Cole had been alone in the bathroom for almost fifteen minutes. Retracing her steps, she hurried into the bathroom and went completely still. Anger and annoyance pulsed through her as the sound of running water filled the space.

Taking the few remaining steps to the shower stall, she flung open the door. David sat on the floor of the stall, water beating down on his head and rinsing a layer of soap from his large body. She reached over and slapped the lever controlling the flow of water.

David's head came up slowly and he glared at her. "What the hell do you think you're doing?"

Serena swallowed back the angry retort threatening to spill from her constricted throat. "What do you think *you're* doing?"

"Taking a shower," he shot back.

"I said you could relieve yourself, not shower."

"I needed a shower."

Resting both hands on her hips, her gaze narrowed. "What you needed to do was keep those stitches dry for at least forty-eight hours."

"I was beginning to smell."

"Let *me* determine whether you smell, Mr. Cole. And if you do begin to smell, I'll wash you."

Bracing a hand against the tiled wall, David pushed himself to his feet. He rested his forehead against the cool tiles as a wave of dizziness gripped him, while managing to swallow back the bile rising in his throat.

"You will not wash me." His refusal came out haltingly, from between clenched teeth.

Her hand went to his thick wrist and she led him slowly out of the stall. "What are you, David Cole? Stubborn, stupid, or maybe just obsessively vain?"

David leaned heavily against her side when she picked up a thick towel and blotted the water from his body. His gaze was fixed on the profusion of curling hair, neatly pinned up off her long neck. As she leaned closer the soft curls brushed his shoulder, causing him to jerk his arm away.

Her head came up and their gazes met. Even with his limited vision he was astounded by the perfection of the face only inches from his own. Her rich, dark beauty was hypnotic, and he couldn't look away. Silken, black eyebrows arched over her large, round eyes, giving her the look of a startled little girl.

But there was nothing girlish about her body. It was

slender as well as lush. The loose-fitting slip dress could not disguise the curve of her full breasts or her rounded hips. From his superior height he could easily see down the bodice of her dress whenever she leaned over, and he felt like a pervert because he liked what he saw. The rich, even layers of browns on her face extended to her shoulders and breasts, reminding him of spun sugar. He didn't know why he thought of her in terms of foods. Perhaps, he mused, because she looked good enough to eat.

"To answer your question, Miss Morris, I am neither of those adjectives. What I am is hungry, thirsty, and in lots of pain. And what I don't like is not being able to take care of myself."

Reaching up, Serena dabbed lightly over the bandages covering his wound, using a corner of the towel. "What you don't have right now is a choice, Mr. Cole. Someone opened your head like a ripe melon, resulting in a severe concussion. You are also running a temperature, which means there is evidence of an infection. You're in my parents' home, where they have assumed responsibility for your safety and recovery. And that means I give the orders and you'll do exactly what you're told to do. Is there anything about what I just said that you don't understand?"

He went completely still, one dark eye focused on her mouth. "Are you in the military?"

His question caught her off guard and she stared back at him, a frown creasing her smooth forehead. "No. Why?"

"Because you give a lot of orders," he shot back.

Her frown disappeared and she gave him a slow, sensual smile. "I only give orders when I have to."

David stared mutely at her smiling face. She'd half-lowered her lids over her hypnotic eyes and stared up at him through her lashes. It was a gesture he'd seen many times when women flirted with him. But this woman was not flirting. What she was doing was ordering him about like a storm trooper.

"Then you must be a supervisor, Miss Morris."

She opened her mouth to come back at him, but didn't. She wasn't going to explain herself. Not to David Cole. He needed her, not the other way around.

Tossing the towel on a chair, she curved an arm around his waist and steered him out of the bathroom. "You're going back to bed and I want you to stay there until I bring you your breakfast. After you eat I'll see if I can't find you something to put on. *La Montaña* is beautiful. However it is hardly the Garden of Eden."

David sat down heavily on the side of the bed, his legs shaking. They weren't shaking because of the weakness wracking his injured body, but because of what Serena had just said.

"Where am I?" he whispered.

Serena eased his legs up onto the bed and waited until he lay back against the mound of pillows cradling his shoulders. Pulling the sheet up to his chest, she said, "You're at my parents' house."

"But you said that this is *La Montaña.*"

"It is."

A fist of pain gripped his temples. Clenching his teeth, he closed his eyes. She was lying to him. Her name was Morris, not Vega. *Raul Cordero-Vega owns La Montaña,* he wanted to shout, but the words never came out. He tried to concentrate on what she'd told him, but his thoughts were a jumble of confusion. She'd said *La Montaña* was her parents' home, and if she wasn't a Vega then what was her connection to the man? Another wave of dizziness accompanied the pain, and within seconds darkness descended and he slipped into a world where there was no pain, no haunting scent of the woman who stood over him.

Serena's fingers grazed David's stubbly cheek before going to his forehead. His brow was moist and clammy. He had overexerted himself by attempting to shower.

"You're a vain fool, David Cole," she whispered softly. He had lied to her, saying he needed to shower, while the scent of cologne and aftershave still lingered on his large, hard body. The scent of his cologne suited him. It was subtle yet dramatic. It was like its wearer—she knew after less than twelve hours of meeting David Cole for the first time that he was powerful and dramatic.

Despite his physical state, he exuded power and confidence. There was no doubt he was used to giving orders and having those orders followed without question. She recalled some of the rich and powerful people who had been invited to social gatherings at *La Montaña*. They came wearing haute couture and priceless jewels, looking down their noses at the household staff as if they were insects who annoyed them.

A smile softened her lush mouth. Many wealthy people had come to Costa Rica to retire, taking advantage of the weather, Central America's purest democracy and highest standard of living, and the highest degree of economic and social progress. Some came to conduct business because of the nation's political stability, strategic location, infrastructure, inexpensive labor force, and various government incentive programs.

Raul Cordero-Vega, as Minister of the Interior, oversaw the Ministry of Economy, Industry, and Commerce like a despot. The president and his cabinet ministers were aware of her stepfather's zealous nationalistic fervor and did nothing to curtail it. Raul protected Costa Rica for all Ticos.

Serena left David and went downstairs to the kitchen to see if his breakfast was ready. As an American, David Cole was a foreign businessman, and even though Raul had taken David into his home she knew it still did not bode well for the younger man. Like her mother, she had never become involved in Raul's work, but like her mother she knew that he detested all foreign businesses. He referred to them as locusts. They swept through his country, devouring everything in sight before they disappeared like apparitions.

It would be best if David recovered quickly so he could conclude whatever business he had come to Costa Rica to conduct, she mused as she walked into a large kitchen. A large assortment of cooking utensils hung from overhead hooks in the brick wall space.

Luz Maria Hernando smiled and handed Serena a covered tray. "It is ready," she said in accented English. The talented cook took every opportunity she could to use the language. She had come to *La Montaña* a month after it was built as an interim cook and never left. She had secretly asked that Serena teach her to speak English, becoming completely bilingual in the twenty years she lived at the house. She remained in residence at *La Montaña* even when Raul and Juanita returned to San José during the intense summer season. She and Serena were alike because they both loved the heat and the surrounding rain forest.

"Thank you, Doña Maria," Serena said, smiling. She had taken to calling the never-married, middle-aged woman Doña out of respect. At first Luz Maria lectured her sternly, saying she was not worthy of the title Madam, but Serena persisted over the years and Luz Maria accepted the title as well as she accepted accolades for her superior culinary skills.

She had not disclosed the identity of the man sleeping in one of the guest rooms to the cook, telling Luz Maria that one of her father's guests was not feeling well and needed a special diet of soft foods and her special tea, which everyone claimed had magical powers of rejuvenation.

"He will feel much better after he drinks my tea," Luz Maria said in a soft, mysterious tone.

"I have no doubt," Serena agreed. Turning, she walked out of the kitchen with the tray.

Luz Maria never disclosed the ingredients she used to make the tea, but openly promised Serena she would reveal the brew's properties to her when she married and had a child. The older woman said she would pass along her secret recipe because Serena would need it when her children encountered the discomfort and elevated temperatures that usually accompanied teething.

Serena *had* married, but hadn't remained married long enough to plan for children, and her future plans did not include marrying again or having children.

Her footsteps were soft on the carpeted stairway as she made her way up to David Cole's bedroom.

Eight

Serena placed the tray on one of the bedside tables, then shook David gently. He didn't stir. It was only after she called his name that he opened his eyes.

Flashing him her sensual smile, she said softly, "It's time for you to eat."

He stared up at her, studying her face as if he had never seen her before. Pushing himself to a sitting position, he ran a hand over his hair. It was still damp from his earlier shower. The sheet had slipped low on his flat belly, and he'd made no attempt to adjust it. When he was fully conscious, his concerns had been where he was and who the woman was who took away his pain and fear and offered him comfort and peace, not his nakedness.

Serena sat down on a chair beside the bed and pulled the sheet up over David's belly. "I'm going to feed you something that is quite similar to oatmeal," she informed him, smiling.

David did not like oatmeal, but he was too hungry to protest. He nodded as she picked up a bowl from the tray. He stiffened noticeably when she spooned a portion of cereal from the bowl and put the spoon to his lips.

"I'll feed myself."

Serena shifted a eyebrow and shook her head. "I

don't think so, Mr. Cole. Not the way your hands are shaking."

He looked down at his long, well-groomed fingers, fingers that floated over the keys of a piano and strummed the strings of a guitar with a skill that had elicited chills and tears from those listening to his playing. They were trembling.

"The shaking should go away along with the headache, vertigo, and delirium in a few days." What she didn't tell David was that it would take a lot longer for the bruises over his eye to fade.

Curling his fingers into tight fists, he opened his mouth and closed his eyes, but just as quickly they opened again. The cereal was delicious. It had a sweet, nutty flavor. Within minutes he devoured the cereal.

He was nearly overcome by the warmth and scent of Serena's body as she moved from the chair to sit down on the side of the bed. He wanted to move, yet couldn't. Watching her intently, he saw her reach for a delicate china cup filled with a dark liquid.

"What is that?"

Leaning in closer, her shoulder nearly touching his bare chest, Serena said mysteriously, "A magic brew."

David managed a lopsided, dimpled smile. "Will it turn me into a prince?"

Serena, stunned by the deep dimples in his lean cheeks, held her breath, her gaze fixed on his wide, generous mouth. Even with one eye nearly closed and bruised and one half of his face scarred, David Cole was a beautiful man. His dark eyes, sun-browned, olive skin, and the heavy, silken hair covering his scalp added to his masculine beauty.

"You're already a prince, David Cole," she whispered, verbalizing her thoughts.

His smile vanished as he felt the warmth of her breath on his face. Her round eyes were unblinking, her slender body rigid. It was as if she were waiting—for what he didn't know. He was also waiting, waiting for the spell she had woven to break.

"Frogs don't become princes until they're kissed by a princess," he countered.

She blinked once. "I am not a princess."

Reaching up with his right hand, he smoothed back a curl from her forehead. "Oh, but you are, Miss Morris."

What he did not say was that all of the men in his family thought of beautiful women as royalty. And all of the men in his family had a penchant for beautiful women.

Serena put the cup to his lips, breaking the spell. "Drink."

He took several swallows of Luz Maria's tea, surprised at the flavor. It was unlike any tea he had had before. As a musician he had visited more countries than he could count on both hands and feet, sampling the cuisine in each of them. There were times when he discovered that the most unappetizing looking concoction was the most palatable. The other band members always teased him about experimenting whenever he ordered the unknown, saying he was going to come down with ptomaine or dysentery. Much to their astonishment it never happened, while some of them did succumb to various intestinal maladies.

He took the cup from her hand, holding it tightly between his fingers, and emptied it. He handed it back to her, nothing in his expression revealing what he was feeling at that moment.

"What do they call you?"

Serena thought it odd that he would use that phrase to ask her her name. "Serena," she replied before standing up.

"Any middle name?" She shook her head as she returned the cup to the tray. "Serena is a beautiful name for a princess." Settling down on the pillows cradling his back, he smiled. *And it's the perfect name for someone sent from heaven to give him back his life,* he mused, closing his eyes.

This time when he drifted off to sleep it wasn't to escape from the pain. It was to sleep and heal. The tea had begun to work its magic.

Serena stared at her sleeping patient, a slight smile softening her mouth. "If I'm a princess, then you are a prince, David Cole." Picking up the tray, she left the room. She had to get some clothes for him. Despite the fact that she was used to naked bodies, there was something about David's that bothered her. Not as a nurse, but as a woman.

Changing quickly from the red dress and mules into a pair of black linen slacks and a white linen, button-front, sleeveless top, she pushed her bare feet into a pair of black, patent leather thong sandals. She wanted to drive into the city and buy something for David to wear before it began raining again. Wherein the rest of Costa Rica experienced two seasons—wet and dry— Limón's Caribbean coastal region was usually wet all the year round. It sometimes experienced less rain in the dry season, which was generally from December to April, when Ticos referred to the dry season as *verano.* The rest of the year was their *invierno,* or winter.

Before she left for her trip she informed Luz Maria that she had invited a guest for dinner. She did not encounter anyone from the permanent household staff as she made her way through a wide hallway running along the rear of the house. However, she did notice several men working diligently on several new trees that had been added to the existing ones surrounding the property.

Other than his family and his country, her stepfather's passion was plants. He was educated as a botanist, and added an enormous greenhouse to *La Montaña* ten years after the house was constructed. It contained every plant, flower, and tree indigenous only to Costa Rica. An aviary was built years later, housing quetzals, macaws, toucans, and tiny pygmy parrots.

Her parents' late-model Mercedes-Benz was not in the four-car garage, and she assumed that Rodrigo had taken it when he drove them to the airport for their flight to San José.

Her first and only car, a bright yellow, 1974 Volkswagen "Bug," was parked in its assigned bay. Raul made certain it was serviced and ready to start up even though it was only driven when she returned to Costa Rica. Gabriel's rugged Jeep was parked in its usual spot, next to a brand new pickup truck. The pickup was used by anyone who needed to navigate the local roads whenever torrential rains made vehicular travel virtually impossible.

The Volkswagen's engine roared to life as soon as she turned the ignition. Shifting into reverse, she backed out of the garage and maneuvered down the paved road leading away from *La Montaña*.

She drove with the windows down, and the muggy stillness descended on her exposed flesh like a heated wet blanket. Dark clouds hovered overhead, foretelling another downpour within the hour. Reaching up, she picked at the damp curls clinging to her moist forehead. For the duration of her stay in Costa Rica she knew she would often have to affect a single braid to keep her hair off her face.

Serena was always astounded by how much the spirit and culture of the Limón region resembled the Caribbean islands. However, Costa Rican history told the story of how the province of Limón had been geographically and culturally isolated for centuries, its Afro-Caribbean population even banned from traveling into the Central Valley until after the 1948 civil war. Communications improved after a major highway was completed in the late eighties, but the region's population was still sparse because of the extreme climatic conditions—constant high humidity and rain interspersed with brilliant sun and clear light.

Tourists found the region fascinating, because it was a naturalist's fantasyland. The whitewater rapids of Río Pacuare, the nesting grounds, marshes, and lagoons around Barra del Colorado, Río Estrella, and Manzanillo for turtles and birds, and the string of seductive, white beaches edged with coral reefs all made it a favorite of thousands who came to Costa Rica for sybaritic vacations.

Parking her car in an area close to the *Mercado Municipal,* she continued on foot to the vast, decrepit building whose vendors and merchandise spilled out onto the streets. All around her she heard the familiar, "Wh'appen, Man?" It was the leisurely greeting of Limón's Afro-Caribbeans.

She headed for a vendor's stall that carried men's apparel. It took her an hour to select underwear, T-shirts, shorts, and a pair of large leather thongs. She'd held up each garment, trying to assess if it would fit David, finally deciding to buy several large and extra-large T-shirts, and shorts and underwear with a thirty-six-inch waist. Stacks of jeans caught her attention, but she decided against purchasing a pair because she was unsure of the length. There was no doubt that David

Cole was tall, as tall as Raul and Gabe, but he weighed more than the two men.

She planned to return to her car when the items on a vendor's stand caught her attention. It took another quarter of an hour to select a comb, brush, and shaving equipment. A mysterious smile curved her lips when she predicted that David Cole would probably appreciate the grooming supplies more than the clothes.

"Vain peacock," she whispered to herself as she stored her purchases in the back seat of the Volkswagen. A roll of thunder followed by an ear-shattering crash of lightning shook the earth at the moment she slipped behind the wheel. Her return trip to *La Montaña* would have to be navigated in a downpour.

Shoppers scurried as the rain began to fall, seeking shelter. They knew the heavy downpour would end almost as soon as it began. Only a few barefoot children lingered, until their parents shouted at them to come in out of the rain.

Serena shifted gears, squinting through the windshield. The wipers were set to the fastest speed, yet it wasn't fast enough to keep rivulets of water from distorting her view.

Maneuvering over to the side of the paved road, she cut off the engine and waited. Her moist breathing fogged up the windows as heat and moisture filled the small car.

Within fifteen minutes the rain subsided and the sun emerged from behind wispy clouds. The heat intensified quickly with the sun, forcing her to roll down the windows. The small car had become a suffocating tomb.

She downshifted as she made her way up the steep incline to *La Montaña*, maneuvering into her parking space at the garage at the same time Rodrigo emerged from the Mercedes-Benz. Vertical lines formed between her eyes. She hadn't seen him on the road in front of her.

"*¡Buenas tardes!* Señorita Serena."

"Good afternoon, Rodrigo," she said, giving the man a warm smile. "Have my parents returned?"

Rodrigo shook his head. "No. They are staying in San José for a few days."

Serena stared at the man who had been Raul Vega's driver for nearly twenty years. He was of medium height and alarmingly thin, despite having a voracious appetite. And even though he had recently celebrated his fiftieth birthday his tanned face was smooth, and his straight, black hair claimed no traces of gray.

It was rumored that when he was in his teens he had fallen in love with the daughter of a wealthy landowner. He knew her parents would never consent to their marrying because he was a common laborer. Rodrigo had worked hard, sometimes holding down three jobs, hoping to save enough money to elevate his status, but when the young woman married a wealthy Costa Rican businessman he left San José for Limón, working on a banana plantation for several years.

When one of the plantation workers mentioned that Raul Vega was hiring men to work on the grounds surrounding the large mountaintop house, Rodrigo had left the plantation for *La Montaña*. He secured a position—not to work the land, but as a driver. It was a position he treasured. He was well-paid and had his own living quarters at the beautiful house. There were times when he had nothing to do. However, there were times when he did things that had nothing to do with his skills as an excellent driver. It did not matter, because no one had ever referred to him as a peasant again.

Rodrigo glanced at the packages on the backseat of the Volkswagen. "May I help you with your purchases?"

"Please," Serena replied, pushing her seat forward.

The driver gathered the bags and waited until she closed the door to the car. "Where do you want them?"

"Kindly take them to my bedroom."

She delayed following Rodrigo into the house. She knew she had to check on David, but she also wanted to survey the land surrounding *La Montaña*. She never tired of listening to the raucous cries of the colorful birds, or staring out at the thick, blue haze that always hung over the rain forest. The cloying fragrance of creeping flowers mingling with the smell of damp earth was like the sensuous scent of a priceless perfume. The scene from the mountaintop retreat was breathtaking, and at that moment she wondered why hadn't she returned to Costa Rica to live.

The air was pure, clean, the forest abundant with natural flora and wildlife. The beaches were pristine and the water unpolluted. The country's natural beauty was overwhelming, and its people at peace.

She was now thirty years old and she had lived sixteen of those years in Costa Rica. And over the time she had asked herself that question over and over since she left to live in the United States. The answer was always the same: *Because I am an American.*

The word reminded her of the American convalescing under her parents' roof. Turning, she made her way into the house.

Walking down the hall, she stepped into the guest room and saw David reclining on a chair, eyes closed, his right foot resting on the ottoman. The sheet, draping his body like a toga, floated to the floor in graceful folds. She knocked softly against the open door.

His eyes opened and he glared at her. "Why did you lie to me about my face?"

Nine

Serena felt as if the breath had been siphoned from her lungs as she struggled to breathe. It was apparent that he had looked at a mirror.

"I did not lie to you." She struggled to control her temper.

David slowly lowered his right leg, the effort it took to complete the motion clearly marked on his face. That he was in pain was evidenced by his grimace and bared teeth.

"I asked about my face and you said it was healing."

"The doctor said it was healing. And it is."

"What he didn't say was that I would be scarred for life."

Suddenly the strain of what she had undergone for the past two weeks swept over Serena. Hearing of her brother's arrest; listening to the charges leveled against him; hearing the judge deny him bail; seeing him hand-cuffed and led out of a courtroom; knowing that if a jury found him guilty that he would die in Florida's electric chair.

Gabriel Diego Vega was going to die, while arrogant David Cole was only concerned about a little scar along the side of his face, a scar which probably could be eradicated by cosmetic surgery. Walking over to the bed, she picked up two pillows and launched them at

David like guided missiles. One landed on his lap, the other at his feet.

Her mood veered from fear to frustration, and then to full-blown anger. "My brother is going to die, and all you can think about is a little scratch on your face." Swallowing hard, she attempted to blink back tears and failed. They overflowed, staining her cheeks. "It sickens me to have to look at you." Turning, she raced out of the bedroom, ignoring David as he called out her name.

My brother is going to die. The six words echoed in David's head like the slow pounding sound of a kettle drum. Closing his eyes, he lowered his head, ignoring the band of pain tightening its vise around his temples.

The image he saw behind his lids was that of Serena's face and her tears. He saw the tears *and* her sadness. He was alive, bruised and battered but alive, while her brother was going to die.

When, he asked himself, had he become so selfish? When had he come to think only of David Cole, and no one else but David Cole?

Resting his head against the back of the wing chair, he slowly opened his eyes and stared at the space where Serena had been. He hadn't been that way when he was with Night Mood. He had been a member of a band who thought of themselves as an extended family. They'd traveled, eaten, slept, and rehearsed together. The six men saw more of one another than they did their own biological family members. The six men thought as one, and performed as one unit.

But his own selflessness stopped once he left Night Mood and took over as CEO of ColeDiz. His focus became productivity and profit margins. All he thought about was winning, at any cost.

He remembered a time when he had not wanted anything to do with business. All he'd wanted, knew, and breathed, was music. And as much as he fought the pull, his instincts for business were predetermined. His maternal grandfather, his own father, and his brothers had been, and were, consummate deal makers. A small amount of capital in their hands proliferated like yeast-filled dough.

His first passion had been, and would always be, music, but over the past nine years deal making had become a priority. And with the deal making came a hardness, a self-centered ruthlessness he hadn't realized he possessed—until now.

Serena Morris had taken care of him, while he only cared about himself. He was alive, while her brother was going to die. He could not retract what he'd said, but he could try to make amends.

Using the armrests as support, he pushed to his feet, swaying, then stood upright. He ignored the pain in his head and foot as he gingerly made his way slowly across the room. Stumbling, he gathered the sheet in his right hand and inched his way out of the bedroom and into the hallway. It took Herculean strength for him to turn his head to the right, then the left. His bedroom was at the end of the hallway, so using the wall as his support he turned left. He had to find Serena. He had to apologize. He also needed answers to a few questions. If this was really *La Montaña*, then what was she to Raul Cordero-Vega?

He ignored the wave of heat and then chills which were sweeping over his face and chest. A rush of dizziness caused him to stumble again. Reaching out, he braced a hand against the wall, steadying his progress and slowing his pace.

Moisture beaded his forehead and coated his upper body. Each step he took weakened him, but he would not give in to the relentless pain stealing whatever strength was left in his battered body.

He slowed his halting steps in front of a door. Leaning

against its solid surface, he knocked. There was no answer and he tried turning the doorknob. It was locked.

He continued down the wide hallway, his bare feet
making no sound on the Moorish style patterned runner. Even though the next room was less than twenty
feet away it could have been all of two hundred. Gritting
his teeth in frustration, David willed the dizziness to
abate. He could abide the pain, but not the dizziness
and weakness.

The door to the next room was open; leaning weakly
against the door frame, David saw Serena. She stood
with her back to the door, staring out the window. She
was motionless, her arms wrapped around her body in
a protective gesture.

With his uninjured eye he noticed the slender lines
of her body in the black slacks. The dark color slimmed
her narrow waist and hips. His gaze moved up to her
hair, and for the second time since he'd come to Costa
Rica he smiled. He liked her hair. Right now it was secured on the top of her head, but he wanted to see it
down, floating around her face and shoulders in a rich
cloud of gold-brown and red curls.

"Lo siento mucho, Serena."

She heard the melodious male voice and spun
around. Her gaze widened when she saw David supporting his sagging body against the door. Crossing her bedroom quickly, she wound an arm around his waist, and
when he attempted to adjust the sheet it fell to the floor.

Leaning heavily against her smaller frame, David
closed his eyes and swallowed back the bile threatening
to make him sick. "I'm sorry," he said, repeating his
apology in English.

Serena saw the beads of moisture dotting his forehead. Never had she encountered anyone as stubborn
as David Cole. *"Usted tiene que guardar cama."*

"I'll go back to bed and stay there," he promised. "It

was just that I wanted to apologize to you. And why is your brother going to die?"

Supporting most of his weight on her shoulder, she turned and led him back to his bedroom. "I'd rather not talk about my brother right now. You can apologize after you're better."

"Okay," he conceded, concentrating on putting one foot in front of the other.

They made it back to the bedroom, David falling heavily onto the bed. She lifted his legs and he lay back against the two remaining pillows. Closing his eyes, he successfully swallowed back the bile, berating his foolishness. Serena was right. He had to stay in bed.

He lay motionless as she took his temperature and blood pressure. The sensual scent of her was everywhere—in the air and on his flesh. His head hurt, his face ached, and his right foot throbbed continuously, yet he could not quell the desire he was beginning to feel for the woman taking care of him.

She barked at him like a storm trooper, issuing orders like a drill sergeant, yet he was drawn to her. She was a princess and an angel, one sent from heaven to save his life.

Serena withdrew a sheet from the chest at the foot of the bed and spread it over David's motionless body. His blood pressure was normal, as well as his temperature. A slight smile curved her lips. He was healing.

Placing the back of her hand against his stubbly left cheek, she stared at the perfection of his face. David Cole had every right to be upset. The scar would mar his exquisite masculine beauty.

"Would you like me to shave you?"

David opened his eyes, staring up at her with large eyes that were so black that she couldn't see into their liquid, obsidian depths. The bruise over the left one was now a deep purple instead of its former crimson.

"I'd like that very much."

Serena realized the deep, melodious quality of his voice for the first time. It was a low, rich, soothing baritone. She also recognized the cadence of a U.S. Southern drawl whenever he spoke English.

"I picked up a few things for you to wear. I don't believe it would be in your best interests to continue walking around in the nude." *Not that you don't have a beautiful body, David Cole,* she mused.

He smiled up at her, displaying his enchanting dimples. "How can I thank you?"

Pulling her hand away, Serena cocked her head at an angle and studied his animated features. "Thank me by getting well, David Cole."

"You've got yourself a deal, Serena Morris."

She returned his smile. "I'll be right back."

It took her less than ten minutes to retrieve the clothes she had bought him and to fill the large crock bowl with hot water. Shaving him while he lay in bed presented a problem. It would have been easier if he sat on the armchair. But she did not want to get him out of bed. Her only solution was to straddle his body.

Removing her sandals, she knelt on the side of the bed, then hoisted a leg over his body. David gave her an incredulous look when she supported most of her weight on the heels of her feet as she perched her lithe body over his thighs.

"Can you think of a better way?" she questioned, reaching across his body for a cloth she had placed in the bowl of hot water on the bedside table.

He couldn't answer her, because his body had reacted immediately to the pressure of her buttocks pressed against his groin. The only barriers between them were cotton and linen, and there was no doubt that she felt the rising of his sex under her rear end.

Serena's hands were shaking as she wrang the water

out of the facecloth and placed it over the lower half of David's face. What was she doing? She was sitting on a naked man who, although injured, was fully aroused. And there was no doubt that she had aroused him.

She wanted David to close his eyes so he wouldn't see her own reaction to his obvious desire. But he didn't, and seconds later his gaze went from her face to her chest, where her distended nipples were visible through the lacy cups of her bra and the delicate fabric of her linen blouse.

Her gaze widened. "Close your eyes," she ordered in a breathless whisper.

He complied, smiling. "That will be a lot easier to do than getting another part of my body to follow your orders. There are times when *it* has a mind of its own."

Serena felt the heat in her face sweep over all of her body. It settled between her thighs, and it took Herculean will to not respond to the pulsing hardness pressing up against her buttocks.

Shaking a can of shaving cream, she pushed the button, and peaks of cream settled on her fingertips. She marveled that she didn't cut or nick David as she drew the razor expertly over his jaw, circumventing the area over his left cheek where Dr. Rivera stitched the flesh together.

She eased herself off his body, noticing that his arousal had not abated. It was apparent that her patient was a healthy, virile male who would be more than sexually adequate when having to perform.

Standing at the bedside, she wiped away all traces of shaving cream and applied an astringent to his smooth, brown cheeks.

David opened his eyes for the first time since Serena had ordered that he close them. He realized that she was as affected by his body's reaction as he was by hers. The softness of her flesh, her sensual scent of flowers and musk clinging to her skin, and the firm roundness of her bottom pressing against his sex had him close to exploding. What he did not want to do was embarrass himself by spilling his lust on the bed instead of in her body. His gaze widened in shock. He hadn't known her twenty-four hours and he wanted her! Wanted to be inside her!

Wanting to sleep with Serena Morris went against everything he believed in. He'd never engaged in gratuitous sex! Not ever! Not as a teenage boy nor as a popular musician. Aside from the nickname of Dracula, the members of Night Mood had also called him "The Monk," because he refused to sleep with women when touring.

He had always been careful to not drink too much for fear of losing control and ending up in bed with a woman who would later claim that he was the father of her baby. His retort when the band members teased him was that he wanted no part of a paternity scandal; even more than avoiding any legal entanglements or entrapments, he wanted the choice to be his when he decided to marry and father children.

David did not know why he thought of marriage and children now. Did his thoughts have something to do with Serena Morris? Was it because she had helped save his life that he felt they were connected? That he owed her something? That perhaps he wanted to repay her by offering to share his life with her?

He touched his jaw, savoring the feel of smooth flesh under his fingertips. A slow smile softened his mouth. "You're much better than my barber. Thank you."

Wiping her hands on a towel, Serena returned his smile. "My barbering skills do not extend to haircuts. Not unless you'd like me to shave your head."

David ran a hand over his close-cut, graying hair. "I don't think so." There had been a time when he wore his shoulder-length hair in a ponytail, and he missed the long hair, black attire, and diamond stud earring from his Night Mood era.

She dropped the razor in the bowl along with the facecloth and towel. Taking a surreptitious glance at her patient, she noticed the expression of satisfaction softening his features.

"I'm going to help you into a pair of boxers. Then I'll see about getting you something to eat," she stated firmly.

He flashed another dimpled smile. "Thank you."

She emptied her purchases on the foot of the bed, picking up a pair of plain white boxers. "I didn't know your size, so I picked up a thirty-six."

Arching a sculpted, black eyebrow, David stared at her. "Excellent guess." He closed his eyes as she drew back the sheet and slipped the underwear over his feet and inched it up his legs. Raising his hips slightly, he facilitated her covering up his nakedness.

The heat in his face had nothing to do with his injury or the extra exertion. For the first time since laying eyes on Serena Morris he was embarrassed. She knew that she aroused him—there had been no way for him to conceal it—and whenever she gazed upon his nude body he knew she was now aware of him not as a patient but as a man.

Opening his eyes, he stared at her staring at his thigh. He knew what had garnered her rapt attention. "It's a bat," he explained.

"I can see that," Serena acknowledged, staring at the distinctive outline of a bat tattooed on the inside of David Cole's upper thigh. "Why a bat?" she questioned, pulling the sheet up and folding it back neatly over his belly.

"I played with a jazz band in my former life. It was called Night Mood. We dressed in black, hung out all night, and slept during the day. I had affected the habit of not going to bed until I saw the sun break the horizon. The other guys got into the habit of calling me Dracula. When we returned to the States after a two month tour of Europe we decided to get tattoos. All of the other guys selected cats."

It was her turn to arch her delicate eyebrows. "Why the thigh, David?" The outline of a bat with its wings outstretched was positioned where his member rested against his hard thigh.

"I didn't want it visible so that I'd have to consider having it removed one day."

Serena gave him a skeptical look. "Is that the only reason?"

"Should there be another one?"

"I think so, David Cole. I think you were so vain that you didn't want to mar your body where someone would see it."

"Someone?"

Gathering the bowl and shaving materials, she gave him a sidelong glance. "Women."

"How wrong you are, Serena," he drawled in Spanish. *"Una mujer.* Yes," he confirmed when seeing her expression of surprise. "You are the *only* woman who has seen it."

She went still, staring at him and seeing amusement in his eyes. "Don't tell me you're—"

"I prefer *women,"* he confirmed, interrupting her. "It's just that I don't make it a practice of sleeping with a lot of them."

"That's unusual coming from a musician."

"Former musician."

"Okay," she conceded, "a former musician."

"Knowing this, does that change your impression of me?"

"No. It still doesn't change the fact that you're obsessed with your looks. I don't know if anyone has ever told you, but you're a vain peacock."

Instead of refuting her statement, he laughed, the sound following her out of the room and down the hall.

Serena laughed softly to herself. David Cole was vain. And sexy; sexier than any man she had ever seen in her life. He was what Latin women called *muy guapo*. He was one *fine* man.

Ten

David sat up in bed, his back supported by several pillows, while Serena fed him spoonfuls of a flavorful chicken soup with rice and vegetables. He hadn't realized how hungry he was until he began eating. He ate all of the soup and drank half a cup of tea. His lids soon fluttered wildly as he fought against listlessness making it almost impossible to keep his eyes open; within minutes he fell into a deep, comforting sleep.

He never knew when Serena eased the pillows from behind his back and shoulders and placed them under his head. He also was not aware that she leaned over his prone form for several seconds before leaning closer and placing a light kiss on his forehead.

"Sleep well, David," she whispered softly, then walked out of the room.

Serena returned to the kitchen, smiling at Luz Maria. "He ate all of the soup, but only drank half of the tea," she informed the cook.

Luz Maria took the tray from Serena, returning her smile. "That's okay. I made the tea a little stronger this time. He only needed to drink a little bit. Is he complaining about pain?"

"No."

"Good." Her tea, with its natural anesthetizing properties, dulled intense pain almost immediately while causing one to fall into a deep sleep. It contained a popular herb used by Costa Rican natives for many centuries to counter infections that attacked the body.

"Are you ready to eat?"

Serena nodded, sitting down at a massive mahogany table that had been crafted more than a hundred years before. The skilled furniture maker had carved his name and the date on the underside of the table.

She watched Luz Maria as she spooned a portion of soup into a bowl. The talented cook was tiny, barely five-feet in height, and weighed about one hundred pounds, and even though she prepared exquisite meals for her employer and his family she made it a practice not to eat any meat. On occasion she consumed a small amount of chicken. However, she much preferred fish and the vegetables indigenous to the region.

Serena looked forward to eating *casabe, yautía,* and *plátanos* whenever she returned to the Central American country. She liked *plátanos,* or bananas, whether they were green or ripe. Luz Maria placed a bowl of soup on the table, along with a small dish filled with *plátano maduro.* The aroma of the lightly fried, yellow bananas wafted above the other tantalizing smells in the large kitchen.

"Will your papa and mother return in time to share dinner with your guest tonight?" Luz questioned, waiting until after Serena had swallowed several spoonfuls of soup.

"No. It will be Dr. Rivera and myself. My parents are going to stay in San José for a few days. They went to meet with President Montalvo and the ambassador from the United States."

Luz Maria crossed herself, saying a silent prayer. When she heard of Gabriel Vega's arrest she'd begun a daily novena of lighting candles and saying prayers for his return. She could not believe he had killed anyone. She'd watched Gabriel Diego Vega grow up, and everyone who met him was taken with his gentleness and sincerity. She, like Raul Cordero-Vega, believed the people in the United States had falsely accused Gabriel of a crime he did not commit.

Serena saw Luz Maria cross herself, knowing that the older woman had erected a shrine in her bedroom for her brother. Caring for David Cole helped to lessen her own heartache. She did not have to spend all of her waking hours thinking or crying now.

She finished her lunch, thanked Luz Maria, then retreated to her room. She wanted to go for a walk but decided against it. The daytime temperature had gone over the ninety degree mark, making the intense heat dangerous for anyone who remained outdoors longer than necessary.

It was time for *siesta*. She would wait for the early evening to walk down to the river. After her walk she would prepare herself to share dinner with Leandro Rivera.

Removing her sandals, blouse, slacks, and underwear, she pulled a short shift over her head, then lay down on the bed. She stared up at the mosquito netting shrouding the large, four-poster bed. Warm breezes swept into the bedroom and over her exposed limbs from the open French doors leading out to the second-story veranda. Her thoughts strayed to Gabe as she willed herself not to cry. She was unsuccessful. The tears welling up behind her lids overflowed and stained her cheeks. Turning her face into the pillow, she cried silently until spent. Then she fell asleep.

David stared up at Dr. Leandro Rivera as the doctor examined his face. "It's healing nicely, Señor Cole."

"When are you going to remove the stitches?"

Leandro smiled, the skin around his eyes crinkling attractively. "They will dissolve on their own. How's your ankle?"

"I can't put too much pressure on it."

That's because you shouldn't be putting any pressure on it, Serena said silently. She stood at the foot of the bed, watching Leandro take David Cole's blood pressure. Then she saw his obvious expression of relief when he registered David's normal body temperature.

"Señorita Morris will assist you when you get out of bed tomorrow. I've instructed her to have you soak your foot and ankle in cold water to take down some of the swelling."

Turning his head, David looked at Serena. When she entered the room with the doctor he was shocked by the change in her appearance. Her hair was brushed off her face and secured in a tight chignon on the nape of her neck. A light cover of makeup illuminated her large, round eyes and highlighted the lushness of her full lips. She had even exchanged her perfume for one that reminded him of woodsy spices. A fitted silk sheath in vermillion red matched the vibrant color on her lips. His gaze lingered on her perfectly rounded face, noting that the large pearls in her pierced lobes were companions for a magnificent single strand draped around her long, delicate neck.

She's going out! And he knew without asking that she was going out with Dr. Leandro Rivera. The doctor's tailored dark suit and silk tie were a departure from his usual linen slacks and jacket.

Not knowing why, David felt a surge of jealousy. It wasn't that he was in love with Serena, or even liked her a lot, but what bothered him was that she'd affected him more than any woman he'd ever met. He'd discovered earlier that afternoon that he lacked control over his sexual urges when near her and that she made him think of marrying and fathering children.

"I hope you two have a good time tonight," he said without warning. Leandro smiled, while Serena frowned.

"Thank you," Leandro returned, confirming his suspicions.

"I'll check on you later," Serena said as she turned and walked out of the bedroom. Leandro replaced his instruments in his bag and followed her.

David's gaze followed her retreating figure. He could see the perfection of her strong legs in a pair of red satin, sling-strap heels. She had elected to leave her legs bare, and the smooth brown color shimmered sensually over firm, lean muscle.

And for the second time that day David felt a surge of desire that left him trembling and shaken with an urgency to bury his sex deep within the softness of her enticing body.

Reaching over for the cup of tea on the bedside table, he gulped it quickly, smiling as sleep overtook him so that he did not have to think of Serena Morris or the man who would command her attention for the evening.

Serena and Leandro walked slowly, side by side, as they made their way along the path leading away from *La Montaña* and toward the Caribbean. He had elected to park his car a quarter of a mile from the house, saying that he needed the additional exercise.

A rising wind swept over her moist face, cooling her bared flesh. She did not know what to expect, but she had not expected her dining partner's wicked sense of humor. They had spent the better part of two hours laughing instead of eating Luz Maria's expertly prepared avocado and mango salad, shredded beef, white rice and black beans, steamed pumpkin, and a chilled dessert made of fresh coconut.

The meal began with her thinking of David Cole's dinner. He'd eaten a bowl of potato soup seasoned with rosemary, tarragon, chives, scallions, and strips of a melted yellow cheese and crispy crumbled bacon. It had pleased her that he ate all that was in the bowl, indicating he was well on the road to recovery. The absence of a fever and his healthy appetite made it a certainty that his period of convalescence would be shorter than she had originally predicted. She knew he was practically pain-free. Luz Maria's magical tea worked as well as Demerol, without any of the addictive properties of some prescribed painkillers.

Leandro caught her hand as he assisted her over the uneven surface of an area of the landscape. Tightening his grip, he smiled down at her upturned face. His four-wheel drive vehicle was parked less than twenty feet away, yet he had not released her fingers.

Rising on tiptoe, Serena pressed her lips to his smooth jaw. "Thank you for coming to dinner."

The skin around his dark, slanting eyes crinkled in an engaging smile. "May I call on you again for dinner?"

"Of course," she replied.

His smile slipped away as he stared down at her. *She's so lovely,* he mused. "What can I offer you to return to Limón and work with me?"

Shaking her head, she forced a smile. "Nothing right now. My life is in the United States."

"Your life or *someone?*"

"My life." There was no mistaking the emphasis on the two words.

Leandro released her hand, leaning over and placing

a light kiss an inch from her mouth. *"¡Hasta luego!* Serena."

"¡Buenas noches!"

Turning, she made her way back up the path, not waiting for Leandro to drive away. She felt the heat of his gaze on her back, and she wondered if she had made a mistake to share dinner with the young doctor. She wasn't vain, at least not as vain as David Cole, but she knew that Dr. Leandro Rivera was interested in her the way a man would be interested in a woman. He was a Tico and she was an American, and never had she felt as American as she did at that moment. Perhaps it had something to do with her stepfather's virulent attack on Americans that made her realize that she, like her mother, truly loved the country of their birth. Or maybe it was because of her date with Leandro, a Costa Rican man, that made her aware of how different he was from American men.

She had not dated before she left Costa Rica for the States, so her introduction to the opposite sex was through the men she met in college. The fact that she had spent sixteen of her first eighteen years of life in a Central American country was undetectable once she fully immersed herself in the culture of her biological parents.

Walking into the large house, she smiled. The thick stucco walls kept the heat at bay and permitted the interiors to remain cool despite the intense tropical heat. She made her way up the staircase, feeling the muscles in the back of her legs pulling. It had been a while since she had worn a pair of heels. She could not remember the last time she had put on a dress and heels and gone out dancing.

Not since Xavier, a silent voice whispered to her. Not since she walked away from her ex-husband and her marriage. Her career had become a priority, and dating something she relegated to her past.

Now her priority was her brother. She'd returned to Costa Rica to bond with her family and do what she could to help secure his release from a Florida prison.

She decided to check on David before going to her own bedroom. Leandro had given her specific instructions. He wanted the American businessman ambulatory. It was important that David get out of bed for longer periods of time. He promised to deliver an adjustable cane to facilitate his patient's walking.

Standing at the open doorway she saw that David was not in bed. Walking into the room, she noticed that he sat on the armchair, his injured foot on the footstool.

The large bedroom was semi-dark, the only light coming from the light of a bedside lamp. David appeared to be asleep, eyes closed, his head resting against the high back of the chair.

She moved quietly toward the doorway, stopping when he said, "Do you like him?"

Turning slowly, Serena stared at David staring back at her, registering the deep, melodious sound of his voice for the first time. Whenever he spoke Spanish it sounded as if he were singing a sensual love song. She much preferred to hear him speak Spanish.

"Excuse me?"

"I asked if you like him."

She laughed in a low, throaty chuckle. Folding her hands on her hips, she shook her head. "Vain and arrogant, too, Mr. Cole?"

A slow smile deepened the dimples in his cheeks. "If you say so, Miss Morris."

"I say so."

Raising a hand, he beckoned to her. "Please come and talk to me."

She did not move. "What do you want to talk about?"

He lowered his hand. "Anything. If I go back to bed I'm going to fall asleep again, and I've slept more in the past two days than I've slept the past month."

Making her way slowly across the bedroom, Serena's eyes sparkled in a friendly smile. "I give you less than a week before you'll be able to go home."

"I have to take care of some business before I return home."

"You'll have to wait for my father to return from San José for that."

David's uninjured eye widened as he felt his pulse quicken. Vertical slashes appeared between his eyes as he stared at Serena standing beside his chair. "Your father?"

Leaning down and gently moving his foot, she sat on the footstool and crossed her outstretched legs at the ankles. "Yes. My father is Raul Cordero-Vega."

He felt as if he had been punched in the gut. His brow furrowed and he wondered if his being at *La Montaña* was a coincidence or was it by design. He knew Vega wanted him in Limón, and for the first time he suspected perhaps Vega was the mastermind behind his assault and abduction. He and Cordero-Vega despised each other, and the woman he was attracted to was the daughter of his nemesis. "But isn't your name Morris?"

"It is. Raul is my stepfather."

David continued to stare at the woman who was the most exotic female he had ever met. The color of her flesh, the blend of her brown and reddish curling hair, and the perfection of her round face and features transfixed him as no other woman had. Her nearness and her fragrant skin heated him until his body reacted violently with a swift rushing desire. He was grateful to be sitting as he placed both hands in his lap.

"How old were you when he married your mother?"

"Two. My father died before I was born."

He examined her closed expression as she stared out the French doors. David did not know how, but he felt what she was feeling, and it was sadness, sadness that was heavy and haunting, knowing all was not right in the Cordero-Vega household. He remembered her tirade about her brother dying.

"Where's your brother, Serena?"

She jumped, startled, even though David's question was spoken softly, caressingly, and what she wanted to do was cry. Gabriel, her brother, the other half of her, was locked away from her. She couldn't hold him or comfort him. Was he treated harshly? Did he get enough to eat? Was he protected from the hardened prisoners who had made incarceration a way of life?

"He's in Florida," she began in a quiet voice.

"Where in Florida?"

Serena did not answer right away as she struggled to bring her fragile emotions under control. "He's in a federal prison," she whispered.

"On what charges?"

Turning her head, she stared up at David. Leaning forward, he stared down at her. David Cole was a stranger, yet she felt as if she had known him for years. Her interaction with him had been impersonal since he had taken refuge in her parents' home, but for some unknown reason she wanted to pour her heart out to him.

Glancing away, she said, "Murder and drug trafficking."

David slumped against the high back of the comfortable armchair. He was a Floridian, and he knew the laws in Florida were harsh and punitive when it came to murder and drugs. Who had her brother been involved with? Was he also an American?

"What happened, Serena?"

She did not answer, could not. Her vocal chords constricted, not permitting her to speak. Closing her eyes, she could see Gabriel's closed expression as he stood in the Florida courtroom while the federal prosecutor read the charges against him.

"He's been charged with smuggling, and killing a DEA agent." Her tone was flat, emotionless. Each time she had to repeat those charges she felt as if someone had pierced her heart with a sharp instrument, allowing the blood to flow unchecked.

"Who was he involved with?"

Her head came up quickly at the same time she rose to her feet. "He wasn't involved with *anyone,*" she snapped angrily. "He went on a sailing trip with a group of college friends. Their boat was intercepted by the Coast Guard and DEA—"

"Was he with Guillermo Barranda?" David interrupted.

She went completely still, her eyes widening in shock. "How did you know that?"

"I'm from Florida," he explained, speaking English for the first time since Serena had come into the bedroom. "The media coverage of the drug bust and the death of a DEA agent was paramount for about a week. The only name I remembered was Guillermo Barranda. The rumor is that his father heads the largest drug cartel in South America." A frown furrowed his forehead. "What was your brother doing with someone like Barranda?"

"They were college roommates."

David grunted, shaking his head. "Someone should've told him to change roommates."

"Since when do you blame children for the sins of their parents?" she shot back angrily.

Her words slapped David as if she had physically struck him. He had no right to judge the younger Barranda. There were enough skeletons in his own family closet to rattle for several generations. There was a time when the Coles were rift with alienation and bitterness for more years than he could count. It was only within the past five years that things had changed and his parents, brothers, and sisters had reconciled with one another.

Lowering his right foot and using the armrests, he pushed to his feet, swaying before he righted himself. "You're right, Serena. *I* of all people should be the last to judge someone else for what his father has done," he replied cryptically.

Standing, she stared at the middle of his hair-matted chest rather than meet his gaze; she had heard rumors about her stepfather—nasty rumors about his abuse of the powers of his office—and had always forgiven him because of his passion for the country of his birth. She and her mother had never permitted themselves to become involved with the political machinations that controlled Raul Vega and turned him into a nationalistic zealot.

Nodding, she said, "The adage is true—those who live in glass houses should not throw stones."

He flashed a slow, sensual smile. "Amen."

Serena wound an arm around his waist, feeling the heat from his body seep into her own through the red silk dress. The natural fragrance of his masculine skin was hypnotic and cloying.

They made their way slowly across the room to the bed. David sat down hard, breathing heavily. The effort it had taken for him to get out of bed and make it over the chair had drained his strength. He had been prepared to spend the night on the chair if Serena hadn't returned.

She raised his legs and eased them onto the bed as he lay down. Pulling a sheet up to his waist, she smiled at him. "Dr. Rivera wants you ambulatory. He's sending over a cane to help you keep your balance. We'll start you with taking your meals out of bed. It may take a few days, but as soon as the swelling in your ankle lessens you'll be able to shower by yourself."

This news pleased him. "Thank you."

Serena stared at David. It was the first time since he was brought into *La Montaña* that he'd shown any measure of humility. "You're welcome." Patting his muscled shoulder, she flashed her winning smile. "Sleep well."

David closed his eyes, a smile curving his lips. He still could see Serena, smell her, hear the sound of her throaty voice, and savor the gentle touch of her healing hands. She was his special angel, sent from heaven to give him back his life, and what he wanted to do when he left Costa Rica was take her with him. He never thought that perhaps it was gratitude that drew him to her, because he knew it wasn't. It was something else; something he could not quite identify. Not yet.

Eleven

June 16

Serena woke as the sun pierced the dark cover of night. Streaks of lavender, mauve, and pale blue had crisscrossed the heavens by the time she had splashed cold water on her face, brushed her teeth, slipped into a sports bra, T-shirt, shorts, and running shoes, and secured her hair atop her head with an elastic headband. The warm rays filtered over her exposed flesh the moment she stepped out onto the veranda. Instinctively she knew she had only another hour before the tropical heat made it virtually impossible for her to jog her daily three miles.

Making her way out of her bedroom, she noticed a black leather garment bag and matching, oversized Pullman outside the door to David's bedroom. She assumed someone had found his luggage and delivered it to *La Montaña.* She would speak to Rodrigo after she returned from her jog.

Rodrigo, along with Luz Maria, was responsible for the day-to-day operation of *La Montaña.* Luz Maria oversaw the kitchen and every aspect of the interior of the large house, while Rodrigo saw to the exterior. He kept the automobiles in working order and made certain the landscaping crew maintained the grounds, greenhouse, and the aviary. He was silent, inconspicuous, and very efficient.

She stretched vigorously, loosening up before she half-walked and half-jogged down the path to the beach. A blue-gray haze hung over the nearby rain forest like a heavy shroud. The raucous sounds of birds filled the air, their differing cries blending like an orchestra warming up before the start of their staged performance.

This was the Costa Rica Serena loved: the heat, the cries of the birds, the clear, blue-green of the Caribbean, the thick, lush world of the rain forest, and the majestic splendor of *La Montaña* rising above the unspoiled perfection of a land not yet defiled by overpopulation or pollution.

Inhaling the cloying fragrance of flowers growing without boundaries, she could understand her stepfather's fervent passion for protecting the land of his birth. It truly was a Garden of Eden. A garden he did not want debauched by the destructive waste that usually accompanied greed and avarice—all in the name of progress.

Dampness lathered her arms and legs long before she reached the beach and began a Smooth, rhythmic running along the pristine, white sand. She had run less than a quarter of a mile when she saw tracks and a large turtle that had apparently come ashore to lay and bury hundreds of eggs in the sand before returning to the sea.

The heat from the rising sun was oppressive, stealing precious breath from her lungs, and she knew it would be impossible to run more than a mile before passing out or becoming dehydrated. Stopping, she rested her hands on her hips and inhaled thick, hot air. She had jogged less than half a mile. She did not know how long she would stay in Costa Rica before returning to the

States, but she knew that jogging every day was not possible. Her running the marathon was contingent on her logging a minimum of twenty miles a week, and she knew she was going to have to train differently if she were to remain in Costa Rica beyond a month.

Instead of running, she walked back to *La Montaña*. Limón was fully awake with the steady hum of cars and trucks traversing the paved roads as its citizens prepared for a day of work. As she neared the house she saw Rodrigo driving away, and wondered whether he was going to pick up her parents. She had wanted to call her mother, but decided to wait. She was certain that if Juanita had encouraging news she would've called her immediately.

Walking into the coolness of the house, Serena made her way up the back staircase to her bedroom. Glancing at the bags outside David Cole's door, she noticed the quality of the leather and the monogrammed *DCC* emblazoned on gold along the sides of the Pullman and garment bag.

There were so many questions about David that she wanted answered. If his family was as prominent and wealthy as Leandro had hinted, why hadn't she heard of them? And where had he learned to speak flawless Spanish?

She forgot everything about David as she stripped off her clothes and stood under the cool spray of a shower while she washed her hair and her body.

A quarter of an hour later she walked into David's bedroom, hair billowing around her head and face in a sensual cloud of red-brown curls. She had applied an oil-based lotion to the damp strands where they crinkled in soft, loose ringlets.

David turned to stare at Serena the moment he detected the fragrance of her perfume. It wasn't the same as the one she wore the night before. The last time he saw her she was wearing the red silk dress, but this morning she wore a pair of khaki shorts with an oversize T-shirt. Again, he was transfixed by the perfection of her legs.

"Good morning."

They shared a smile. They had spoken in unison.

"Good morning, David."

His smile widened. "Good morning, Serena." Pushing himself up, he supported his upper body on his elbows. "Can you help me to the bathroom?"

She arched an eyebrow, returning his winning smile. "Of course."

Slipping an arm under his knees, she swung his legs around until his feet touched the floor. Moving to his right side, she provided the extra support he needed when he gingerly placed his weight on his injured foot. They made it to the bathroom and she help him over to the commode.

"I know," he began as she opened her mouth, "I'll call you when I'm finished."

"You learn quickly. I like that," she teased.

I like you, David said silently as he stared at her retreating figure. And he did. He had awakened early and he lay in bed thinking about Serena. She yelled at him and bullied him, and these were traits he did not like in a woman. The women he found himself involved with were typically submissive and compliant. They did not challenge him or issue demands. And he usually told them from the onset that he could not promise more than he was able to give at the time, and most knew he had no intention of marrying or fathering children. Some accepted his stance, while many did not. As a result he had had very few serious relationships that continued beyond two years.

It was said that men usually married women much like their mothers, and David had come to the realization that he was looking for a woman like his mother. Marguerite Cole was quiet and extremely tolerant. She had permitted her much more effusive husband to see to her every need and desire, while she concentrated on nurturing her children and safeguarding her household. Any issues aside from her home and children she left to Samuel Claridge Cole. What he didn't understand was his attraction to Serena, because she was *not* like his mother.

When he had reluctantly left his world of music behind and assumed control of ColeDiz International, Ltd., David found, much to his chagrin, that he took to business like a duck to water. It was less than a year after he'd become CEO that he realized that he was a much more astute businessman than a natural musician. Music was a passion he worked hard at, while business came naturally. What he wanted to do was conclude the sale of the banana plantation and return to the States.

He did not know why, but when he left Costa Rica he did not want to leave Serena Morris behind. He wanted her to return with him.

She assisted him as he washed his face and brushed his teeth. It frustrated him that he was unable to perform the mundane tasks of maintaining the most basic of hygienic functions without help. His head throbbed painfully as he hobbled back to the bedroom and fell across the bed, wondering how long it would take before the pain vanished, along with the accompanying weakness.

Serena observed David's closed eyes and clenched teeth. He was putting up a brave front while suffering silently in pain. She realized whoever had assaulted him probably intended serious injury, or death. But who, she wondered, wanted him dead? And for what reason?

"I'll bring you something to eat," she informed him

softly. Giving him a lingering stare, she turned and walked out of the room.

The dull pain that radiated along the left side of his face would not permit him to nod or speak. He did not want anything to eat. What he wanted was for the pain to go away—for good.

Serena walked through the narrow hallway at the rear of the house that led to the kitchen. Instinctively she utilized the rear of the house to gain access to the kitchen. She realized it was something she and Gabriel, did as children on many occasions. When their parents entertained guests in the living room or formal dining room, they had sometimes left their beds and cajoled Luz Maria into giving them samples of the fancy concoctions she had prepared for the elegantly attired visitors.

There were times when she'd spent more time with Luz Maria than she had with her own mother. She loved the fragrant aromas wafting from the large pots on the massive stove and broiling meat in the oven. The cook taught her to bake her own bread, cure meats, and prepare a dish of perfectly steamed white rice whose grains shimmered with the olive oil used during its cooking process.

Built-in shelves along the kitchen walls claimed jars filled with dried herbs and spices grown in *La Montaña's* greenhouse. Luz Maria had been given her own section in the structure where she carefully tended the medicinal plants she used to counteract fever, pain, boils, and a plethora of infections and ailments.

Luz Maria Hernando glanced up when Serena walked into the kitchen. Her dark gaze softened as she studied the woman she'd watched flower into a natural beauty. Since she hadn't married or had children, she'd secretly claimed Serena as her own. And the younger woman could have been her daughter because there was a marked resemblance between them: similar coloring and curly hair. At fifty-two, Luz Maria was ten pounds heavier than she had been at twenty-two, yet her body retained a slender firmness that still turned many a male head.

"*¡Buenos dias!,* Doña Maria."

"*¡Buenos dias!, Princesa.* How is your guest?" she continued in English.

"He's better, but still in some pain."

"A lot of pain?"

Serena shook her head. "I don't think so. I believe it comes and goes."

Luz Maria smiled. "I'll fix him a different tea. It will take away the pain and not make him sleep so much."

Serena watched as the cook walked over to a shelf and selected a jar with a length of yellow yarn tied around its neck. She smiled. Luz Maria had chosen to identify her herbs with colored yarn.

Sitting down on a tall stool near the thick, mahogany table, she studied Luz Maria as she spilled the contents of the jar onto the table and counted out four leaves. Crushing the leaves with her fingertips, she placed them in a small piece of cheesecloth, tied it with a length of thin, white cord, and put the bundle in a large ceramic mug. Ladling hot water from a large, simmering pot on the stove, she poured it over the cheesecloth, permitting the leaves to steep.

"He is young?" Luz Maria asked without taking her gaze from the steaming cup.

Serena smiled, studying the dark head streaked with shimmering strands of silver. "Yes, Doña Maria, he is young."

Luz Maria glanced up, smiling. "He is married?"

"I don't know," she answered truthfully. Seeing the

knowing smile curving the cook's mouth, Serena leaned forward, resting her hands on the table. "What aren't you telling me?"

Shifting an eyebrow, Luz Maria stopped smiling, and her expression grew serious. "Do you really want to know, *Chica*?" she questioned, using her stepfather's term of endearment. "Do you really want to know what's in your future?"

There were rumors that Luz Maria Hernando could tell one's future, but Serena had always shied away from such superstition. She felt knowing one's future could not prevent whatever was destined to happen.

Shaking her head, she said, "No."

"I'll respect your wishes, but one thing I'll say is that the young man you're taking care of will be a part of your future."

A rush of blood heated her face. She did not want David Cole in her life. The fact was that she did not want any man in her life—now or in the future.

"What about Gabriel? What is going to happen to him?" Her scathing tone mirrored her fear and frustration for her brother.

Luz Maria's smooth, dusky-brown face creased into a sudden smile. Her novena had been answered. "Gabriel is safe."

"Safe from whom?"

"Safe from himself, and those who seek to take his life."

Slipping off the stool, Serena curved her arms around the older woman, inhaling the differing smells clinging to her body. She savored the fragrance of cloves, mint, and bergamot, while Luz Maria's large, dark eyes narrowed in a smile. The blending of her African, Native Indian, and Spanish blood made for a seductive attractiveness that made Serena wonder why some man hadn't claimed Luz Maria for his wife.

"Thank you, Doña Maria." The woman had never lied to her.

"You want to know about your brother's future, yet you hesitate to know your own."

"Maybe before I leave Costa Rica again I'll ask that you tell me."

"You won't have to ask, *Chica*. I *will* tell you whether you ask me or not, because you will need to know what to do."

Serena pondered her cryptic statement as a chill raced down her spine, causing her to shiver noticeably. *Bruja*, she said to herself. Luz Maria had been called a witch by many of the people connected with *La Montaña*, but it was only now that she was inclined to believe them.

The iciness had not left her limbs even after she'd carried a tray with the tea, a bowl of creamed rice cereal, and a glass of tropical fruit juice to David's bedroom. Luz Maria's prediction that Gabriel's life would not end in a Florida prison cheered her, while the prophecy that her own would be inexorably entwined with David Cole's unnerved her.

There was no doubt that she was attracted to him—only a blind woman would not be—but she wanted that attraction to be a superficial one. He was good-looking. No, she admitted, he was gorgeous. His rich, olive-brown coloring, liberally gray-flecked, black silky hair, delicate features, and dimpled smile were mesmerizing. His tall, muscular body was exquisitely formed, and his deep baritone voice was soft and melodious. The fact that he was wealthy, vain, and arrogant only added to his overall masculine appeal. In his arrogance he was very secure with who he was and what he had become.

She placed the tray on a small, round table next to the armchair, then helped David from the bed over to the chair, noticing that he continued to clench his teeth. It was obvious that his pain had not disappeared completely. After raising his right foot onto the stool, she positioned the tray over his lap.

He fed himself while she changed his bed. She felt his gaze watching her every movement, and wished that she had not worn the shorts. Whenever she turned she saw his one uninjured eye fixed on her legs.

Crossing the room, she stepped out into the hallway and picked up his leather garment bag and Pullman. The leather was soft and supple as heated butter. The bags were well used, yet had retained the distinctive smell of newly tanned hide. Walking slowly under the weight of the bags, she made her way into the bedroom.

David had just drained a large mug filled with a sweet, fragrant tea when he saw Serena laboring under the weight of a garment bag she had slung over her shoulder and another large case she pulled along the floor.

"Let me help you," he offered, putting the tray on the nearby table. He attempted to rise to his feet, then halted. He had put all of his weight on his swollen foot, nearly losing his balance.

"I've got it," she insisted, breathing heavily and dragging the Pullman.

Recognizing his own luggage, David hobbled slowly across the room, favoring his right foot. He knew the weight in the leather pieces, because he'd packed enough clothes for his two-week stay.

All of his suspicions about Vega were now confirmed. He'd thought perhaps someone had assaulted him in a robbery attempt, and if that had been true then he never would've seen his luggage again. Any knowledgeable thief would have sold the two pieces and contents for a tidy sum. Blinding rage surpassed all of the pain torturing his body.

"Put them down, Serena! Now!"

Registering the deep, angry command, she let go of

the Pullman and eased the strap of the garment bag off her shoulder. It landed heavily on the floor beside the Pullman. Folding her hands on her hips, she glared up at David as he gingerly made his way over to her. Moisture lathered his face with the effort it took to put one foot in front of the other.

"What are you trying to do?" he questioned. His tone had softened considerably.

Her stance did not change as she stared up at him looming above her.

"Don't ask a dumb question if you don't want a dumb answer," she snapped angrily.

"I wouldn't have to ask if you hadn't shown me what a fool you are to try to move something that weighs more than you do," he countered.

Her gaze widened. "Are you calling me a fool? Maybe I am," she continued, not giving him a chance to come back at her. "I am a fool for taking care of someone who's too stubborn and much too ignorant to acknowledge that I'm only trying to help."

Reaching out, he caught her shoulders and pulled her against his chest. "I'm not calling you a fool. I—"

"Do I have to add liar to the list of your other sterling qualities?" she interrupted.

The warmth, softness, and scent of Serena seeped into David, making him forget who he was, where he was, and the pain wracking his body from head to toe. He held onto her as if she were his lifeline. He wanted and needed her to take away his pain, the yearning surpassing every craving he'd ever known, while defying description.

His outstretched fingers covered more than half her back, and she was certain he felt her slight trembling. Her face was pressed against his shoulder, and as she shifted her head the end of her nose grazed the thick, crisp, curly hair on his broad chest.

He closed his eyes, languishing in her female heat and feeling the white hot pain slipping away. Swaying slightly, he managed to keep his balance.

"Let me go, David." Her voice was muffled in his chest.

Drawing in a deep breath, he let it out slowly. "Not yet."

"Please."

He heard the husky plea, but he would not release her. What he wanted was for her to offer him what all of the women in his past had not been able to do—he wanted Serena to relate to him not because he was David Cole, but because he was a man; a man whose name and family mattered naught to her.

His hold on her slender body eased as he pulled back. The tense silence multiplied and surrounded them with an awareness that had not been apparent before. Without a word of acknowledgement, their roles changed from that of nurse and patient to that of man and woman—male and female.

Serena's arm tightened around his waist, and he leaned docilely into her as she led him back to the bed. She spent the next half-hour bathing and shaving David while he lay motionless, eyes closed. Seeing his nude body did not disturb her as much as Luz Maria's prediction which had caused confusion in her head.

The young man you're taking care of will be a part of your future.

No! a voice in her head screamed. All she wanted was for him to heal, conclude his business with her father, then return to the States.

All she wanted for herself was her brother's freedom.

Twelve

David spent the morning and early afternoon drifting in and out of a painless sleep, giving Serena the opportunity to unpack his luggage. She hung up eight pairs of lightweight summer slacks, two dozen monogrammed shirts, four jackets, a half-dozen silk ties, six pairs of shoes, and a month's supply of briefs and socks, most bearing the label of Ralph Lauren or Façonnable.

A leather shaving kit contained Façonnable scented soap, deodorant, aftershave balm, and cologne. The masculine, woodsy scent was well-suited to its wearer. A small flannel bag contained a gleaming, sterling silver razor with *DCC* inscribed on its delicately curved handle. She slipped the razor back into its sack, smiling. The disposable razors she'd used to shave him had not even come close to the elegant, engraved shaving instrument.

Emptying the contents of the shaving kit, she discovered an ultra-thin Piaget watch. Examining it closely, she read the back of the timepiece. There was no doubt that the watch's exquisitely thin case in solid eighteen karat gold and black lizard strap cost more than some farm workers earned in a year harvesting crops. There was no question that David Cole spared no expense when selecting his wardrobe and accessories.

Returning to the bed, she stared down at his relaxed

face. His bare chest rose and fell gently in sleep. The discoloration over his left eye had changed from an angry purple-red to a shiny, dark blue. Some of the swelling had faded so much that he would soon claim full visibility. The sutures along his cheek held the flesh tightly with no sign of swelling or redness. There was no doubt that his face would be scarred, but she suspected that it would not detract from the natural male beauty which made him devastatingly handsome.

She decided to let him sleep. She needed to contact her parents in San José to find out what progress they'd made in securing the release of her brother.

The phone rang a half dozen times at the Vegas' San José residence before someone picked up the telephone.

"Hola," came a softly modulated female voice.

"Mother?"

"Serena? Have you heard anything?"

"No. That's why I'm calling you."

A soft sigh filtered through the receiver. "Nothing has changed. Raul met with President Montalvo twice, but there's been no word from the American ambassador about a formal discussion. All we can do is pray."

"Doña Maria says Gabe is safe."

There was a moment of silence before Juanita spoke again. "Are you certain she said that?"

"She said 'he's safe from himself and those who seek to take his life.' You know I'm not superstitious, but I believe her, Mother."

"I don't know what to believe anymore. All I want to do is . . ." Her voice broke, and she was unable to continue.

Serena felt her own eyes fill with tears. "Mother, please—don't." The soft sobbing coming through the wire shattered her control. It pained her to hear her mother's anguish. "Call me when you hear something." She ended the call, hanging up and cutting off the sound of Juanita's weeping.

Blinking back her own tears, she berated herself for telephoning and upsetting her mother. She made a silent promise not to call her parents again. She would wait for them to contact her.

She felt a strange restlessness that wouldn't permit her to lie or sit down. What she wanted was for everything to be a dream, and when she awoke all of the horrors of the past two weeks would disappear like a lingering puff of smoke. Something unknown whispered that she should believe Luz Maria's prediction that Gabe wasn't in any danger, but she would not believe it fully until she touched him without the barriers of shackles or the presence of criminal justice officials.

Her anxiety made her want to jog. However, that was impossible in ninety degree tropical heat. Whenever she ran she gloried in the rush of wind across her face. It made her feel as if she were flying, soaring high above the noisy crowds and burgeoning traffic, and made her free—free from the painful memories of love found and lost.

Love lost. Why was she thinking of Xavier? Was it because of what Luz Maria prophesied about her future being linked with David Cole's?

Why him, when they did not even like each other? Why did she find arrogance and vanity unappealing traits in other men, but not in David?

Walking over to the French doors, she opened them and stepped out onto the second story veranda. The humidity swallowed her whole in a cocoon of weighty, wet warmth. Low-hanging dark clouds indicated an imminent downpour. She sat down on a cushioned bamboo chaise, staring out at the landscape surrounding

La Montaña and remembering the first time she had stepped out onto the veranda. The view of the mountains, ocean, and the dense growth of the rain forest had made her feel as if she had flown up to heaven, where she looked down and saw all that God had created. A smile had curved her lips and she had whispered, "It is good."

And it was still good. The panoramic vistas had the power to soothe and erase her anxiety. She had waited until four months after her marriage ended to return to Limón, and the moment the small plane touched down at the airport the healing had begun.

Closing her eyes, she listened to cries of the birds calling to one another in the towering trees. The cacophony of sounds was nature's orchestra serenading life. She lost track of time until a rumble of thunder, followed by a driving downpour, forced her off the veranda.

She returned to the bedroom and glanced at a clock on the beside table. It was only eleven-forty. She had been up for hours, and felt as if she had accomplished nothing. Some of her restlessness was because she truly had nothing to do.

Taking care of David had not taken up much of her time. She changed his bed, gave him his shots, brought him his meals, and assisted with his grooming. Other than that he was now a patient who had required very little attention. She had only to give him injections of antibiotics and check his stitches.

Her role at the hospital, although supervisory, was hectic and demanding. She was responsible for scheduling rotations, supervisory staff meetings, and weekly conferences with hospital administration. There were times when she complained about the responsibility, but she truly loved her profession and marveled at the ongoing successes of modern medicine.

She made her way quietly into David's room. A smile crinkled the skin around her eyes when she saw him leaning against the wrought-iron balustrade, eyes closed. He'd shifted most of his body's weight to his left foot. The now softly falling rain pasted his hair to his scalp and molded his boxers to his hips and thighs. Seeing the moisture bathe his golden-brown body, droplets of water clinging to the hair on his chest, caused a rush of heat to sweep over her body like a backdraft of fire from a launching rocket.

Serena felt like a voyeur, watching numbly as David raised his arms and right foot while slowly turning his face heavenward. He kept the position for a full minute, then lowered his arms, foot, and head. She wondered if he were perhaps meditating, or possibly praying?

Her gaze was fixed on the perfection of his tall, muscled physique, noting the symmetry of his wide shoulders in proportion to his waist and hips. She visually measured the trim lines of his torso's proportion to the length of his legs.

And it was in that minute that she realized that she ached, needing him to physically make her a complete woman.

It had been more than two years since she had lain with a man, and what she had denied, had been denying, was that she missed the intimacy.

She missed the furtive glances, caresses, kisses, missed lying in bed, touching, missed waking in the morning to a warm, hard body next to her own, and she missed the complete possession when she accepted a man into her heart and into her body, when for a short time they would become one and she could claim him as her own.

Moving silently across the space, she stepped out onto the veranda. Ignoring the moisture seeping into her hair and clothing, she stood inches from David, watching the serenity softening his delicate features. He had to know that she was there, but he gave no indication, he did not open his eyes.

Something foreign, unknown, gripped her hand as she touched the center of his chest. The heat from his body almost caused her to pull her fingers away, but she did not.

Drawing even closer, she pressed her chest to his, her arms encircling his waist. She felt a wave of embarrassment heat up her face as he stood rigid, hands at his sides.

"Why don't you come in out of the rain?" she urged softly.

"I love being out in the rain," he countered in the deep melodious tone she had come to savor. "For me it's a renewal, a rebirth."

"A renewal of what?"

Opening his eyes for the first time since Serena touched him, David stared down at her damp, curly hair. He knew the exact moment she had stepped out onto the veranda. He could detect her scented body over the redolent essence of flourishing flowers and fauna surrounding *La Montaña*. He realized he would be able to identify her even if blindfolded. His breathing deepened as he felt the outline of her firm breasts against his bared chest.

"A renewal of life, Serena. Without the rain life would cease to exist. Each time it rains I think of it as a promise that the world and all that is in it will continue until the next time. Unfortunately, most of us take rain and life for granted."

"How true." Her voice was a breathless whisper, lulling and pulling David in. He felt a rush of desire that he wasn't able to control.

The evidence of his desire was apparent. There was no way he could hide his aroused state—not with her body molded to his.

Serena felt his heat melt into her. She wanted him, and it was more than obvious that he wanted her. It had taken only two days for her feelings and her role to change from caretaker to that of caregiver.

She remembered his statement that he had not made it a practice to sleep with a lot of women. That may have been so, but she also instinctively knew that David Cole certainly could attract a woman.

Her own sexual experience was limited. There were usually extended periods of time between her relationships, and if she did enter a relationship it usually was long-term.

Her hands dropped as she attempted to pull away, but David's hands moved quickly up to her shoulders. "Don't leave me—not yet." His gaze dropped to her chest, seeing the outline of her breasts against the damp T-shirt. "I want to hold you."

She felt his hardness pressing against her middle. She did not want him to hold her because she feared her own lack of control. How could she tell a man she'd known for two days that she wanted him to kiss her? That she wanted him to remind her that she was a woman who wanted and needed the intimacy of physical contact.

Flashing a nervous smile, she said, "This is very unethical, David. I'm your nurse."

He smiled his lopsided, dimpled smile. "That's because you've been unethical. Nurses normally would not share a patient's bed, nor do they sit on their patients' laps when shaving them."

Her jaw dropped. She hadn't realized that he was aware that she had slept next to him his first night at *La Montaña*. "That protocol could not be avoided," she countered.

"And neither can this one." Without giving her chance to analyze his statement, he slipped his arms down her body, his fingers encircling her waist as he lifted her off her feet until her head was even with his.

Her hands moved up his shoulders, her arms slipping around his neck. Holding tightly to keep her balance, she wasn't given the opportunity to protest as David angled his head until his mouth moved over hers, staking its claim. She felt the demanding pressure of his mouth, savoring the heated contact of flesh meeting flesh.

Then it was over as quickly as it had begun. He lowered her until her sandaled feet touched the solid surface of the veranda floor, unaware of the effort it took for him to maintain his balance while picking her up. If he hadn't used the wrought-iron railing for support, the action would've proved disastrous. If he had fallen forward he would have crushed her. Not only would he have caused further injury to himself, but her as well.

"I'm ready to go in now." His breathing was labored, as if he had run a grueling race. Tasting her mouth confirmed that his body was in concert with what he was beginning to feel for her. It wasn't gratitude for her caring for his injuries, but his wanting her the way a man wanted a woman.

Pulling out of his loose embrace, Serena turned and reentered his bedroom. "Aren't you going to help me?" he called out to her retreating back.

Not turning around, she curled her fingers into tight fists. Her body was going through all of the familiar changes associated with sexual arousal. Her breasts felt hot and heavy and the pulsing center between her thighs made her knees tremble.

"Who helped you get out of bed and walk out there?" Tension hardened her sultry voice. She was angry and annoyed that she had lost herself in the man and in the moment.

The erotic vision of watching him standing in the

rain, wearing only a pair of white, cotton boxers lingered in her mind. She could still see the contrast of his rich, brown body against the white fabric, recall the definition in his arms as he'd raised them above his head, and remember the warmth of his body when she'd placed her hand against his chest. The sights were enough to make her lower her guard so much that she would permit her own body to ache for a man.

David stared at her petite figure. There was no doubt that she was angry with him.

And he was surprised at his own reaction to Serena. It wasn't that he was celibate. What he was was *very* controlled. He had gotten used to women coming on to him and learned to counteract their advances before he entered his twenties. He always wanted to want a woman, not the reverse. He did not want to want Serena Morris, though, but his body would not follow the dictates of his brain.

And he found it ironic that while he lay under Raul Cordero-Vega's roof he coveted the daughter of the man he despised most in the world. How could he tell her that her stepfather ordered his assault? That he was responsible for him being in Limón? That in a fit of rage Vega could possibly threaten to take his life? And why would she believe him—a stranger—if he disclosed his suspicions?

He couldn't tell Serena that it had taken him the better part of a quarter of an hour to make his way out of the bed, to half-limp and half-crawl out to the veranda. He had fallen twice before he was able to support his sagging body against the balustrade.

Serena made it to the door before she realized David hadn't moved. Turning around, she saw in the distance separating them that he held onto the elaborately swirling wrought-iron design. He hadn't moved because he couldn't move.

Retracing her steps quickly, she moved to his side. "Lean on me." The command was soft and comforting. He did lean against her—heavily. Again, it was apparent that he had overexerted himself.

"Not the bed. Please," he added, breathing heavily when she stopped and stared up at him.

"Okay. Then you can sit on the chair." She led him over to the chair where he sat down, his lips drawn back over his teeth. She watched him massage his left temple. "Do you want something for the pain?"

He shook his head slowly. "No. It's not too bad," he lied smoothly. The pain had returned, this time with a blinding fury. It slashed across his left eye, making it difficult for him to focus clearly. Closing his eyes, he willed it gone.

Watching him intently, Serena saw what David would not admit. His rapid breathing and the absence of natural color in his face indicated discomfort—extreme discomfort. Raising his feet to the footstool, she sat down on the floor and cradled his left ankle. Manipulating the foot, she began with his big toe and massaged it with the pads of her thumbs. She listened, rather than saw, as his breathing slowed and the tension in his foot eased. She massaged each toe, feeling the grainy pressure under the flesh give way, then proceeded downward to the ball of the foot, along the arch to the heel.

David opened his eyes when the debilitating pressure over his eye eased. He stared down at Serena massaging his foot. Her dampened hair had begun to curl around her face and shoulders. A few wayward curls fell over her forehead and he yearned to reach over and push them away so they could not obscure the perfection of her features. He wanted to study the shape of her pouting mouth, committing it to memory. Everything about her face was flawlessly young and virginal.

He'd only brushed his mouth over hers and she had

not responded, prompting him to believe that perhaps she was quite inexperienced, or might even be a virgin. He wondered how old she could be. Twenty-two? Twenty-three? If she was in her early twenties, then she was too young for him. At thirty-six he wanted a woman secure enough and mature enough to deal with his decision not to commit to a relationship which would eventually end in marriage.

He believed in marriage, respected its sanctity, yet he was not ready for it.

Serena, finished with the left foot, turned her attention to the swollen right one. She repeated the manipulations she'd used on his left foot, exercising a minimum amount of pressure.

"You have magical hands," he said in a quiet tone. "Where did you learn to do this?"

Raising her head, she stared up at him, smiling. "Reflexology? My ex-husband taught me."

He did not know why but a rush of relief settled in his throat, making him momentarily speechless in his surprise. *Ex-husband.* She had been married. She was not a virgin.

"How long have you been divorced?"

"Annulled," she corrected. "It's been two years."

He leaned forward on the chair. "How old were you when you got married? Eighteen or nineteen?"

Serena laughed, the low haunting sound caressing him as if he had reached out and placed her hand over his heart. "I'll accept that as a compliment, but I'm sorry to disappoint you. I was twenty-eight."

His expression stilled, growing serious. "You're thirty?" The question was a statement.

"Yes." The single word lingered like a sigh.

Serena watched David watching her. It was as if he were photographing her with his eyes, seeing her for the very first time. His gaze slid smoothly from her face to her chest before reversing itself. Something foreign, unknown, erupted in the entrancement, and she knew that the man whose foot she cradled so gently saw her in a whole different light.

"How old did you think I was?"

"Early twenties."

"I'd hardly be a nursing supervisor at twenty-three."

"You could be if you graduated from nursing school while still in your teens."

She managed a sultry laugh. "I happen not to be that gifted." Her smile faded as she studied him studying her. The seconds ticked off until more than a full minute elapsed. "How old are you?" Her husky voice broke the pregnant silence.

"Thirty-six."

She arched a sculpted eyebrow. "You appear older."

He noticed she'd said *appear,* not look. "Perhaps it's the gray hair. Most people in my family gray prematurely."

Serena shook her head. "It's not the gray hair at all. You seem to have a weariness not usually associated with your age. It's as if you're living two lifetimes simultaneously."

A slight smile softened his mouth and deepened the lines at the corners of his large, dark eyes. "How right you are. I'd planned for this business trip to be the last time I'd ever come to this country. I'm here to sell off the last of ColeDiz's Costa Rican investments."

Her gaze widened at this disclosure. "How long do you think that'll take?"

"I've given myself fourteen days. And if it doesn't happen within the two weeks, then I'm going to walk away and leave it unresolved."

A slight frown furrowed her smooth forehead. "But won't you lose a lot of money for your investors?"

His frown matched hers. "There are no investors.

ColeDiz is privately and family owned. I'll have to offset the loss by giving up a portion of my personal resources." The banana plantation was worth millions, but he would willingly forfeit the money to rid himself of Raul Cordero-Vega's domination. Vega's claim that the workers at the banana plantation polluted the environment was totally unfounded. All the plastic casings were recycled.

She remembered Leandro saying that the Coles were one of the wealthiest black families in the States, and David had just confirmed that fact.

Releasing his foot, she stood up. "I'm going to change out of these damp clothes, and I'm going to suggest that you also change. I'll check to see whether Dr. Rivera sent over the cane. If he did, then I'll help you walk around before *siesta*."

She moved over to a chest of drawers and withdrew a pair of shorts she had purchased and another pair of boxers. Retracing her steps, she handed the clothes to David.

He took them, saying, "I think I can dress myself."

She nodded and walked out of the room, closing the door behind her.

Thirteen

David sat staring at the space where Serena had been, his thoughts a tangle of ambivalence, not understanding why his emotions fluctuated from one extreme to the other. He did not know why he felt drawn to Serena when in pain, then indifferent once he was free of pain.

He knew he needed her, but he did not want to want her. But even that was beyond him whenever he stopped seeing her as a nurse and saw her as a woman.

He was shocked when she revealed her age. She looked much younger, but looking back he realized that she exhibited an air of confidence atypical of a woman in her early twenties. And that confidence had not come from her career; it came from living thirty years of life.

Leaning forward and using the armrests, he pushed to his feet. He managed to change his clothes with a minimum of effort. The shorts fit perfectly, even though the style was not one he would have selected. As soon as he was able to put on a shoe he would begin wearing the clothes he'd packed for his trip.

He led off with his right foot, and amazingly it wasn't as painful as it had been. What Serena had called reflexology was miraculous. His entire body felt loose, fully relaxed, and his mind was clear for the first time in days.

Walking slowly across the bedroom and putting most

of the pressure on his right heel, David managed to keep his balance. He made it to the door at the same time Serena appeared with an adjustable aluminum cane hanging over her wrist. She had brushed her hair and secured it off her face with an elastic band. A jumble of damp curls floated over the crown of her head, causing the breath to catch in his chest at the innocent sensuality of the provocative disarray. She had exchanged her shorts and shirt for a pale orange cotton dress with narrow straps crisscrossing her shoulders and back. When she shifted slightly he could see that her back was bared to the waist, displaying an inordinate amount of flawless, sable-brown flesh.

He went completely still, unable to move. Desire, hot and rushing, exploded, and he closed his eyes briefly, hoping to shut out the erotic vision of the petite woman standing inches from him.

What was there about Serena Morris that made his body react with such reckless abandonment? He'd seen women much more classically beautiful and voluptuous. The fact that she was shorter than the women he normally found himself attracted to was also puzzling.

Opening his eyes, he stared down at her staring up at him. What he had to admit was that even though Serena appeared young and quite virginal she projected an aura of sensuality that most women could never claim. Her provocative voice, the way she looked up at him through her lashes, and the way she moved were all as measured as a choreographed dance. The entire package screamed silently for him to take her. Take her and enjoy whatever she was willing to offer.

But was she offering? He shook his head. *No.* She'd offered him the knowledge of her profession, and nothing more. It was he who wanted more.

Why now? What could he want from Serena that he

hadn't gotten from other women in his past? And why her? Why the daughter of his nemesis?

Arching her sculpted eyebrows, Serena smiled. "Are you ready for your walk around the block?"

Returning her smile, David revealed a mouth filled with large, white, straight teeth. "Lead on, MacDuff."

She handed him the cane, watching as he adjusted its length. Gripping the rubber-padded handle with his right hand, he took a step, then another. Satisfaction lit up his dark eyes. He extended his left hand, and he was not disappointed when she grasped it.

Serena felt the strength of his long fingers curled around hers. "I think we'll begin with walking the length of the hall. If you get tired let me know, and we'll stop."

Side by side, they made their way out of the bedroom and down the carpeted hallway. David passed the room with the locked door, pausing momentarily. "Whose room is this?"

Serena glanced at the door, then closed her eyes. When she reopened them she saw David staring at her with an expectant look on his face. "It's my brother's."

He nodded, wondering why the Vegas had elected to lock the door. He still maintained a bedroom suite at his parents' West Palm Beach residence, and the door to the suite remained open and available to him whenever he returned.

Thoughts of his own unoccupied Boca Raton house elicited a wry smile. It had taken him two years to locate the architect who could design the house he sought, and another two years from the time the plans were drawn up to the time the towering structure was completed.

His home was configured in three sections—the main house, running vertically from the local road, and two additional "bookend" structures that made up a guest

house and a recording studio. The rooms were volumi-
nous, with twenty-foot high ceilings, permitting ample
height for the intense Florida heat to rise above the
tiled and carpeted floors. The main house contained
living and dining rooms, a master bedroom, a smaller
bedroom, and the kitchen. Guest bedrooms with private
balconies were situated within the one "bookend" structures, which were fully accessible from the courtyard. A
series of French doors displayed a bougainvillea-covered
pergola bordering the courtyard.

He thought of the last time he stood in his home,
staring out at the swimming pool, noting his approval
of the dark finish inside the pool which allowed the
water to absorb as much radiant heat as possible during
the winter months. What had pleased him most about
the structure's overall design was that screens were designed to slide into walls, so that when the house was
open, it was truly open.

The only thing that had prevented him from moving
in was its lack of furnishings. He was to meet with his
oldest brother's wife once he concluded his business
with Cordero-Vega to begin the process of selecting furnishings and accessories. The delight in Parris Cole's
green-flecked brown eyes was apparent once she strolled
through the massive empty spaces. She'd promised to
decorate it with furnishings that would make it a de-
signer's showplace worthy of a layout for *Architectural Di-
gest*.

He had waited four years from design to construc-
tion, and he was willing to wait another six months to
complete decorating its interiors.

"What are the chances of your brother being found
not guilty?"

Serena chewed her lower lip before answering. "I
don't really know at this point. My father hired one of

the best criminal attorneys in Florida, but he wasn't able to persuade the judge to let Gabe out on bail."

David saw the anguish on her lovely face and registered the pain in her words. He had brothers, and he wondered how he would feel if they were to spend days, months, or even years incarcerated.

Tightening his grip on her slender hand, he glanced down at her enchanting profile. "I can't promise you anything, but when I return to Florida I'll see what my father can do. He no longer wheels and deals like he used to, but he still has enough clout to make a telephone call to Florida's inner circle of power brokers."

Stopping, she turned and smiled at David with an open, expectant expression. "You'd do that?"

A smile brought an immediate softening to his battered features. Inclining his head, he said quietly, "Yes, I would."

Rising on tiptoe, she pressed her mouth to his. "Thank you, David."

The warm sweetness of her mouth stoked the smoldering fires burning within him. David was certain that if he had not been holding onto the cane or her fingers, he would have taken Serena in his arms and allowed her to feel the sense of sexual urgency that made him want to take her to his bed.

He did not want to make love to Serena as much as he wanted to copulate. He did not want emotions to enter into the act. What he wanted was for their coming together to be as primitive and unbridled as an act of mating, and once he entered her body he would hold nothing back. There was something about her that touched the most primeval core of his existence, and he wanted to assuage the savage craving by using her body as a receptacle for his seed. The thought that he wanted to use her body for his lust caused him to stumble.

"Why don't we stop and rest?" Serena offered, thinking perhaps that David had tired.

"It's okay. I can make it to the end of the hall." He was breathing heavily, but it wasn't because he had overexerted himself.

Why was he thinking of using her, when he'd never used any woman to slake his sexual frustrations? *I'm losing it,* he berated himself. The last thing he wanted to do was take advantage of Raul Cordero-Vega's daughter while under the man's roof. And if he did, he doubted that he would leave Costa Rica with his head intact.

Continuing down the hall, he noticed an alcove and the door to another room. "What's there?"

"My parents' bedroom."

"How did they meet?"

"His first cousin was my mother's roommate in college."

"Had your mother gone to college in Costa Rica?"

Serena shook her head. "No. Gabriella came to the States to major in English, while my mother majored in Spanish. Both were foreign language majors. My mother came to Costa Rica during a holiday recess and met Raul at a family gathering.

"It was apparent that they were attracted to each other, but Juanita was engaged at the time. Family gossip says that Raul followed her around like a lovesick puppy, telling her that if she broke her engagement he would marry her the following day. Juanita did not break her engagement and married my father Hannibal Morris a month after she graduated college.

"They waited five years before starting a family, because my father wanted to finish medical school. It wasn't until she was twenty-seven that Juanita found herself pregnant. They were overjoyed with the news, but their joy was short-lived. My father died instantly in a head-on accident when a teenage driver lost control of his car during a severe thunderstorm. My mother, who was eight months pregnant, woke up in a hospital's recovery room to find that she had become a mother and a widow.

"She moved in with her parents for a while. Then, when I was six-months old, she took Gabrielle up on her offer to spend some time with her in San José. She and Raul met again and he pursued her like a man possessed. There were rumors that he took advantage of her grief, but no one would deny that he didn't love her. A year and a half later she agreed to marry him. Juanita presented Raul with his first and only child the day I celebrated my fourth birthday."

"It appears that your stepfather was a patient man."

What he did not say was that Raul Cordero-Vega was also tenacious, stubborn, and obstinate. Each time they met it was he who had compromised, until the last time. But not this time. This time the Interior Minister wouldn't walk away a winner.

"He's not perfect, David. That was something I realized years ago. But he is the only father I have, and I know he loves me as much or more than I love him."

They made it to the top of the staircase, turned, and retraced their steps. The sounds of their feet were muffled in the carpeting which ran the length of the hallway. David's right foot throbbed slightly as he walked into his bedroom and sat down heavily on the side of the bed.

Serena took the cane from him and rested it against the bedside table, where he could reach it if he needed to get out of bed. "Do you want anything to eat or drink?"

He barely moved his head and she knew instinctively that his headache had returned. "No," he managed between clenched teeth. "I just want to rest now."

Swinging his legs into the bed, she covered him with a sheet. She ran her fingers down the left side of his face, noting that the flesh over his cheekbone had tightened considerably. Her fingers moved to his temples and she massaged them gently, releasing his tension. She felt the muscles easing with her tender ministrations.

He stared at her, his gaze as soft and loving as a caress. "Thank you for taking care of me, Miss Serena Morris."

She met his gaze with a gentle one of her own. "You're quite welcome, David C. Cole."

He smiled, his dimples winking at her. "The C stands for Claridge. It's my father's middle name."

"Why don't you try to get some sleep, and when you wake up we'll share lunch and you can tell me all about your family."

His lids fluttered before a sweep of long black lashes lay on his high cheekbones. "You've tucked me in but haven't given me a kiss," he teased.

"Nurses don't kiss their patients."

"You did before."

"When?"

"When I told you that I'd contact my father on your brother's behalf," he reminded her.

Serena felt her face heat up. "That was different. It was a kiss of gratitude."

Rising on an elbow, he reached out his right hand and he held her face gently. "Let me show you how grateful I am that you helped save my life."

Before she was given an opportunity to protest, Serena found herself lying across David's bare chest, her mouth fused to his. This kiss was nothing like the one they'd shared on the veranda, or the one she had given him in the hallway.

His firm lips moved like watered silk over hers, coaxing her to respond as she felt the blood coursing through her veins and arousing the passion she had locked away when her marriage ended.

She felt the dormant strength in his body as his arms curved possessively around her waist, while his broad shoulders heaved as he breathed in the scent of her bare flesh welded to his. Her breasts grew heavy, the nipples tightening from the shivers of delight igniting between her thighs and journeying upward. She gasped, giving him the advantage he needed, and his tongue slid sinuously between her parted lips.

His heat, the intoxicating smell of his aftershave, and the protective feel of his arms around her pulled Serena into a cocoon of wanting where she forgot everything but the man whose mouth was doing things to her she had not thought possible.

Her hands went to his head, where her fingers played in the short, silky strands lying close to his scalp. Moaning softly, she shifted, feeling his hardness searching against her thighs through layers of cotton.

"Da—vid," she moaned, his name coming out in a long, lingering sigh of complete satisfaction.

"Mi vida, mi alma," he groaned, answering her. And that she was. She had become his life because she had helped give him back his life. And now that he'd kissed her she had become a part of his soul. A soul he did not and could not afford to lose.

Tightening his grip on her slender body, David reversed their positions, devouring her mouth. He pulled back, giving both a chance to catch their breaths before taking her mouth again in a kiss that made her surrender to his unyielding, relentless assault as her tongue met his.

Serena welcomed his weight, throwing her head back and baring her throat. He rained passionate kisses along the column of her neck, moving down to her breasts. One hand searched under the bodice of her dress and closed over a full, firm breast.

Seconds later, his mouth replaced his hand at the same time she arched off the mattress. His teeth closed gently around a turgid nipple. A low, keening sound escaped from her open mouth. Not recognizing the sound as her own, she froze as a rush of moisture bathed the secret place between her legs. Her eyes widened in shock. No! She couldn't! Not with a stranger!

"No, David!" She tried rising, but couldn't because of his greater weight bearing down on her down. "Let me go."

Through the thick haze of desire making him a prisoner of his own passions, David heard her desperate cry. Raising his head, he stared down at the fear shimmering with the tears in her large, rounded eyes. What had he done to frighten her? All he did was kiss her.

Cradling her face between his palms, he pressed a kiss on the tip of her nose, then released her and rolled off her body. She slapped his hand away when he attempted to adjust the bodice of her dress.

He stared at her lowered head as she smoothed out the wrinkled fabric after she'd pulled the narrow straps up over her shoulders. "Don't expect me to apologize for kissing you." Her head snapped up at the same time her jaw dropped. "I kissed you because I wanted to," he explained softly. Her expression shifted from one of shock to anger. "If you hadn't wanted it, then you should've said so, and not kissed me back."

Serena scrambled off the bed and glared at him, her hands folded on her hips. "You arrogant son of a—"

"You liked it, Serena," he snapped, cutting off her angry tirade. "Otherwise you wouldn't have had your tongue down my throat."

She went completely still as her mind replayed his accusation. *You liked it.* And she *had* liked it. No, she loved it. The feel of David's hands and mouth had taken her beyond herself. And for the few minutes she lay in his arms she'd forgotten every other man who had ever touched her, wondering what it would be like for him to possess her totally.

Tilting her delicate chin, she stared down her nose at him. "You're right, David Claridge Cole, I liked it. I liked you kissing and touching me." It was her turn to watch his expression change from cockiness to bewilderment, and she decided to challenge his arrogance. "And I'm willing to bet that you want more than a kiss or a feel." Hooking her thumbs under the straps of her dress, she took a step closer to the bed. "You want all of me, David?" she crooned. "Do you feel up to burning up the sheets? Do you think you can handle me?"

He watched, mouth gaping, as Serena slipped the straps of her dress off her shoulders and gathered the skirt and pulled it above her knees, baring her slim, muscled thighs. Her lids lowered over her eyes, not permitting him to see their clear gold depths.

"Do you mind me being on top?" she questioned, her voice dropping to a lower register where it sounded like a muted horn in a thick fog. "I like submission in *my men* when I make love."

The blood rushed to David's head, tightening the vise of pain around his temples. He wanted the blood in another part of his body so that he could take the seductive witch up on her challenge, but it was not to be. The heat and pain stabbed him behind his left eye, nearly blinding him.

"I can't," he admitted. He shook his head, then chided himself for doing so as the pain intensified. Easing down on the bed, he lay back and placed a muscled forearm over his forehead. "Please go."

Serena pressed her attack. "I'll go, but I want you to remember something, Sport. Don't ever tell me what I

want or like. I'm quite capable of verbalizing my wants
and my dislikes. If I want you to kiss me or decide I
want you in my bed I'll come out and tell you. Do I
make myself clear, or do you need the Spanish transla-
tion?"

"Lo siento mucho," David apologized, breathing heavily
and wishing she would leave him alone.

"So am I," she countered, turning and walking out
of the room. And she *was* sorry, sorry that she had permitted him to kiss her, sorry that she enjoyed it so
much, and sorry that it reminded her of how sterile
her life had become.

Fourteen

Serena spent the afternoon berating herself for her wanton exhibition in David's bedroom. For a brief, crazed moment she had become a *puta*, displaying her wares and offering herself to a man for his sexual pleasure. What had saved her was that he had not been able to follow through with the blatant seduction.

Walking slowly through the greenhouse, she barely noticed the many plants and trees as she recalled David's gasp when she'd bared her thighs. A smile softened and curved her lush mouth when she remembered telling him that she liked being on top. Just for that brief instant she feared that he would faint. It was only after he lay down that she realized that he was in pain.

But something also nagged at her, telling her that David Cole was not a man who would permit a woman to openly challenge him. If he was anything like her father, she knew he would exact punishment at another time, and by his own methods.

Shrugging a slender shoulder, she continued her tour of the enormous, enclosed, glass structure. She and David had not shared lunch because she told Luz Maria to have one of the women assigned to *La Montaña's* housekeeping staff bring him his lunch. Deciding to forego her own meal, she telephoned Leandro and suggested that he come by after office hours to check on his patient. She wanted him to discharge David so that he could conclude his business matters with her father, then leave Costa Rica. Having him live at *La Montaña* had become too encompassing and distracting.

She stopped at a tree whose bark was covered with a profusion of rare orchids so dark that they appeared black instead of an inky purple. These orchids were only one of Raul Cordero-Vega's many prized hybrids. Raul, a highly educated botanist, had said on occasion that he missed teaching and lecturing. However, he preferred to work for the government, wherein he was responsible for protecting Costa Rica's natural environment for the generations to come after him.

In a corner of the greenhouse was a plot with Luz Maria's herbs. None of them were labeled like her father's, so Serena had no idea what the plants were nor their purposes.

Luz Maria had promised that when she had children she would teach her what commonly grown plants she could use to cure or heal boils, fevers, to counteract the discomfort associated with headaches, menstrual and teething pain, and insect bites, and to slow down the poisonous effects from venomous reptiles or spiders.

Walking the perimeter of the greenhouse, Serena decided it was time for Luz Maria to fulfill her promise now. She had planned to spend three months in Costa Rica, while waiting for an assurance that her brother could be released on bail. She would use the time to her advantage.

She left the greenhouse and spent the remainder of *siesta* in the aviary. Most of the exotic birds were housed in enormous cages, some from floor-to-ceiling, but others were left to fly about with reckless freedom. A brightly colored pygmy parrot lighted on her bare shoulder and pecked at the tiny, gold-hoop earring dangling from her left lobe.

Shooing him away, she watched the antics of the other birds, who had realized a stranger had invaded their habitat. Most fluttered wildly, calling out to one another. The flash of bright color was blinding, ranging from brilliant yellow and vermillion red to seductively deep blues, purple, and black.

La Montaña, the greenhouse, and the connecting aviary represented Raul's material wealth and pride. His wife and his children were his priceless treasures, second only to his love of his country.

David lay across the bed, staring up at the ceiling. A tiny, dark-skinned woman had brought him his lunch on a tray and he had sent her away, along with the food. His seething anger overrode his need to eat.

He had made a fool of himself, and Serena humiliated him. She had offered him her body and he hadn't accepted what she was so willing to give him. And he wanted her more than he had wanted any woman up to that moment.

It was said that when women became sexual aggressors men usually could not perform because of the reversal of roles; he had become an example when her brazen exhibition stunned and frightened him. He'd found himself inept.

Impotent! How could he be at thirty-six? Sitting up and swinging his legs over the side of the bed, he reached for the cane. Making his way slowly across the bedroom, he opened the French doors and limped out to the veranda. The tropical heat was brutal, sucking the breath from his lungs and making breathing a labored exercise. Squinting against the rays of the brilliant sun, he stared out at the stretch of ocean in the distance. His gaze swung around to the tops of the dense trees shading the cool, dark undergrowth of the jungle. Despite the heat he shivered slightly when he thought of what prowled along the jungle floor. Closing his eyes, he imagined the teeming life inhabiting the rain forest. The cries of the birds, the growls of the jaguars, and the screeches of the monkeys became music, notes strung together to form an exotic, rhythmic composition.

For the first time in nine years he heard music in his head. Notes, harmonies, and melodies he wanted to capture before they floated into nothingness. A smile filtered across his face as he opened his eyes. He needed paper. He wanted to write down the hauntingly beautiful sounds reverberating in his mind.

Turning, he limped from the veranda, closed the French doors to keep out the heat, then walked out of his bedroom to Serena's. Her door was slightly ajar, and he heard a man's voice. Listening intently, he realized she had the radio on. He knocked on the door and waited. He knocked again, then pushed it open.

His earlier anxiety quickly vanished. He knew he was not impotent when his body reacted quickly to the sight of Serena coming out of the adjoining bath wearing only a pair of tiny, white-lace, bikini panties.

Serena saw him at the same time he stepped into her bedroom. Startled, she stood still, hands frozen at her sides. Her eyes widened as she watched David staring at her half-naked body. His chest rose and fell heavily in unison with her own trembling breasts.

Somewhere, somehow, she found her voice. "Get out."

Instead of leaving, he turned his back, shutting out the vision of her flawless body. He could still see her perfectly formed, full breasts resting high above her narrow rib cage. The legs he had only glimpsed before were exhibited with slim thighs flowing into strong calves and slender ankles.

"I knocked but didn't get an answer, so I walked in," he said, apologizing.

Serena stared at his broad back as she inched over to a chair and picked up a sleeveless smock dress. He had elected to wear one of the T-shirts she had bought for him.

"What do you want?" she asked, slipping her arms through the sleeves.

"I need paper. Preferably unlined."

"What for?"

"I want to write down some music."

After buttoning the many buttons lining the front of the dress, she walked over to David and stood in front of him. She wanted to scream at him for making her aware of how much she needed him, and for being so damned attractive.

"Before I give you the paper I think we should talk."

Sighing heavily, he nodded. "You're right."

Her gaze moved from his face down to his right hand, which held the cane in a punishing grip. It was apparent that he had shifted most of his weight from his injured foot.

Taking his left hand she led him slowly over to an alcove in the room, where she had set up a sitting area. "Come and sit down."

David eased himself down to a cushioned bamboo rocker, permitting the cane to slide to the sisal area rug covering the terra-cotta floor. The furnishings in the alcove were delightfully attractive. The orange, black, and yellow print on the cushions and matching table-cloth on a small round table and the carved ebony masks and pieces of sculpture on a bamboo bookcase mirrored the blending of African and Caribbean cultures of Puerto Limón.

Serena claimed a chair facing David. She studied his dark eyes watching her every move as she smoothed out the flowing fabric of her dress. Glancing away, she stared out through the French doors.

"I'd like to apologize for my wanton behavior earlier this afternoon," she began. Her gaze swung back to his. "But I won't retract what I said about letting you know what I like or dislike."

David lowered his head, successfully concealing an emerging smile. The forefinger of his left hand traced the rapidly healing scar over his left cheek. "Did you enjoy kissing me as much as I enjoyed kissing you?" His head came up and she was rewarded with the full force of his dimpled smile.

Her lips twitched as she tried holding back her own smile. "You don't quit, do you, David Cole? Are you ever humble?"

Pursing his mouth as if in deep thought, he shook his head. "Nope."

This response made her laugh, and to her surprise so did David. When she recovered she realized it was the first time she had laughed in weeks.

Pressing his head against the back of the chair, David flashed a sexy, lopsided grin. His bruised eye and scarred cheek made him appear less pretty. The scar marred his face just enough to give him a rugged look.

"How does it look?"

"What?" she questioned, not knowing what he was referring to.

"The scar?"

"I find it kind of sexy."

He arched a sweeping eyebrow. "Sexy? I don't think so."

"All you need is an earring in your ear and you can masquerade as a pirate for Halloween."

He leaned forward. "Give me one of your earrings, and we'll see."

Her hand went to her right ear. "They're pierced."

"So is my left ear."

She stared, wordless. She had shaved and bathed him, and not once had she noticed that his ear was pierced. She removed the earring from her right ear and walked over to where he sat. Leaning over, she inserted the small hoop in his ear.

David closed his eyes, savoring her scent and the warmth of her body. "How does it look?" he queried when she stepped back to survey his ear.

Her smile gave him his answer. "Very sexy."

He returned her smile. "Thank you."

Serena took her seat, shaking her head. "Earrings and tattoos. Have they become the latest accoutrements for an international businessman?"

"You forget that I was a musician first, businessman second."

"Which do you like better?"

"Music, of course. However, it seems as if I have a natural bent for business, while I have to work my butt off to get my music just right."

Crossing her sandaled feet at the ankles, Serena realized she wanted to know more about the man who disturbed her in every way. "Why did you leave the band?"

"My older brother Martin resigned as CEO of Cole-Diz to go into politics, and I was next in line so I took over the reins."

"How long ago was this?"

"Nine years."

"Then you were very young."

"Twenty-seven. I was responsible for enterprises in at least a half dozen countries. We own vacation properties in Puerto Rico, St. Thomas, and Aruba, and coffee, sugar, and banana plantations in Belize, Mexico, and Costa Rica. I intend to divest ColeDiz of its only remaining Costa Rican venture."

"What do you plan to do with it?"

"I'll use the proceeds to set up another banana plantation in Belize."

She stared, unblinking, at this disclosure. If he was going to meet with her father, then the sale was not to be a private one. "You intend to sell it to the government?"

He glanced at her from under lowered eyebrows as his expression changed. His mien grew cold, hard, making him look as if he been carved out of dark marble, while his blatant masculine beauty faded behind a mask of angry loathing.

A consortium of businessmen had been willing to make an offer for the property until Raul Cordero-Vega intervened. What Vega wanted was for ColeDiz to sell the plantation to the government for half the consortium's agreed upon price. He then planned to sell the plantation to the consortium, yielding a one hundred per-cent profit for his government's coffers.

"That all depends on your father."

"Why my father?"

"I can't discuss that with you." David did not want to draw Serena into the undeclared war he'd been waging with her stepfather ever since he'd taken over as CEO of ColeDiz International Ltd.

Serena's expression also changed. For the first time she saw David Cole for what he was—a businessman; one who shifted millions, perhaps billions, of dollars from a country or an account as easily as one moved a piece on a chessboard.

She nodded slowly. "I'll respect your decision." Rising to her feet, she said, "I'm going to the kitchen. Would you like me to bring you something?"

"Yes, please. Something to drink."

"Don't run away," she teased, hoping to alleviate the tension that had sprung up between them with the mention of Raul Cordero-Vega's name. .

"I wouldn't even if I could."

The instant the statement was out of his mouth David knew that his feelings for Serena were deepening, intensifying. The taste of her honeyed mouth and viewing her naked body were imprinted on his brain for a lifetime. He stared at her staring back at him, and in a breath of a second both knew what the other was thinking and what the other wanted. She had accused him of being arrogant, and he had no intention of changing her assessment of him.

"You have to know that I *want* you, Serena," he said quietly in Spanish. "And it's not for a quick lay," he continued in English. "And don't think I want you out of gratitude for saving my life."

Serena was certain he could hear her heart pounding in her chest as it resounded loudly in her own ears. All she knew about David Cole was that he was wealthy and he had been a musician. And all she could see was that he was gorgeous and arrogantly charming. What she did not want to acknowledge was that he was the most sensual man she had ever encountered. His delicate dark looks, pierced ear, and tattooed, muscled body stimulated her imagination so much that she was certain that sharing a bed with him was certain to become an unique experience.

"I sleep with you, and what am I left with? Memories of a few days or nights of spilled passions, while you go back to Florida and take up where you left off with your wife or your girlfriend. Thanks, but no thanks."

He smiled, shaking his head. "I have no wife or girlfriend."

"Yeah, right. And I'm a prime candidate for a hair transplant."

David's gaze went to the profusion of hair secured at the top of her head. He managed a tight smile. "I may be many things, but a liar is not one of them."

Serena wanted to accept his offer. She wanted to lock
her door, then lead David to her bed. She wanted to
undress him and undress herself, baring all of her body
for his approval. Never had she wanted to lie with a
man and offer up all that made her a woman. She
wanted and needed to be reminded why she was born
female. And if only the situation were different she
would willingly do it and not have any regrets.

She did not want them to be in Costa Rica, and she
did not want the anguish of her brother's imprisonment
casting a pall over the happiness she was certain she
would find in David's embrace.

Managing a wry smile, she said quietly, "Perhaps in
another time and another place I'd lay with you, but
not now."

"You have to know that your stepfather and I don't
get along, but that's because we're much too much
alike. And like Raul Cordero-Vega, I am also a patient
man. I'll wait for you."

"You may have to wait a long time," she whispered.

"I really don't give a damn how long it'll take, Miss
Morris." He shrugged a broad shoulder. "I have nothing but time."

Turning on her heel, she stalked out of the room,
cursing under her breath. *I don't want him. I don't need
him,* she told herself over and over. If she said it enough,
she was certain to believe it.

She made it to the kitchen in record time. Luz Maria
was nowhere to be seen. Walking over to the refrigerator, she yanked open the massive door. She took out a
gallon container filled with fruit juice and placed it on
the table. Her sandaled feet slapped angrily on the brick
floor as she made her way over to the cabinet housing
the glassware.

"He makes you very angry, no?"

Serena swung around at the sound of Luz Maria's

voice. "What are you doing, spying on me?" she questioned in rapid Spanish.

Luz Maria folded her arms under her breasts and wagged her head. "There's never a need for me to spy on you, *Chica*. When are you going to believe what I tell you? You and the young man are destined to be together."

"I don't love him, Doña Maria. I don't even like him," she protested.

"Not yet," she predicted. "He's nothing like the other one."

Serena knew who she was referring to. Luz Maria never referred to Xavier by name, saying that he was not worthy of his name coming from her mouth.

Sighing audibly, she let her shoulders slump. "There are very few like Xavier. But why David Cole?" she asked, identifying him to Luz Maria for the first time. "He's— he's so sure of himself. I don't like arrogant men," she continued, trying to rationalize why she should keep David at a distance.

"He's sure of himself because he knows and sees what he wants. He wants you, *Chica*, and he's going to have you. Do not fight what is planned by a power greater than we are."

Throwing up both hands, Serena wondered why she was listening to superstition. *Why?* a silent voice answered. *Because you know she's right. She told you about Xavier, but you refused to listen.* Luz Maria had predicted her failed marriage, saying that she'd had a vision that the altar where she was to stand exchanging vows with Xavier was shrouded in darkness.

She'd married Xavier believing they would remain together forever. But it ended in days, and she ceased being Mrs. Xavier Osbourne eight months after she promised to love him until death parted them, with the annulment, and became Serena Morris again.

She retrieved the glasses and filled them with the juice, feeling Luz Maria watching her. "I don't fight it, then what? I live happily ever after?"

The older woman nodded slowly. "He'll make you happier than you can imagine. He will offer you a life filled with things most women only dream about. He will give you your heart's desire."

"Because he comes from a wealthy family?"

"It's not only money, *Chica*. He will give you children, many beautiful children. He will cherish you the way most people worship precious jewels."

Closing her eyes and shaking her head, Serena breathed heavily through her parted lips. "I can't, Doña Maria."

"Why not?"

"Not while Gabriel is—"

"Forget about your brother," Luz Maria said harshly, forcing Serena to open her eyes and glare at her. "Have you listened to anything I've been saying? Your brother is safe!" The two women stared at each other for a long, suffering moment. "He is safe," she continued, this time her voice soft and comforting. "He will be happy, *Chica*. It is time for you to seek your own happiness."

She did not know why, but she believed Luz Maria. She had quickly analyzed every word and believed. But she had to convince herself that she wanted David enough to share her future with him.

Placing the two glasses on a tray, she smiled at Luz Maria and walked out of the kitchen. She intended to try to see David in a whole new light. She would open her heart and mind to the man who had just promised to wait for her.

Fifteen

Serena delivered the glass of fruit juice, a pad of un-lined paper, and a pencil to David. A mysterious smile played about her lush mouth when he thanked her with a smile that made her pulse quicken with its sensuality.

He sipped the juice slowly, watching Serena over the rim of the glass. She reclaimed the chair vacated earlier and picked up a book from the table. Once he'd drained the glass, he gathered the pad and pencil, drawing horizontal lines for treble and bass staffs. Notes appeared on the lines and in spaces in rapid succession as he half-sang and hummed softly under his breath.

The sound of his singing prompted Serena to glance up from her novel. His hand moved rapidly across the pad, drawing more staffs and filling them with notes just as quickly. She was transfixed with his intense concentration. After more than half an hour he put down the pencil and massaged the area over his left eye.

Closing his eyes, David clenched his teeth and prayed that the dull, throbbing pain would disappear so that he could complete the first phase of his music project. When he opened his eyes he found Serena staring at him.

"I think you've overtaxed yourself," she stated, rising fluidly from her chair to settle down on the floor beside him. Peering at the page, she noticed it filled with a profusion of sharps and flats as well as notes. "It looks very complicated." He had written a musical composition that included parts for piano and guitar, horn and drums.

He stared, complete surprise on his face, his pain temporarily forgotten. "You read music?"

"My mother would be very disappointed if I didn't, after eight years of piano lessons."

Leaning over, David cradled her face between his palms. "You're perfect. We're going to make a wonderful couple. Will you collaborate with me?"

She shook her head. "Surely you jest, David. I'm not an accomplished pianist."

"Let me evaluate how accomplished you are. I assume you have a piano at *La Montaña*?"

"Yes. There's one in the living room."

"Help me downstairs."

"Not today."

Releasing her, he reached down and picked up the cane. "Either you help me or I'm on my own."

Pulling away from him, she rose to her feet. "You're impossible. I've never met a man more stubborn, more vain—"

"And more arrogant than you, David Claridge Cole," he intoned, finishing her statement.

"I don't believe you. Now you're finishing my sentences."

Using the cane for support, he stood up. "Help me, Serena, or you'll be responsible if I fall on my face and—"

"No." She maneuvered close to his right side, then without warning snatched the cane from his loose grip. He nearly lost his balance, but managed to right himself. "I said not today."

David glared down at her from his impressive height, seething. He knew he could easily take the cane from her, but decided it would serve no purpose. He was more than aware that he could not navigate the staircase without her help.

Vertical lines appeared between his dark eyes. "You win." *But only today,* he added silently.

He did not protest when she led him back to his bedroom and settled him into bed. "Stay with me," he whispered when she turned to leave. He patted a space beside him. "Lie down with me."

Her eyes widened noticeably with his unexpected request. "Why?"

"I want to talk."

"Is that all?"

"Yes, that's all. Right now I don't want to be alone."

David felt a lump rise in his throat when Serena turned and walked to the door. He'd verbalized his vulnerability. He did not want to be alone because it reminded him of how alone he had been for the past nine years.

Since he left the band he'd felt adrift, flying from one country to another, sleeping in a different bed every month, and adjusting to different cultures and speech patterns within minutes after the company jet touched down on airport tarmacs.

He always returned home to Florida, reconnecting with his sisters and brothers, their husbands, wives, and children, yet feeling estranged from all of them. Both of his sisters were now grandmothers, while his brothers were fathers with four children between them. He was always "Uncle David" to the many grand and great-grandchildren belonging to Samuel and Marguerite Cole.

Whenever there was a family gathering he was looked upon as the "loner" because he had never brought a woman with him. He had not wanted to send double messages to his family and whomever he was seeing at the time. Introducing a woman to the Cole clan was viewed as an announcement of the imminent exchange of marriage vows.

But did he want to marry? *Yes.* Did he want children? *Yes.* He wanted that, and more. He wanted to marry, and get it right the *first* time, because he had taken a solemn oath that when he married it would be *for life*.

He closed his eyes, sighing audibly. What he wanted to do was wipe his mind blank in the same manner one erased a chalkboard. He could not understand why the urge to marry and have children was now so strong that it taunted him whenever he and Serena were together.

He wanted her. And the want had changed, become an aching need. He needed not just a small part of her, but all of the woman. He heard the soft click of the door as it closed, squeezing his eyelids tightly while welcoming the pain radiating along the left side of his face.

He lay, eyes closed, listening to the sound of his own heart beating loudly in his ears. The ache in his face slipped down to his chest, to his heart, and for the first time in his adult life he wanted to shed tears over a woman. And it was the first time that he hadn't gotten what he wanted from a woman.

He detected her fragrance, then the warmth of her body. David's eyes opened. He smiled and held out his hand. Serena stood next to the bed, smiling down at him. She'd removed her dress and sandals and stood clad only in her panties.

"Would you like me to share your bed?" she asked in the low, husky voice he'd come to adore.

"Por favor." His smile matched the brilliant rays of the tropical sun coming in through the French doors as she placed her hand in his. Pulling her gently down to the bed, David shifted until she lay beside him.

Serena rose slightly and draped herself over his chest,

positioning her legs between his outstretched ones. "I told you I like being on top," she whispered in his ear.

He laughed, the sound rumbling deep in his broad chest. "And you also like your men submissive."

"Not too submissive." Angling for a more comfortable position, she rested her head on his shoulder and closed her eyes at the same time his arms tightened around her waist.

There was a comfortable silence, both of them listening to the even, rhythmic sound of their own breathing. Serena's breath caught in her throat when one of David's hands moved down to cradle a hip between his splayed fingers.

"You must think me very brazen to—"

"You're not brazen enough," he countered, interrupting her. "A passive woman is boring—in and out of bed."

"Are you saying that I'm exciting?"

"Just looking at you is exciting, Serena."

Raising her head, she rested her chin on his chest and stared down at him smiling up at her. "Should I take that as a compliment?"

"*Sí, mi alma.*"

"Where did you learn to speak Spanish?"

"My mother taught me."

"With the name Cole?"

"My mother was a Diaz before she married my father. She was born in Cuba, and migrated to the States with her family when in her teens. The Diaz wealth was the result of producing some of the finest cigars to ever come out of Cuba.

"Marguerite Josefina, or M. J., disgraced her very proper family when she became a photographer's model at sixteen. She redeemed herself four years later when she married my father."

"Are you an only child?"

"No." He laughed. "I'm the youngest of five. My mother gave Samuel Claridge Cole two sons and two daughters. My father claims a third son from an illicit affair. It's taken many years, but both my parents have redeemed themselves."

"That's a lot of redemption."

"Fifty years ago having five children was the norm. Having more than three is considered a lot nowadays."

Lowering her chin, Serena pressed her cheek to his shoulder. Why were they talking about children? And why, she thought, was she lying practically naked on this man? Was it because of Luz Maria's prophecy that their destinies were linked?

She knew the answers even before her mind formed the questions. She was in David Cole's bed and in his arms because she had fallen into the sensual trap he had set for her.

It had nothing to do with his looks, his name, or wealth. It was the man. A man whose kisses took her beyond herself, and whose arrogance made her angry enough to lose whatever self-control she had so that she came on to him like a whore offering up her body. She'd shocked him, but he had come back for more. A man who said he wanted her, and had promised to wait for her. But could she afford to take the chance and lose her heart to him? *Sí*, whispered a voice that sounded like Luz Maria's.

Smiling, she rubbed her chin sensuously against his shoulder, the crisp, black hair sprinkled over his chest tickling her nose. She gasped loudly when she felt David's hand slide under the waistband of her lace panties. The heat from his fingers warmed her lower body.

She stiffened once, then relaxed as his fingers traced the outline of her bottom, lingering along the indentation separating the two spheres of firm muscle.

"David!" Serena did not recognize her own voice

when his hand moved to capture the heat from her sex hidden under a mound of tight, moist curls.

The fire raging throughout her body swept to his, and David could not stop the lust and his aching need to claim Serena for his own. Every nerve in his body screamed with the fury of a storm battering everything in its wake as he tightened his hold on her body and reversed their positions.

Staring down into her large eyes, he saw the pinpoints of gold darken with her rising passion. He lowered his head and tentatively tasted her mouth with soft, nibbling kisses, while his hands were busy undoing the waistband of his shorts. He shed the shorts and boxers within seconds, but was forced to pull his mouth away when he reached down to pull the T-shirt over his head.

Serena felt his loss when he pulled back, even though his gaze had not strayed from hers. She refused to acknowledge that she was offering her body to a man she'd known less than a week, or that she was going to sleep with a man under her parents' roof for the first time in her life. All she craved was the man looming above her, who with his possession would sweep away the pain and distrust of her short-lived, failed marriage.

Naked and resplendently aroused, David knelt over Serena. A wolfish, lopsided grin creased his cheeks. Afternoon shadows flooding the room, outlined the perfection of his golden-brown, hard body and glinted off the gold earring hanging from his left lobe.

Holding up her arms, she welcomed him to partake of the feast laid before him. He looped his fingers in the waistband of her panties and pulled them down her hips and legs. His large eyes widened once he gazed upon all of her.

"Me gusta ésta," he whispered, touching one breast. "And I like this one, too," he continued, leaning over and dropping a kiss on the other.

Serena closed her eyes and gave herself over to his slow and tender lovemaking. His mouth charted a path from her mouth to her throat and lower to her aching breasts. Supporting his greater weight on his elbows, he drew one breast into his mouth, biting gently on a swollen nipple.

"You're so beautiful," he whispered over and over, placing moist kisses down the length of her body.

She thought she was going to explode when his hand searched between her thighs and found the distended bud of flesh hidden under the tangled curls. Arching off the bed, she shivered and shuddered violently as his hand closed, holding her tightly.

"David," she moaned when the flame he'd ignited in her threatened to consume her, leaving nothing but minute particles of cinder.

He answered her plea, positioning his sex at her wet, pulsing entrance and pushing gently. His own groan echoed hers as he felt her body opening, stretching to accommodate the length and width of his blood-engorged maleness. It appeared to be minutes, but in actuality it was only seconds before he buried himself up to the root of his manhood.

He fit into her body like a glove a half size too small, and he feared exploding if he attempted to move. Her body was small and tight—inside and out. But he had to move or succumb to the lust and desire merging in a conspiracy to drive him crazy.

Serena alleviated his dilemma when she searched for his mouth and pushed her tongue between his parted lips. Her kiss was nothing like the one they'd shared earlier that morning. Her thrusting tongue unlocked the control he had always maintained when he took a woman to his bed.

Her conditioned body was like the taut skin stretched over a conga, and the rhythms coming from her body were the sounds of primal Africa—wild, unrestrained. He rolled his hips, answering the call of the drums of his ancestors, pounding out a rhythm so ancient that no one knew from whence it had come; their moist bodies writhed in an uncontrollable frenzy. Her body moved in concert with his, arching to meet his powerful thrusts.

Everything faded for Serena—everything except the man lying between her legs and taking her to a place where she soared with the eagles to escape the volcanic eruption spilling lava and incinerating everything in its wake.

Whimpers of ecstasy escaped her when the first ripple of release swept through her. The pressure built steadily as David's hardness swelled until there was no more room for it.

He felt her wet flesh close around him in long, measured, pulsating intervals at the same time that his own passions spiraled beyond his control. "Let it go, Baby," he pleaded hoarsely.

But Serena did not want to let it go. She wanted the fire and passion to last until she burned or drowned in a raging torrent of uncontrollable ecstasy.

"No," she moaned under the unrestrained assault of his powerful thrusting hips.

Holding her head firmly between his hands, David pulled back and drove his swollen flesh into her wet pulsing body, quickening his rhythm until the dam broke for both of them. Burying his face between her scented neck and shoulder, he bellowed his explosive triumph of surrender into the pillow, while Serena sobbed out her shivering delight against his shoulder.

Both lay motionless and breathing heavily, savoring the aftermath of completion. Serena closed her eyes and trailed her fingertips over his damp back.

David's breathing finally slowed and he gathered

enough strength to reverse their positions. Pulling her close to his moist body, he reached down and drew the sheet up over Serena and himself. "Let's take our *siesta* now," he whispered against her ear. "We'll talk later."

Nodding, she pressed her bare hips against his groin and smiled. She did not want to talk, because she couldn't talk. Not when she wanted to relive the smoldering passion she'd found in the arms of the man cradling her to his heart.

She drifted off to sleep, and minutes later David found his own solace in a sated sleep reserved for lovers. What he wanted to say to Serena could wait, but he wondered how long he would have to wait to make her his wife.

Sixteen

David woke hours later to find himself alone. The space where Serena had lain was cold even though the scent of her body lingered on the linen and on his body.

Rolling over on his back, he could barely make out the furnishings in the bedroom. Lengthening shadows from the setting sun shrouded everything in an encroaching darkness, and it was obvious that his *siesta* had exceeded the normal two to three hour limit.

Stretching like a big cat waking from an afternoon of rest, he smiled, recalling the passion Serena had offered him. What surprised him was that he'd offered all that he had, too, holding nothing back. Once he'd entered her he knew he was lost, lost to the ecstasy she aroused by their just sharing the same space.

Serena had come to his bed, soft and purring, and their brief moment of shared ecstasy would remain with him always. He closed his eyes and relived the feel of her smooth skin, the heat radiating from between her silken thighs, and the exact moment when he touched heaven where his heart opened to the love he had saved for the woman he would share his life and future with.

He could not have imagined when he boarded the jet for this last business trip to Costa Rica that he would also negotiate a deal that would include an affair of the heart—his heart.

An audible rumbling from his stomach reminded him that he hadn't eaten anything since early morning, and he knew he had to leave the bed where he had placed his invisible claim on a woman. When he looked at her he saw his unborn children in her eyes.

Serena hummed to herself as she added a half-dozen *culantro* leaves to a large pot filled with soup stock. She radiated a glow that was obvious to all who saw her.

Luz Maria was surprised when she walked into the kitchen and offered to help her cook. Even though she'd noticed the tiny, dark red abrasion at the base of the younger woman's throat she did not say anything. She quickly reminded herself that Serena was the daughter of her employer. Even though she lectured the younger woman on occasion, she knew when not to overstep the invisible boundary set up for employer and employee.

But she did not have to say anything to Serena, because she knew she had taken her advice and opened her heart to Señor Cole.

Serena added a coarsely chopped onion, green pepper, and two sweet chili peppers to the pot. "How long will it have to simmer?"

"About an hour and a half," Luz Maria answered.

"Señorita Vega, Dr. Rivera is here."

Serena and Luz Maria turned at the sound of a man's voice. Rodrigo stood less than five feet away, his dark eyes missing nothing. Neither woman had detected his approach, and both were unsettled by his silent stalking.

Serena recovered first. "Thank you, Rodrigo. Please have Dr. Rivera wait in the *sala.*"

"*Sí,* Señorita."

Luz Maria arched an eyebrow at her employer's driver. She had always considered him a strange man, but something unknown communicated that he was also a dangerous man. What it was she had not been able to discern.

After washing her hands in a large, stainless steel sink Serena dried them, then walked out of the kitchen to the living room. She had forgotten that she'd summoned Leandro. Her reason for calling him had changed quickly since she slept with David. A gentle smile softened her mouth when she thought of their session of passionate lovemaking. That smile was still in place when she entered the living room and saw Leandro rise to his feet.

Extending both hands, she pressed a kiss to his cheek. *"¡Buenas noches! Como está,* Leandro?"

"Consado. I'm more than tired," he admitted. "I'm exhausted. I don't think I had a moment to myself from the time the clinic opened this morning. Too many emergencies, including a woman who delivered on my examining table. It was an easy birth, but I would've preferred handling the procedure in the hospital."

"How was the baby?"

He smiled a tired smile. "Beautiful. A big boy. A very *big* boy."

"Momma and baby doing well?"

"Luckily, yes. Enough about my day. How's our patient doing?"

"He appears to be healing quickly. He has headaches, but that's to be expected after a concussion. What's good is that he's ambulatory." She smiled at Leandro. "I will have Luz Maria bring you some refreshments while I check on Señor Cole."

Serena retreated to the kitchen to instruct Luz Maria to bring Leandro a cup of tea that would ease his stress, then she went upstairs to see David.

Leandro's mention of delivering a baby sounded a warning bell in her head. She had slept with David without benefit of contraception. The realization had come to her only after she woke up in his bed hours after they'd made love. She had mentally calculated when she last had her period, and her apprehension increased. She had picked the most fertile time of her cycle to engage in sexual intercourse.

Perhaps, she'd prayed, just perhaps, fate would be on her side. Even though Luz Maria had predicted that she and David Cole would have children, she did not want them now.

Knocking softly on the closed door to David's bedroom, Serena waited, then knocked again. There was no sound of movement behind the closed door. She turned the knob, eased open the door and walked in. Her gaze went to the bed where they'd made love. The twisted sheets were blatant testimony of their passionate encounter.

She walked across the bedroom and toward the adjoining bath, smiling as she considered how quickly her feelings had changed since sharing her body with David Cole. She was certain she wasn't as sexually experienced as David, and of the few men she had slept with none had aroused her to the level of carnality that he had— not even when she'd thought herself in love with Xavier.

Luz Maria's prediction replayed in her mind: *He will offer you a life filled with things most women only dream about.* And she was right. She'd always wanted a satisfying sexual experience with a man. She wanted to be able to lose herself in the man and in the moment without guilt or shame. She always wanted, from the first time she offered her body to a man, to be able to tell him what pleased her and what did not please her. Even though she hadn't verbalized her desires to David, she was certain now that he was worldly enough to accommodate her sexual entreaties without intimidation.

She found David leaning with his back against the

shower stall for support while he slowly and methodically dried his body with a thick, thirsty bath sheet.

"Do you need a little assistance?"

His head snapped up at the same time a slow, sexy smile displayed the attractive dimples on his lean cheeks. He hadn't heard Serena come into the bathroom. His gaze lingered on her lush mouth as she moved closer. Her hair, pulled off her face, was pinned in a tight chignon on the nape of her neck, allowing him to view her unobscured features. She had exchanged her dress for a pair of jeans and a blue and white striped cotton camp shirt. The denim fabric hugged her compact body, displaying the indentation of her narrow waist and the womanly flare of her rounded hips.

It was as if he were seeing her for the first time. Her exotic beauty was breathtaking, and he loved listening to her smokey voice. Everything about her evoked music. A bluesy Latin-jazz composition with a subtle, English/Spanish voice-over chorus.

He'd tried analyzing what it was about Serena Morris that made him crave her; why did he feel the urge to write music again, and why had he taken her to his bed when he hadn't known her a week? He'd rationalized it was gratitude, but knew that gratitude usually would not elicit the urge to marry.

He had more than ten days before he concluded his stay in Costa Rica, and he planned that Serena would agree to leave with him when he left for the States. They would fly back to West Palm Beach, Florida, where he would enlist the aid of his family to intervene on her brother's behalf and introduce her to his family as his future wife.

Dropping the towel to the floor, he moved over to a stool and sat down; he selected underwear, a T-shirt, and

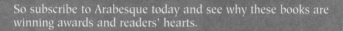

WE HAVE 4 FREE BOOKS FOR YOU!

FREE BOOK CERTIFICATE

Yes! Please send me 4 *Arabesque* Contemporary Romances without cost or obligation, billing me just $1 to help cover postage and handling. I understand that each month, I will be able to preview 4 brand-new *Arabesque* Contemporary Romances FREE for 10 days. Then, if I decide to keep them, I will pay the money-saving preferred subscriber's price of just $16.00 for all 4...that's a savings of almost $4 off the publisher's price with no additional charge for shipping and handling. I may return any shipment within 10 days and owe nothing, and I may cancel this subscription at any time. My 4 FREE books will be mine to keep in any case.

Name _____

Address _____ Apt. _____

City _____ State _____ Zip _____

Telephone ( ) _____

Signature _____ AR0698
(If under 18, parent or guardian must sign.)

Terms and prices subject to change. Orders subject to acceptance by Zebra Home Subscription Service, Inc. .
Zebra Home Subscription Service, Inc. reserves the right to reject or cancel any subscription.

ZEBRA HOME SUBSCRIPTION SERVICE, INC.

120 BRIGHTON ROAD

P.O. BOX 5214

CLIFTON, NEW JERSEY 07015-5214

||..|..|||....||..|.|..|.|..|.|..|||..||..||..||..|||..|

a pair of shorts from the stack of clothes on a table near the stool. "I think I have everything under control."

Serena realized that he was in control. He was now able to wash and dress himself without her help, and she had no doubt that all David had to do was wait for her father to return from San José before he concluded his business dealings in Costa Rica.

She did not know why, but she did not look forward to his leaving even though she knew he was emphatic about dissolving his family's holdings. Maybe, just maybe, she prayed, something would prevent him from leaving as planned. She hadn't had her fill of him—not yet.

"Dr. Rivera is here to examine you."

David gave her a lingering stare; vertical lines appeared between his eyes. "Where is he?"

"Downstairs. Why?

"I don't want to compromise your reputation. There is noticeable proof that I wasn't the only one sleeping in my bed. The smell of your perfume is all over the linen, along with other telltale signs that we did more than take *siesta* together."

"Of course," she whispered, feeling the rising heat flare in her face and chest when she remembered what they'd offered each other only hours before.

She had slipped out of his bed while he slept, retreating to her own bathroom, where she washed away the scent of his body and their lovemaking. She returned and found him still asleep, and loathed waking him to change the bed. She felt no shame about sleeping with him, but she did not want to openly advertise their liaison.

"I'll help you down the staircase," she offered, walking over and picking up his cane.

Curving an arm around his waist, she led him slowly out of the bathroom and into the bedroom. Both glanced at the rumpled bedclothes, then at each other. They shared the kind of secret smile usually reserved for lovers only before continuing out to the hallway.

David pushed off the first step, holding the wrought-iron banister tightly and making certain not to put too much pressure on his right foot as he switched the cane to his left hand. Soon he was able to coordinate his movements so that he was able to navigate the stairs unaided. At least he knew he would not require Serena's help if he wanted to leave the boundaries of his bedroom.

The beauty and splendor of *La Montaña* lay before him as he made his way down the curving staircase to the living room. Thick, pale plaster walls provided the perfect backdrop for terra-cotta floors and heavy mahogany furniture in distinctively Spanish style tables and chairs. His gaze lingered on a massive concert piano and several guitar cases resting along a wall in a far corner of the room. Serena had mentioned that she played piano, and he wondered if she also played the guitar.

Leandro Rivera placed a fragile china cup and saucer on a side table and rose to his feet. A wide grin wiped away all traces of fatigue as he visually examined his patient. David Cole's recovery was remarkable.

Only a slight swelling was noticeable over his left eye, while the angry, purple bruise had faded to a shadowy, yellow-green. The swelling had diminished in his right foot although he leaned heavily on the cane for additional support. He stared at Serena as she settled David on a straight-back chair. His gaze lingered on her until she walked out of the room, leaving the two of them alone.

"Cómo está, Señor Cole?"

"Very well, Dr. Rivera."

Leandro picked up his black bag and walked over to David. A noticeable silence filled the room as he checked David's eyes, respiration, and blood pressure. His forefinger traced the healing scar.

"How's the pain?" he questioned, putting away his stethoscope.

"I'm coping."

Leandro shifted an eyebrow. "I can always prescribe something if it becomes unbearable."

David's gaze lingered on Leandro's features. The slight puffiness under his slanting eyes marred his youthful appearance, indicating he hadn't had much sleep.

"I'd rather not take any painkillers."

"What I'll give you is not addictive if you follow the prescribed dosage."

"I'm not concerned about becoming addicted. I've always made it a practice not to take any drugs."

He'd seen drugs destroy the lives of more musicians than he cared to enumerate. Some began taking pills to help them sleep before progressing on to pills to help them wake up. Then there were the recreational drugs— the ones that took away the anxiety so that the fear of performing before a live audience vanished along with inhibitions. Because of the flagrant use of drugs among musicians, the members of Night Mood had taken an oath that any drug abuse was tantamount to expulsion from the band. Not even a single offense was tolerated.

"It's up to you, Señor Cole. But if you change your mind let me know."

"I'd like you to let me know how much I owe you for your services."

Leandro secured the lock on his bag with a loud snap. "That has been taken care of."

"By whom?"

"El señor Cordero-Vega."

A shadow of annoyance crossed David's face. He did not want to owe Raul Vega. "How much did he pay you?"

"That I cannot tell you. It is privileged information."

David's temper exploded. "Like hell it is! I'm your patient, not *el señor Cordero-Vega*. Give him back his money. I'll pay for my own medical expenses."

Leandro could not understand what had angered the American. Most people would be more than pleased to know that someone had graciously paid their medical bills. Since he'd opened his clinic some of his patients were unable to pay the fees he charged, and had taken to paying them out over several months, while the brash *Americano* openly insulted Minister Cordero-Vega's selfless generosity.

Grasping his bag tightly, he inclined his head. "There is no need for me to come to see you again unless you request it. Good night, Señor Cole."

David sat rigidly, watching Dr. Leandro Rivera's ramrod-straight back as he crossed the living room, opened the door, and stalked out of the house. He was still in the same position when Serena returned.

Glancing around the room, she said, "Where is Dr. Rivera?"

"He left."

"Without saying good-bye?"

"He said good night."

Folding her hands on her hips, she glared at David. "What did you say to him?"

Closing his eyes and resting his head against the back of the chair, he compressed his lips. "Nothing."

"David!"

He opened his eyes and met Serena's angry expression with one of his own. "All I did was ask him for a bill."

She tapped her foot impatiently. "And—"

"And he told me that your father had paid him."

"So? What's the big deal?"

"The big deal is that I want nothing from your father," he hissed between clenched teeth. *"Nada."*

Her mind reeling in confusion, Serena moved over

to the sofa, sat down, and stared at David. There was no mistaking his hostility.

"What's this all about, because it can't be about money."

He shook his head. He could not tell her of the enmity between him and her father. He did not want her to choose between them, because he was certain he would come up the loser.

"You're right. It's not about money. Your father and I have never seen eye-to-eye where it concerns business and . . ." His words trailed off. He would not tell her that they despised each other.

Studying his impassive expression, she recognized a trait in the man she'd just slept with that was so apparent in her father. They were more alike than dissimilar. "You don't see eye-to-eye because you both want control. It's about power, David." She waved a slender hand. "You men and your asinine *machismo*. When will it ever stop?"

"Don't blame me, Serena."

"I'm not blaming you. My father is not exempt. Both of you are stubborn and hardheaded."

He managed a half-smile. "Don't forget patient." She snorted delicately under her breath while cursing him. "Did you say something, my love?

"I'm not your love," she retorted, sticking her tongue out at him. Why was it that she couldn't remain angry with him?

"Are you offering me your tongue again, Darling?" he asked, his drawling cadence verifying that he was a product of the American south.

"You're disgusting."

"I'm honest, Serena." Picking up his cane, he pushed to his feet. Limping over to the sofa, he sat down beside her. Leaning closer, he studied her steady gaze. "I want you. Not just your body, but all of you."

Her eyes widened, while she searched his battered face

for a sign of deceit. "You want more than I can offer you."

His lids lowered over his near-black eyes. "Are you saying that you can't love me?"

"I tried loving once and it didn't work."

"I'm not your ex-husband," David countered.

"That you aren't."

"Should I take that as a compliment?"

"Take it any way you want. I can't give you what I don't have."

They stared at each other, neither speaking, until they realized they were not alone. Serena turned and found Rodrigo staring at her and David as they sat on the sofa with less than a foot between them.

"*Si?*" she asked sharply, finding her voice.

"Your father called while you were taking *siesta*," he said with a knowing grin on his face. He was aware that when her parents called she had slept not in her own bedroom, but in that of the *Americano*. "He and your mother will be flying back tomorrow morning. I will pick them up at the airport at eleven-thirty."

"Thank you, Rodrigo."

"*¡De nada!* Señorita Vega."

Serena waited until Rodrigo left the room before she threw her arms around David's neck. "It worked! It had to, or else they wouldn't be coming back so soon."

Pulling back, he stared at the excitement shining from the depths of her brilliant eyes. "What worked?"

"My brother's coming home."

Her joy overrode her realization that Rodrigo should have given her the message from her parents when he announced Dr. Rivera's arrival. Her happiness was boundless as she permitted David to share the moment as he held her to his heart.

Seventeen

David relished the warmth of Serena's body and her spontaneity. He wanted her again, but needed nourishment first.

"Can you give me the number for the nearest take-out restaurant?" he whispered close to her ear.

Pulling back, she stared up at him. "Luz Maria Hernando's food is better than that of any take-out restaurant in the world." A smile ruffled her mouth. "I take it that you're hungry, Sport?"

"Starved."

"You should be. You sent your lunch back."

"I wasn't hungry."

"It wasn't that at all. You sent it back because you were pouting."

He managed to look insulted. "I don't pout."

"You don't realize you do. When you don't get your way you affect an expression that looks very much like a pout to me."

He gave her a pained expression. "Why are you torturing me, *mi alma?* You know that I'm weak and in pain."

"You weren't so weak during *siesta,*" she teased with a winning smile.

Shrugging his broad shoulders, he waved a hand. "That was different."

Rising to her feet, she crossed her arms under her breasts. "How different?"

He stood up, towering above her. His mood changed and his expression sobered. "That was different because I wanted you so much. And I'll want you even as the breath leaves my body for the last time."

Her pulse quickened, sending a shiver of chills over her flesh. She did not know why, but she felt a wave of fear settle in her chest. David's words echoed Xavier's. Her ex-husband had stated that he loved her so much that he did not want to live without her, and in the end his obsessive behavior was responsible for destroying their marriage.

"Don't want me *that* much, David."

"Don't tell me what to want or feel."

Serena knew he was spoiling for a confrontation, but refused to rise to his bait. The knowledge that her brother was coming home soothed her quick temper.

"Either you can stay here and mouth off, or come and eat."

David clenched his teeth and cursed himself as soon as he did. A wave of pain radiated up the left side of his face. Serena might not share Raul Vega's genes, but she had acquired his quick, biting tongue that stung as sharply as any whip.

"You like your men submissive and I like *mi mujeres* docile."

She arched an eyebrow. "I'm not your woman."

"Yes, you are," he stated confidently. "You just haven't accepted it yet." She spun around on her heel, leaving him to follow.

Everyone was more certain about her future than she was. David wanted all of her, and Luz Maria predicted she would marry him and give him children.

Why was it so difficult for her to accept the inevitable?

Was it because of Xavier? Or was it because she did not want to love and lose again?

David limped into the large kitchen behind Serena, returning the warm smile of a petite woman stirring a large pot.

"Doña Maria, this is Señor David Cole. Señor Cole, Doña Luz Maria Hernando."

David took Luz Maria's right hand and placed a kiss on her knuckle. "My extreme pleasure, Doña Maria."

The older woman blushed furiously as she stared at the tall man's bowed, graying, black head. Her vision had manifested itself. She hadn't seen David Cole's face clearly, but she recognized his smile immediately. It was his dimpled smile she had seen in her vision; a smile his children would inherit, along with Serena's eyes.

"Me gusto conocer por primera vez, Señor Cole," she returned shyly. What she wanted to say was that she'd already met him several times in her dreams—and it was indeed a pleasure to finally get to meet him in the flesh.

"Señor Cole will no longer take his meals in his bedroom," Serena announced, watching the warm interchange between the cook and her father's guest.

"I'm glad you're feeling better," Luz Maria stated, withdrawing her fingers from David's loose grip.

"Much better. Thanks to your tea and soups."

Luz Maria turned her attention to Serena. "Will you be taking your meals in the dining room?"

"No. We'll eat here in the kitchen. Please sit down," she said to David. "I'll join you in a few minutes."

He nodded and sat down, unaware that Luz Maria watched him as his gaze followed Serena as she left the kitchen, disappearing from his line of vision.

"Tea, Señor Cole?"

His head came around slowly and he stared at Luz

Maria as if he had never seen her before. *"Sí,"* he replied absentmindedly

Serena retreated to David's bedroom and stripped the bed of the soiled linen. She quickly and expertly remade the bed, then dimmed the lamp on the bedside table before drawing the silk-lined, pale drapes over the French doors. She repeated the motions in her own bedroom before she returned to the kitchen.

David's gaze never left Serena's face as he spooned portions of *sancocho*—a flavorful Caribbean stew laden with yellow and white *yautía, ñame,* pumpkin, sweet potatoes, green and ripe plantains, beef, and corn—into his mouth. He ate everything except for the small chunks of meat. The sensitivity in his left cheek would not permit him to chew without experiencing some discomfort.

She speared a slice of ripe plantain, wiggled her eyebrows at him, then popped it into her mouth. His gaze moved slowly down to her mouth, visually tracing the outline of her lips. His smile faded when he recalled the texture and taste of her moist, hot mouth. Within the span of a second he relived the sensual encounter that had left him gasping and dizzy with spent passion. And what he wanted to do was relive that passion with Serena over and over again. He watched her form words, not hearing any of what she was saying.

"Are you all right?"

He nodded, blinking rapidly. "I'm sorry. My mind was elsewhere. What did you say?"

"I said that if you don't want dessert we can go into the living room, where you can try out the piano."

Wiping his mouth with a napkin, David stood up. He'd reached for his cane and taken several steps before she attempted to rise. She waited, watching intently as he took several steps, then waited for her to proceed him.

"What other instruments do you play aside from the piano?" Serena asked once they were seated side by side on the piano bench.

"Guitar and percussion." David rested his fingers reverently on the keys as if he feared contaminating them.

"That explains the calluses on your fingers."

"They come from hours of playing the congas."

Seeing his fingers poised over the keys made her aware of the breadth of his large hands. He struck a chord, the sound resonating melodiously throughout the space. It was apparent that her mother had the piano tuned regularly.

She was mesmerized as he went through a series of scales, his fingers skimming over the keys like a waterfall. Her gaze shifted from his fingers to his face. He'd leaned forward, eyes closed as if he were in a trance, and played everything from Joplin to Handel. When she registered the distinctive notes from Gershwin's *Rhapsody In Blue* she joined him in a duet.

David's piano playing was masterful, and it was the first time since she'd sat down to take lessons that she'd actually enjoyed playing the piano. They shared a wide grin as the last note lingered, then faded into a hushed silence.

Curving an arm around his waist, Serena rested her head against his shoulder. "You're incredible."

The fingers of his right hand encircled her neck. "You're pretty good yourself."

"Not half as good as you are."

"That's only because I have longer fingers."

"Don't be modest, David. It's not becoming."

Lowering his head, he brushed his lips against her ear. "When are you going to change your opinion of me?"

"Never," she whispered. "I've gotten used to your arrogance." *And it wasn't his arrogance she liked. She liked the man.*

"How often do you play?" he questioned, his warm breath sweeping over her bare lobe.

"Not often. But I usually play here at *La Montaña* because I like this piano."

David nodded, his fingers caressing the side of the Steinway. "It should be played every day, because it's truly a magnificent instrument."

"Was your transition from musician to businessman difficult?"

"No," he admitted with a smile. "I had majored in music education and minored in business administration."

"Why business?"

Lowering his eyebrows, he glared. "Because my father deemed it. He expected business to be my major, but after a somewhat passionate altercation we decided to compromise."

A knowing smile trembled over her full lips. "I take it you're used to winning?"

He arched a sweeping eyebrow. "I don't know what it is to lose," he admitted quietly.

She shuddered as if a breath of cold wind had swept over her body. At the same time, a warning voice whispered in her head that David Cole could be a formidable adversary, as was Raul Cordero-Vega. She shook off her uneasiness.

"Did you always want to be a musician?" David did not answer her right away, and she thought perhaps he hadn't heard her question.

"Always." Another hushed silence ensued. "There was a time when my parents thought I was hard of hearing because I didn't respond when they spoke to me.

What they didn't know was that instead of hearing people speak I heard music notes, notes in perfect pitch.

"Whenever my older brother and sisters sat down for their lessons I lingered in the room, memorizing every note. A week after my sixth birthday I began my own lessons. Everyone was shocked, including the instructor, when I went through the beginner's book in four weeks."

"Were you a musical prodigy?"

"Oh, no. I was just a possessed pianist who practiced a minimum of three hours each day."

"It paid off, because you play beautifully."

"Will you let me play for you when we return to the States?"

"Where?" she whispered, her husky voice lowering seductively.

"At my home in Boca Raton."

"Will I need a special invitation?"

"Of course not, Serena. My home is yours. You can come to stay—forever, if you so choose."

She slipped off the piano bench and walked over to the floor-to-ceiling windows, her gaze fixed on the all-encompassing darkness punctuated by strategically placed lights illuminating the perimeter of *La Montaña*.

Screams of frustration and fear echoed in her head. Fear that she knew her own destiny, and frustration that Luz Maria's gift had become her curse because she was unable to rally the defenses she needed to stave off David's deliberate seduction.

She found it eerie—no, unnatural—to know that the man sitting at the piano would be the one she would marry even before she was given the chance to fall in love with him.

But could she love him? Could she trust him, or any man, enough to open her heart to love again?

Turning slowly, she met David's gaze as he sat watching, waiting. Her mind told her to resist his pull, but her body refused. If she hadn't lain with him, then she would be able to turn and walk away. Something within her called out to him, and she could not and would not walk away, because she knew he was to be a part of her life. He was her destiny!

David reached down and retrieved the cane resting beside the piano. He managed to find his footing with greater ease than he had since he woke up and found himself at *La Montaña*. What he wanted to do was fling the object across the room and walk unaided. He wanted to sweep Serena up in his arms and climb the staircase to his bedroom for an encore of what they'd shared that afternoon.

He wanted to relive the blinding passion, merging with an uncontrollable lust, that made him fuse his flesh with hers, and his former trepidation about having unprotected sex vanished the moment he filled her body with his seed. In that brief, dizzying moment of lingering lust he wanted Serena Morris as his wife and the mother of his children.

"I'm ready to go back to my room."

Serena nodded, moving quickly to his side. "I thought you would want to try out the guitars before going back upstairs."

"Tomorrow." The single word denoted finality. Tomorrow Raul Cordero-Vega would return to *La Montaña*, and tomorrow would be the time for him to reveal his innermost wishes to Serena.

Tomorrow, she repeated to herself, leading David past the living room staircase, along a narrow passage off the kitchen, and through a door that led to the staircase at the rear of the house.

"My brother and I used to sneak in and out of the house using this route."

Following her lead, David trained his gaze on her back. "Were you ever caught?"

She smiled at him over her shoulder. "Once. I stayed out past my curfew and thought I was going to get over when I managed to slip in the back door that Gabe left unlocked for me. What I didn't count on was my father waiting for me in my room. He'd waited so long that he fell asleep on my bed."

David chuckled, remembering his own youthful escapades. "What happened?"

"I undressed in the dark, and when I got into bed I startled him and he swung at me and bloodied my nose. My screams woke up the entire household. Mother thought he'd deliberately hit me, and she let loose with a stream of colorful expletives closely resembling profanity, shocking everyone. Poppa stared at her as if he'd never seen her before, then walked away without saying a word to defend himself.

"They avoided one another for several days before I went to my mother and confessed what had happened. She told me that I had come to her just in time to stop her from leaving her husband. She showed me the tickets she'd purchased. She was going to return to the States, taking us children with her.

"I begged her not to leave, because I realized at that moment I loved my stepfather too much not to have him in my life."

"How was it resolved?"

"I apologized to him, while my mother grounded me for a month. Gabe was given two weeks for being an accomplice."

"How old were you?"

"Sixteen."

Wincing, David thought of how he'd acted out at sixteen. He'd gotten into situations that his parents claimed had turned their hair white.

He chuckled under his breath. "Did you ever break curfew again?"

She shook her head. "No way. Not after seeing my mother go off like that."

They reached the top of the stairs and stood outside the door to his bedroom. The sound of a clock on the drop-leaf table in the hallway chimed the hour. It was ten o'clock, and she couldn't believe that they'd spent more than ninety minutes playing the piano.

For a reason she could not explain, Serena could not look at David. She felt like a breathless girl of eighteen, away from home for the first time. What she felt was similar to what she'd experienced when she went on her first college date. She hadn't known whether to kiss the young man or unlock her door, then close it quickly, before he could kiss her or ask to come in. In the end she'd closed the door.

And that was what she should've done earlier that afternoon. She should've walked out of David Cole's bedroom and shut the door behind her and stayed out. But she hadn't.

She had consciously denied that she felt anything for David—that he was someone whose life she helped save; it was only after she had permitted him to make love to her that she realized that she did feel something, something deep and so profound that she offered more than her body. She had offered up her heart.

"Good night, David." She turned and walked to her bedroom, feeling the heat of his midnight gaze on her back.

David watched her walk away, wanting to go to her, but didn't. He knew she was uneasy about what had passed between them earlier that afternoon, and he wanted to give her time to sort out her emotions.

Sleeping apart would also give him time to assess his own feelings; he had to admit that Serena Morris claimed a part of David Claridge Cole that he hadn't offered any other woman, for it was the first time he'd ever engaged in unprotected sex. He could've stopped to protect her, but a force beyond himself would not permit him to. A force and a power that shattered his rigid self-control.

He stepped into his bedroom and closed the door. Leaving the cane on the doorknob, he moved over to the bed and sat down. Smothering a groan, he lay across the firm mattress and closed his eyes. He ached from head to foot, but that pain was bearable. He wasn't certain whether he could bear the pain of rejection, though, if Serena decided not to share his future with him.

She helped save my life. She offered me a second chance and I owe her. And because I owe her my life I want to share it with her. His eyes flew open and he stared up at the faint shadows on the ceiling. Owing Serena had nothing to do with falling in love with her. *You love her!* The admission whispered in his head like a song's refrain, and before the sun rose to signal the beginning of another day he believed it.

Eighteen

June 17

Serena woke early the following morning and managed to run two miles before returning to *La Montaña* to begin her day. She walked into her bedroom and found David sitting on the rocker in the sitting area. The scent of his aftershave filled the room, and she noticed that he was already groomed and dressed. Instead of the shorts and T-shirt she'd purchased for him he had selected his own shirt and slacks. The swelling had gone down, and he'd slipped on the leather sandals.

He stood up and suddenly the space seemed dwarfed by his impressive height. "Good morning."

Removing the elastic band from her hair, Serena shook out her damp curls, smiling. "Good morning to you, too. How are you feeling?"

His inky-dark gaze moved slowly over her face and body before a slow smile crinkled the skin around his large eyes. "Wonderful."

Her eyebrows arched. "I see you've managed to wash and dress without help.

He held his arms away from his body. "I've given up the cane."

"You'd better not move too quickly, Sport."

His smile widened. "I'll take it slow for a couple of

days." He closed the distance between them, taking slow, measured steps. He noted her wet tank top and shorts. "Where do you jog?"

"Along the beach."

"How many miles do you do?"

"I was lucky to get in two miles this morning. The heat is too oppressive to try for more."

David stood in front of her, admiring the dewy softness of her moist face. Reaching up, he cradled her face between his hands and lowered his head.

She pulled back. "Don't. I'm wet."

He tightened his gentle grip on her delicate face, inhaling the scent of her perfume under the layer of moisture lathering her body. Ignoring her protest, he moved closer and brushed his lips over hers.

Pulling back, he studied her intently before again flashing his winning smile. "I just wanted to give you a proper good morning."

Her fingers curved around his strong wrists. She unconsciously counted the strong, steady, beating pulse. Lowering her gaze, she smiled up at him through her lashes, causing his breathing to falter slightly. "Thank you."

The seductiveness of the gesture jolted David, igniting the all-consuming passion welling within him. He'd awakened unable to believe the emotions assailing him whenever he thought of Serena. The realization that he'd made to love to her, and the vivid recollection of her response, left him reeling. He thought his mind had conjured her up. He'd recalled the deep, velvety softness of her skin, the scent of her perfume mingling with the aroma of her body's natural fragrance, the weight and feel of her firm breasts in his hands, and the moist heat of her femininity as it closed around him in a strong, gripping pulsing that threatened to propel him from his bed and into hers.

He'd left the bed, flung open the French doors, and stood on the veranda watching the sun rise, waiting for his traitorous body to return to a state of calmness.

And in the full sunlight he became fully cognizant of the changes within himself. He'd laughed aloud when he realized that a little slip of an American born, Costa Rican bred woman had stolen his heart. He'd traveled the world to the adoring screams of thousands of women, and not once had he taken any of them into his bed or into his heart. It had taken a business trip, his last business trip to Costa Rica, for him to fall and fall hard, and for the daughter of his nemesis.

He'd admitted that he was used to winning, and he was. However, he was prepared to lose the Limón banana plantation if negotiations with Cordero-Vega failed. But he was not prepared to lose Serena. He'd taken an solemn oath that he would not return to Florida without her.

Her lashes swept up, her gaze fusing with his as shivers of an awareness passed between them. It had gone beyond the physical urgency to join her body to his. It was now a realization that their future was inexorably entwined, and Serena knew and accepted the reality that the man holding her to his heart would become her husband and the father of her children.

"Why did you leave him?"

The quiet sound of his questioning voice startled her. She flashed a nervous smile. "How do you know he didn't leave me?" she asked, answering his query with one of her own.

His right eyebrow lifted slightly. "Any man who'd leave you is either insane or a fool."

"He became a fool, so I wasn't given much of a choice."

She related the bizarre changes in her ex-husband's behavior only days into their honeymoon and how he had begun stalking her because he suspected she was involved with other men. Without disclosing Xavier Osbourne's name, she revealed the terms of her annulment and the legal restraints that were imposed to keep him away from her.

"He's never attempted to bother you since the annulment?"

Serena shook her head. "He may have loved me, but he loves practicing medicine more. There was no way he would've jeopardized having his medical license revoked or suspended."

What David did not want was a man from her past threatening their future, or a repeat of the scenario that had kept his older brother and sister-in-law apart for ten years.

A shy smile softened his features. "Do you think you can put up with a scarred, vain, arrogant, frustrated musician-turned-businessman for the next fifty years?"

She felt a spurt of heated blood rush through her veins as she took a breath of astonishment. Luz Maria had predicted it, but a small part of her hadn't believed—until now.

"What are you asking, David Cole?"

His hands moved from her face to her waist, pulling her flush against the solid strength of his body. "I think you know what I'm asking, Señorita Serena Morris."

Her gold-flecked, clear brown eyes locked with his jet-black gaze. "No, I don't," she countered, unwilling to make it easy for him.

A scowl marred his beautiful male face. "Yes, you do."

She would not back down. She couldn't with David, because if she did she would always have to defer to his authoritative personality. He was born into wealth, and was no doubt spoiled. He'd admitted that he was used to winning, and there was no question that he considered her one of his many conquests; she was also aware that she could not escape her destiny, that she would marry him, but she did not want him to think he could negotiate and close the deal on their future within four days of their meeting.

"Tell me," she taunted. "You can say everything else that comes to your mind."

The words lodged in his throat. What was he afraid of? That she would laugh at him? That she would reject his offer? That she would think him foolish because he'd confused gratitude for something more?

Swallowing painfully, he forced a dimpled smile. She returned his smile, and in that instant the vain arrogance she'd accused him of claiming returned.

"I want you to marry me."

Serena's smile faded at the same time her lids fluttered wildly. *He'll make you happier than you can imagine. He will offer you a life filled with things most women only dream about. He will give you your heart's desire.*

Luz Maria's words attacked her at the same time she replayed David's proposal over and over in her head. *I want you to marry me.*

"Why me?" she asked, refusing to relent. What frightened her was that Luz Maria's prophesy had manifested itself within days.

"Why not you?"

Her lids flew up and she glared at him. "I asked the question first."

David shook his head in amazement. "Why are you so stubborn?" he whispered.

"I'm no more stubborn than you are," she retorted.

"We are going to have very willful children," he predicted with a wide grin.

He sobered quickly. "Speaking of children," she said, "what happened yesterday cannot happen again. I'll expect you to protect me whenever we sleep together until—"

"Until what?"

What she was beginning to feel for David was nothing like she'd felt for Xavier. And she'd believed she loved her ex-husband. With David it was confidence, safety, and security. She knew that once joined to him she would be protected. She was also realistic enough to know that their living together would be volatile and passionate—in and out of bed.

"Until we're married," she whispered.

He wanted to shout out his joy. She had accepted his proposal. It was a backhanded acceptance, but that did not matter. What mattered was that she was willing to become a part of his life.

His mint-flavored breath fanned her moist face seconds before his mouth covered hers in a kiss that branded her his possession. Parting her lips, she rose on tiptoe to meet his kiss with her own fiery imprint.

"Why me?" she asked again, between his soft, nibbling kisses.

"Why not you," he mumbled, planting tender kisses at the corners of her mouth. "Because you're the other half of me. You're what I need to make me whole. You symbolize what I appreciate most about life—rain, music, and the splendor of the rising sun. Your tears are rain, washing away a fear that leaves a comforting peace. Your body throbs with a rhythm that beats in perfect harmony with mine, and your smile reminds me of the rising sun, so that I look forward to sharing everything I have with you.

"What I feel with you I've never felt with any other woman," he continued in the musical Spanish she'd come to love listening to. "You wanted to know about someone else seeing the tattoo." She nodded numbly. "After I got it I felt exposed because of where it is. I did not want to become that vulnerable to a woman. Any woman."

"But I've seen it."

"That should tell you something about the power you hold over me."

"I don't want power, David. I want trust. Without the trust we have nothing."

He froze, his expression impassive. "What about love?"

She blinked once. "That'll come with time."

Nodding, he released her, taking a step backward. "Thank you for accepting me."

She also inclined her head. "Thank you for asking."

Both had retreated behind a facade of formality, where the shock of what they'd agreed to shook them to their very core.

Serena gave him a half-smile. "Now, if you'll excuse me I'd like to take a shower."

David studied the woman who was to become his wife, committing everything about her to memory before he limped past her and out of her bedroom, closing the door softly behind him.

Serena didn't know she'd been holding her breath until she heard the soft click of the lock. "What have I done?" she whispered to the silent space at the same time tears filled her eyes.

Her brother had been charged with drug trafficking and murder, she'd slept with a man she'd known for three days, her parents were expected home within hours, and it was incumbent upon her to inform them that their houseguest had proposed marriage *and* that she had accepted.

"*Soy loca.*" And she *was* crazy. As crazy as the events going on behind the closed doors at *La Montaña.*

Serena heard the angry sound of her father's voice before stepping into the living room. He was pleading with his wife, who held her head aloft as she climbed the staircase without giving him a backward glance.

"You can't leave me!" Raul shouted to her back.

Juanita stopped, turned and glared down at his angry features. "I'm not leaving you, Raul. I'm going to *my son!*"

"He's also my son."

"What's going on here?" Raul and Juanita froze, their gazes registering the bewilderment on Serena's face. "I thought Gabe was going to be released."

Raul's hands tightened into fists. "He will not be released."

Serena bit down hard on her lower lip. "Why not?" There was no mistaking the tremor in her query.

Raul's angry gaze swept from his daughter to his wife. "Because the U.S. ambassador refuses to get involved."

"That's why I'm leaving," Juanita explained. "My son can't come to me, so I'm going to him." Turning, she continued up the staircase at the same time Raul stalked off to his study.

Serena clapped a hand over her mouth to stifle the screams of frustration threatening to escape. *No, no, no!* She shook her head, refusing to believe what she'd just heard.

Willing her legs to move, she raced up the staircase and to her mother. The door to the enormous bedroom stood open. As she waited in the doorway watching Juanita Vega rip dresses, blouses, skirts, and slacks from the closet racks, she discerned an emotion in the older woman that she'd seen only once—rage. The other time she'd seen her this enraged was when she thought her husband had hit her daughter and bloodied her nose.

"What happened, Mother?"

Juanita gave her a quick glance before she went back to the closet, withdrawing a large Pullman bag. "I'm going to Florida."

"Without Poppa?"

"*Sí!*"

"Why?"

Juanita's hands stilled as she turned and stared at her daughter. "I don't want him with me. I can't accomplish what I need to accomplish with a foreign-born husband in tow."

"What are you talking about, Mother?"

"I'm still an American, while Raul and Gabriel are foreigners in the States. U.S. officials don't look too kindly on foreigners who commit crimes against their country."

"I'm going back with you."

"You can't. I want you to stay with Raul. I don't want him here alone. As it is, he thinks I'm leaving and never coming back."

"But, Mother—"

"Don't Mother me, Serena! Please, Baby Girl, don't add to the madness affecting this family," she added in a softer tone. "Help me keep *nuestra familia* together."

If her mother wanted her to help keep their family together, then why was she leaving her behind? She'd acknowledged Raul Vega as her father, but the reality was that they shared no blood ties. Juanita and Gabriel were her family.

She did not know how, but she felt her mother's pain, pain that had torn her life and her family asunder. "How long will you be gone?"

Juanita placed a small leather case containing her passport on the bed beside her luggage. "As long as it takes for me to get answers to a few questions, questions that the American ambassador to Costa Rica will not or cannot answer."

"Will you call me?"

Walking over to her daughter, Juanita pulled her close. "I'll try to call every day."

Serena kissed her scented cheek. "Thank you for that." She forced an artificial smile. "Do you need help packing?"

"Yes, Baby."

It took the two women less than half an hour to pack and double check everything Juanita Vega needed to return to the land of her birth.

Juanita made her way to the first floor and informed Rodrigo to take her bags out to the car. She had less than two hours to take the commuter plane out of the Limón airport for a flight back to San José, where she would take a connecting one to Miami, Florida.

Serena waited in the car with Juanita for Rodrigo. The two women were silent, wondering whether Raul would come to see his wife off.

The seconds slipped into minutes. Serena exited the spacious Mercedes-Benz sedan when the front door to *La Montaña* opened and only the driver appeared. She did what she had never done before—she silently cursed Raul Cordero-Vega for his stubborn pride.

Rodrigo took his position behind the wheel, started the engine, and drove off without a backward glance. Serena watched as the car made its way down the curving, winding road, disappearing from view, then turned and walked back to the house.

Raul walked into David Cole's bedroom, slamming the door violently behind him. He struggled to control his temper when the American did not move from his lounging position on the bed.

"I see you've recovered very quickly."

David's impassive expression did not change as he

stared out across the room. "I had excellent care," he drawled, his voice a monotone.

As he crossed his arms over his chest Raul's features hardened with a sinister grin. "Lucky for you, Señor Cole, because I need you alive and well. I'd like you to make an international telephone call for me."

David sat up, swinging his bare feet to the floor. "To whom?"

"Your father."

"My father retired from ColeDiz years—"

"This has nothing to do with ColeDiz business," Raul interrupted, his voice escalating with his mounting tension. "This little matter has to do with progeny. A son for a son."

David's forehead furrowed at the cryptic statement. "What the hell are you talking about?"

"I want you to call your father and tell him that if my son is not released from that stinking Florida sewer within the next sixty days he will lose *his* son, body part by body part. I don't care how he does it, but I want my boy out of that hell-hole."

Every nerve within David's body vibrated with a liquid fire that rendered him unable to move, speak. He couldn't believe he was being held hostage for crimes Gabriel Vega had committed more than three thousand miles away from where he stood. A slow smile flitted across his battered face when he realized that Raul Vega was crazy, a madman drunk on his own power.

Resting his hands on his slim hips, he shook his head slowly. "You're sick."

Raul's face darkened with a rush of blood. "And how do you think your father will feel when I amputate your precious fingers and send him one for each day he exceeds my sixty day deadline?" He noted David's expression of horror. "Fingers, toes, ears. I really don't give a damn, Señor Cole. I'm willing to wager your father will bankrupt ColeDiz to buy and sell the politicians who are responsible for putting my son behind bars if it means getting you back in one piece. And despite your obvious shock, I know you're going to agree to my proposal, because if you don't I'll make certain you'll never father children. Yes!" he ranted as his eyes took on a glazed look. "I'll have you castrated before the sun sets on this very day."

The fingers Vega threatened to amputate curled into tight fists. David longed to wrap his hands around the man's throat and squeeze until he pleaded for him to spare his life. And the truth was he would probably spare the lunatic's life, while Vega would take his as easily as he would swat a bug.

Folding his arms over his chest, he stared down at the floor before his head came up slowly. A hint of a smile touched his mouth. "You really have a lot of confidence in my father."

"What I have is confidence in his name and his money. Enough talk. I'll bring you a telephone and you will make the call. I shouldn't have to warn you that what we've discussed in this room stays between us. Or else—"

"Or else you'll geld me? Or better yet, kill me?" David whispered savagely.

Raul leaned in close to his face. "I won't kill you, but when I'm finished with you you'll pray for me to put you out of your misery."

"You would do it? I doubt that, Señor Cordero-Vega. You're too much of a coward, or too smart, to dirty your hands with murder and mutilation."

"That's for me to know and for you to find out. I can reassure you that I'm not a man without scruples. I'm prepared to make your stay bearable. Everything at *La Montaña* is at your disposal. Think of it as your home away from home. The only exception is that you won't be able to leave until I receive confirmation that Gabriel has been released."

"And if he isn't?"

"Then the drama of an eye for an eye and a son for a son will play out until the final curtain."

David thought about his father's failing health. Samuel Cole had suffered a life-threatening stroke four years before, and David was certain he would never survive another if he had to undergo the strain of negotiating for the life of his child.

"I'll make the call. But not to my father."

"If not him, then who?"

"My brother Martin."

Raul's top lip curled under his neatly barbered, gray mustache. "No good. Call your father." Turning, he opened the door, walked out, and returned within minutes with a cordless phone.

David took the instrument, staring at it before dialing the area code for West Palm Beach, Florida. A chill of foreboding numbed him when he heard the break in connection.

"Cole residence," came a familiar female voice.

"Mother, it's David. I have to speak to Dad."

"No 'how are you'?"

"How are you, Mother?" he queried impatiently.

"Well, for an old woman."

"You're not an old woman, and you know it."

"When are you coming home?"

"I don't know. Mother, please put Dad on the phone."

"He's resting."

"Wake him up."

"David—what's wrong?"

"Nothing. I just need to talk to him."

There was a soft sigh before Marguerite Cole spoke again. "I'll get him."

David felt the throbbing pain in his head for the first

time in hours. All he'd shared with Serena faded with her stepfather's threat against his life.

"David," came the wavering male voice in his ear.

"Dad, I want you to listen to me and listen good. I need for you to—"

His conversation with Samuel Claridge Cole lasted less than two minutes. He pressed a button and ended the call, then flung the phone across the room, bouncing it off the solid mahogany door before it fell to the floor.

Rage darkened David's eyes, making them appear even blacker, while Raul gave him a satisfied smile. "Very nice, David," he stated quietly, using his given name for the first time.

"I've done your bidding. Now get the hell out of my sight."

Raul bowed slightly from the waist, picked up the telephone, then straightened and walked away, leaving David shaking with a fury that surpassed the pain threatening to bring him to his knees.

His trembling had not subsided when Serena knocked on the door and walked into the room. "Go away," he ordered, unable to look at her.

A frown creased her smooth forehead. "What's wrong?"

"Nothing. I just need to be alone."

She couldn't believe him. He'd asked her to marry him and now he wanted to be alone. "Not a problem, David. You want to be alone? You've got it!" Spinning on her heel, she walked out of the room.

Sinking down to the mattress, he covered his mouth with his hand to keep from blurting out how much he loved and needed her. He lost track of time as he lay on the bed, trying to sort out his exchange with Vega and the telephone call to his father. Vega's threat did not bother him as much as the croaking sounds that his father made when he told him what he needed to do to save his last born.

Then he did what he hadn't done in years—he prayed. He prayed not for his own life, but for that of Samuel Claridge Cole's.

Nineteen

Serena changed her sandals for a pair of running shoes, stopping long enough to inform her father that she was leaving the house.

"Wait, *Chica.*" He rose from his chair behind the massive desk in his study. A gentle smile softened the harsh lines in his face. "Perhaps we can talk."

Her gaze swept over the tall, slender, stern man whom she had grown to love despite his gruffness. At sixty-two he was more attractive than he'd been at thirty-two. The weight he'd gained filled out his face, softening the sharp angles of his chin and cheekbones. His hair had grayed, along with his clipped mustache, and the overall effect was one of graceful elegance.

"I'm going for a walk, Poppa."

"Would you like company?"

She wanted to say no, but couldn't. What she wanted was to be alone to sort out what had just occurred between her and David. It was apparent something or someone had upset him; what, she didn't know. But she did not intend to become was a scapegoat for his bad moods.

She gave Raul a gentle smile. "Of course."

They left through the rear of the house, waiting for their eyes to adjust to the brilliance of the tropical sun behind the lenses of their sunglasses.

Raul reached for his stepdaughter's hand and held it protectively in his larger one. "Her flight hasn't even left San José, and I already miss her."

Serena registered the fleeting glimpse of weakness in Interior Minister Raul Cordero-Vega for the first time in her life. She'd wanted to think that Gabriel was his Achilles heel, but he wasn't. It was his wife. Juanita Morris-Vega held the power that could destroy the man so many feared with a single word.

"She'll be back, Poppa."

"I keep telling myself over and over that she'll be back, but something won't let me believe it."

"Who are you afraid for? Yourself or Mother?"

Leading her towards the greenhouse, he wagged his head. "Both of us, *Chica*. If they don't let Gabriel go, then Juanita won't come back. She'll stay with him un-til—"

"Don't say it, Poppa. Don't bury him."

Dropping her hand, he curved his arm around her shoulders, pulling her close to his side. "You're right."

They wandered through the greenhouse, stopping to examine and inhale the sweetness of the many flowering plants. Serena picked a variety of white and pale pink blooms for the bedrooms and the dinner table, filling a large wicker basket from the dozen or more stacked on a shelf. Before she'd left Costa Rica to attend college, she'd assumed the responsibility of selecting flowers for the house.

It was when they entered the aviary that she decided to bring up the fact that David still resided at *La Montaña*. "When will you conclude your business with David Cole?" she asked quietly.

Raul stopped suddenly, his eyes narrowing suspiciously as he stared at her. "Why? What has he told you?"

She shrugged a slender shoulder and shifted the basket filled with flowers from one hand to the other. "He mentioned that he'd planned to stay two weeks. But with his injuries I just wondered whether you've changed your schedule."

"Nothing has changed. We will discuss the sale of his banana plantation as planned."

What he did not reveal was the price he'd set for David Cole's freedom. A sixth sense also warned him that his daughter's interest in his houseguest was more than that of a nurse for a patient.

"I trust you and *David* are getting along?"

Nodding, she smiled. "Well enough. I find him a little arrogant, but then so are you, Poppa." Much to her surprise Raul threw back his head and laughed. "Well, it's true," she confirmed.

He sobered, his eyebrows lowering. "A successful man must possess a bit of arrogance, while David Cole has amassed a monopoly on it. I much preferred conducting business with his older brother. Martin Cole was quiet, but lethal, whereas David is loud like a clanging bell."

"He is as lethal?"

Raul hesitated, trying to come up an fitting metaphor for the Cole brothers. "Yes. Martin was like a shark, circling beneath the surface before he struck, while David is a rattlesnake. He sounds a warning, then strikes while he's still rattling."

"Wouldn't you prefer to be warned?"

"Not from someone so young and disrespectful. He wasn't quite thirty when he came to see me for the first time. I rearranged important meetings to accommodate him, and when I would not agree to his demand that I rescind the additional tariff on his banana crop, he walked out of the meeting. It had taken me three weeks to bring all of my ministers together, and we sat like stunned jackasses staring at one another. I swore

from that day that David Cole would pay for his imper-
tinence."

A flicker of apprehension coursed through Serena.
"Pay how, Poppa?"

"I don't know, *Chica*. But his time is coming."

How could she tell her stepfather that she'd slept with
his most combative challenger and planned to marry
him? That she would eventually make him a grandfather and that his grandchildren would carry the blood
of his archenemy?

She stared at Raul, unable to disclose the secret she
held close to her heart. She knew the time would come
when she would be forced to choose between the two
men in her life, and because she knew her destiny the
man whom she called Poppa would be the loser in the
undeclared war. She jumped when the sound of thunder shook the earth.

"I'm going back to the house to put the flowers in
water."

Leaning over, Raul kissed her cheek. "I'm going to
stay here for a while to wait out the storm and talk to
my feathered friends."

Serena stared at Raul as he turned to a cage of toucans, and for a brief second she felt like sobbing. Life
had thrown Raul Cordero-Vega a cruel curve. He'd temporarily lost his wife and son, leaving him to grieve in
silence.

David stood on the veranda, watching Serena and
Raul. He noted the tenderness in the older man's touch
when he wound an arm around his stepdaughter's
shoulders, wondering how one man filled with so much
venom could be that gentle. Was it possible that Raul
Cordero-Vega was schizophrenic?

Seeing Serena lean against her father while smiling

up at him reminded David of his own response to her hypnotic feminine sensuality. They'd argued more than they'd made love, but the one passionate encounter had obliterated all of the acrimony that preceded it. And instead of holding her to his heart he'd sent her away. Her father's unexpected threat swept away the promise of his taking her for his wife, since his existence was now dependent upon her brother's freedom.

He stood motionless, watching the dark clouds roll across the sky, obscuring the brilliance of the tropical sun. He listened for the first rumble of thunder, followed by the distant rustling and screams of jungle wildlife scurrying for shelter.

Closing his eyes, he registered the same ancient rhythms in his head and in his veins that he'd experienced when he entered Serena's body. Why did he connect a tropical thunderstorm, jungle sounds, the pounding rhythms of ancient Africa with making love to her?

What was there about her that reached deep inside of him to make him want her? Just being who she was unlocked his heart and his soul to make him fall in love with a woman for the very first time in his life.

A large drop fell, landing on the tip of his nose. Then another. The heavens opened up, the rain pouring down on his head and soaking his clothes. It cooled his warm flesh and washed away the madness turning his life upside down.

Closing his eyes and raising his arms, he gloried in the wrath of nature's untamed fury for the span of time it took the rains to sweep over *La Montaña*. It washed away the stench of evil pervading the enormous structure erected on the mountain overlooking the sea and jungle, and it also cleansed him.

His lips mouthed the words that the wind tore from his silent tongue: *Forgive me. Father, for I have sinned."*

* * *

Serena walked into her bedroom, her bare feet making no sound on the cool, wood floor. She'd returned to the house before the storm broke, filling the vases in the dining room and bedrooms with the freshly-cut flowers. After settling a vase on the table in the sitting area, she opened the French doors. The refreshing scent of rain-washed earth filtered through the space. The soil soaked up the moisture like a thirsty sponge, unwilling to give back a drop. Waiting until the downpour subsided, she stepped out onto the veranda, turning her face skyward. The moisture cooled her face and seeped into the light fabric of her sleeveless dress. Her eyes opened, and at the same time she shifted to her left. Then she saw him.

The sight of him on the veranda, arms raised, sucked the breath from her lungs as she inhaled audibly. The vision of his finely woven, white shirt pasted against his chest was more sensual than if he'd stood completely naked. The rich, deep brown of his wet flesh showing through the fabric elicited a familiar throbbing in the lower portion of her body.

David felt, rather than saw, Serena even before he opened his eyes. An invisible force propelled him from where he stood until he was next to her, a secret smile curving his mobile mouth as he registered her delicate beauty. She did not move when he reached out for her. Burying his face in the hair swept atop her head, he pressed his mouth to the fragrant curls.

"Forgive me, *Mi amor.* I didn't want to send you away."

Serena fused herself to him, becoming one with him. She wanted to refuse him, reject him, but she couldn't. Her life was entwined with a stranger she'd lain with after three days of their meeting. A stranger whom it was prophesied she would marry. A stranger who would fill her womb with his seed. A sensual, passionate stranger she was falling in love with.

Her trembling fingers feathered over his mouth. "Shh-hhh, David. There's nothing to forgive."

"Yes, there is," he insisted. "I sent you away when all I wanted was to hold you to my heart. Everything was perfect until—" His words trailed off.

"Until what?" Her voice was muffled against the solid heat of his chest.

He couldn't tell her what had transpired between him and her father. She would never believe him. And he did not trust Raul's mental state not to go through with his proposed threats to mutilate him.

"Until I called my father," he began, deciding to tell her half the truth. "He's not doing well."

Pulling back, Serena stared up at his wet face. "What happened?"

"He suffered a stroke four years ago that left him with limited use of his right side and some speech impairment. Extensive therapy restored his speech so that you can understand him, but when I spoke to him this morning his words weren't clear. They came out garbled."

He wanted to say it was because of what he was forced to tell him. That if Samuel Cole didn't use his money and influence to have her brother released from prison he would lose his own son.

Compassion softened her delicate face. "I'm sorry, David. When are you planning to leave?"

His sweeping eyebrows lifted. "Leave?"

She blinked in bewilderment. "Yes. Aren't you going back to Florida to be with him?"

I can't, because your father has made me a prisoner, he replied silently. "No. My family will take care of him. I'll stay and finish what I have to do here." His head came down slowly, and he wasn't disappointed when her lips met his. He drank deeply from her soft, hon-eyed mouth, and when he pulled back both were breathing heavily. A wild, untamed fire burned in his coal-black eyes, searing her face. "When I leave here, you're coming with me."

Serena felt a surge of elation, followed by a shock of despair. "I can't leave, David."

"Why not?" The two words sounded like a crack of a whip.

"My mother just left for Florida. I promised her that I'd stay with Poppa."

What he wanted to shout at her was that her *Poppa* had threatened his life. That her Poppa had made her an unwilling prisoner so that she had to wait for her mother's return before she could go back to the States.

His lean jaw hardened. "I'll wait for you," he said instead.

Her gaze swept furtively over his face. "It may take a while."

"I have time." What he had was a sixty-day reprieve so that Gabriel Vega could be released from prison. He refused to think beyond the sixty days. Cradling her face between his hands, he brushed his mouth over hers. "Lock your door, but leave your window unlocked. I'll come to you tonight," he whispered.

Serena nodded, pulled out of his embrace, and reentered her bedroom. She glanced briefly at the flowers on the table, a secret smile touching her face. Everything was going to be all right. The voice in her head confirmed that fact.

Twenty

West Palm Beach. Florida

Martin Cole leaned in closer to hear what his father was saying, his deeply tanned, golden brown face darkening with the rush of blood from the twin emotions of rage and fear. Samuel Cole's garbled telephone message, *David's in trouble,* had sent him racing up from Fort Lauderdale to West Palm Beach, exceeding the state's speed limit by more than twenty miles.

He stared at his father's deeply lined forehead. "Does my mother know about this?"

Samuel raised a partially withered right hand, waving it slowly. "No. I can't tell her," he replied slowly. "I don't want any of the women to know."

Martin nodded, wondering how his mother and sisters would react to the news that David Cole was being held hostage in Costa Rica by a madman. His midnight gaze shifted to the vaulted ceiling of the loggia of his childhood West Palm Beach home. Closing his eyes, he recalled the madness sweeping through the Cole family nine years before. There had been another kidnapping—that of his own daughter.

Ten-year-old Regina Cole had been kidnapped from her grandparents' home by a man who needed the money to pay off his gambling debts. Regina was res-

cued, unharmed, but not without the lingering effects
of a fear of close, dark spaces. For six long, anxious
days the child had been locked in a closet. Her captors
let her out only to eat and to relieve herself.

What had pained Martin most was that his own father
had been indirectly responsible for his daughter's captivity. He'd contracted with a hit man to kill Martin's
wife. When his many attempts were thwarted the hit
man decided to take the child. What the kidnapper
wanted was an exchange: the mother for the daughter.

It had taken years before Martin's heart softened
enough to forgive Samuel Cole for his loathsome behavior. An adulterous affair with a young woman more
than forty years before had left the elder Cole with
enough guilt to swallow him whole, and he'd confused
Martin's wife with the woman he'd seduced.

The affair resulted in a son, a son Samuel refused to
accept or acknowledge; a son who hated his father as
much as his father hated him; a son who finally forgave
his father, but only when the older man begged forgiveness as he lay dangerously ill.

It had taken the Cole family forty years to reconcile;
forty years to sweep away the remnants of their dirty
family secrets, only to be faced with another crisis now.
However, this crisis did not start from within. It was from
an outsider with a vendetta.

Martin combed his fingers through his steely-gray,
curly hair before his gaze shifted to his father's face.
The stroke had aged Samuel, making him appear much
older than seventy-seven. It had taken the healthy color
from his sienna-brown face, the shine from his once-
thick white hair, and most of all his vibrant spirit. The
bluster that had made Samuel Claridge Cole one of the
most feared African-American businessmen was gone.
His quick mind, his business acumen, and his uncanny
instinct for turning a profit in a failing enterprise had

also vanished. He appeared to be a broken man who lived each day to interact with his children, grand-children, and now great-grandchildren.

However, age was more than kind to Martin Diaz Cole. At forty-nine he was a man in his prime. His tall, large body bore no evidence of softening. Laps in a pool, twice daily, helped him retain the muscle he'd acquired in his mid-twenties. He'd married at thirty-nine, fathered three children, and spent his time man-aging his own investments with his half-brother.

Lacing his fingers together, he smiled at his father. "I'll take over, Dad. I'll call the governor's office and Senators Epstein and Velasquez."

Samuel nodded slowly. "You do that. But there's someone else I want involved."

"Who?"

"Joshua."

A slight frown creased Martin's forehead. "He's re-tired, Dad. He no longer has security clearance. You can't ask him to leave his family and go back into intel-ligence again."

Sighing heavily and pressing his head back against the chaise cushion, Samuel closed his eyes. "I'm not asking him to come out of retirement. I just want him to help his brother."

Martin stared at his father, seeing a glimpse of what had made him who he'd been. He recognized the de-termination of a half-dozen men, and he recognized that Samuel would do anything to protect his family, including going outside of the law.

"I'll call him." Rising to his feet, he leaned over and kissed his father's withered right cheek.

Martin returned to his car without stopping to see his mother. He could not see or talk to Marguerite Cole without lying to her. He'd never lied to her, and he did not want to begin now, not with her youngest child's life at risk.

He picked up a cellular phone and dialed his half-brother's residence in Santa Fe, New Mexico. Drumming his fingers against the steering wheel, he counted off the rings and the seconds.

"Hello," came a deep male voice.

"Josh." There was obvious relief in Martin's voice.

"What's up, Buddy?"

"Can you talk?"

There was a noticeable pause. "What's going on?"

"Can you talk?" Martin repeated.

"Yes. Vanessa and Emily went out about an hour ago. Why?"

"Raul Cordero-Vega is holding David hostage. He won't let him go until Gabriel Vega is released from prison. His kid is charged with murder and drug trafficking, so we both know there's no way he's getting out."

A long, violent stream of profanity burned the wires as Martin listened to his brother's virulent tirade. "I should've eliminated Vega before I retired. The army traced that cache of weapons stolen from Fort Sam Houston to Vega, but they could never prove it."

"Are you going back in?"

"No. Vanessa threatened to leave me if I came out of retirement." There was another pause. "We can't afford to wait sixty days with this lunatic."

"What do you suggest?"

"Give me time to put something together. I believe it's time Vega and I meet. I'll go as a businessman, even though I'm not certain what I'm going to be selling."

Martin's features softened with his trademark dimpled smile. "Thanks, Josh."

"Remember, Buddy, he's my brother, too."

"I'm going back to Fort Lauderdale. Call me there."

"Do M.J. or the girls know about this?"

"No. Sammy says they don't need to know."

"He's right. I'll be in touch."

Martin heard the dial tone when Joshua ended the connection. He turned on the ignition in his car, his mind filled with details of what lay ahead for the Cole family, and as he left the local road for the highway south he prayed they would be able to rescue David before sixty days elapsed.

Twenty-one

Puerto Limón, Costa Rica

David stared at the space where Serena had been. A muscle flicked angrily at his jaw, eliciting a dull throbbing along the left side of his face. He welcomed the pain, as it aroused anger rather than compliance. There was no way he was going to remain at *La Montaña* for sixty days to await his fate, like a calf fattened for slaughter.

He returned to his bedroom, opened the closet, and retrieved his empty garment bag. Running his fingers along a hidden seam, he found the invisible opening and withdrew his passport and a slim billfold filled with credit cards and Costa Rican currency in large denominations. Letting out his breath, he sighed in relief. At least he could leave the country without being detained at customs. He returned the passport and the billfold to their hidden compartment and closed the closet door.

Running a hand over his close-cut hair, he made his way over to the armchair, sat down, and elevated his right foot. Most of the swelling in his toes and instep was gone, leaving only a noticeable puffiness and discoloration around the ankle. It would take a while before he would be able to put full pressure on the foot.

He'd managed to walk unaided, but with an obvious limp, and he knew he was going nowhere without being in peak physical condition.

He thought of the U.S. ambassador's reluctance to intervene in the release of Gabriel Vega. David doubted whether he would be as reluctant to become involved for an American citizen. He had to solicit Raul's aid to contact the ambassador again, this time persuading the man to come to Puerto Limón. It would be ironic if his last trip to Costa Rica would be for the purpose of negotiating on Raul Cordero-Vega's behalf rather than for ColeDiz International Ltd. Both of them would emerge winners. Vega would get his son back and rid himself of the Coles, while David would divest ColeDiz of its remaining Costa Rican enterprise *and* claim a woman and a love that promised forever.

He also mentally catalogued what he would need if he planned to leave *La Montaña* without notifying his host of his departure, refusing to acknowledge his fate if legal arbitration failed.

Serena lay on her bed, recognizing an emotion she hadn't felt in twelve years—a restless waiting.

Then she had been waiting to return to the country of her birth. She had applied to several universities in the States with nursing programs, and within weeks of mailing off the applications she checked the mail daily. It took months before the first response came, and then the others followed in rapid succession. Every school she had applied to had accepted her. Her joy was short-lived when she had to select which school and where. In the end she'd decided on New York. It was close enough for her to see two sets of grandparents in Ohio during holidays and school recesses.

Peering up at the mosquito netting draped over the

four-poster bed, she recalled the joyous occasion when she graduated from nursing school at the top of her class. Her grandparents flew in for the celebration, along with her parents and brother. Gabe fell in love with the land of his mother's and sister's birth, and confided to Serena that he also wanted to attend college in the United States.

Her smile faded when she thought of how her brother's life had been turned upside down. She did not and could not believe Gabe was involved in drugs or murder. Her very straightlaced brother did not smoke, drink, or swear, and she, too, wondered on occasion why he'd taken up with Guillermo Barranda.

The younger Barranda's reputation of throwing wild parties at his off-campus residence with unlimited supplies of women and liquor was well documented in the Dade County vicinity. Serena had questioned her brother about his intense social activities when she met him in Florida during a three day holiday weekend. Gabriel confessed that he had fallen in love with a girl who was the sister of a close associate of Barranda. She'd smiled and warned her brother to think with his head and not his heart. Gabe flashed his sensual smile and ducked his head, nodding.

But what was she doing now, if not thinking with her heart and not her head, when it came to David Cole? She had compromised her professional ethics by sleeping with him, because he *was* her patient. Even if David hadn't been her patient, she'd never slept with a man she'd known only three days. Perhaps if Luz Maria hadn't predicted she would marry David, then she would have resisted him.

No, the silent voice crooned in her head. There was no doubt that she'd been attracted to David Cole from the moment she glanced at him; and she could not deny the powerful, invisible force that drew her to him whenever they occupied the same space. Within days the force had pulled her into him, so that she did not know where he began and she ended. In or out of bed, they had become one.

The soft chiming of the telephone interrupted her musings. Reaching over, she picked up the receiver. *"Hola."*

"Hola, Amiga."

"Evelyn!" Serena screamed. "How did you know I was back?"

"I had to hear it secondhand, Miss Morris. And you know I hate secondhand news."

Serena's large eyes sparkled with excitement. "Are you calling from San José?"

"I'm here in Limón at my mother's."

"Give me time to change my clothes and I'll—"

"Stay where you are, *Amiga.* I'm coming to *La Montaña.* I have something to show you. *Adiós.*"

Serena heard the sound of the dial tone as her high school friend hung up abruptly. Replacing the receiver on its cradle, she propelled herself off the bed. She met Evelyn Perez when they both were ten, and they had become fast friends. As they approached adolescence they made up stories about finding the perfect man, marrying him, and settling down to have a beautiful home filled with lots of babies.

Evelyn had married her high school sweetheart a month following their graduation, but hadn't had any children.

She combed her hair, securing the curly strands in a single plait, slipped into a sarong style cotton skirt in a vibrant, sun-gold and black print and a gold tank top. The color emphasized the rich, warm, brown undertones of her flawless complexion.

The black ballet slippers on her feet muffled the sound of her footsteps as she descended the staircase just as the front doorbell chimed melodiously. "I'll get it, Isabel," Serena said to the petite, dark-skinned, silent woman who came to *La Montaña* three times a week to clean and maintain the routines Juanita had set up for the smooth management of her household.

Her delicate jaw dropped when she opened the door and stared at a grinning Evelyn holding a tiny infant in her arms. "You did it!"

Evelyn Perez-Comacho handed Serena her daughter. "Meet Señorita Serena Lupe Consuela Comacho."

Serena's eyes filled with tears, and she blinked them back before they could fall on the sleeping baby girl. "You kept your promise to name your daughter after me."

"I always keep my promises, *Amiga.*"

Cradling the child to her breast, Serena stepped aside. "Come in out of the heat."

Evelyn moved past her childhood friend and into the cool magnificence of *La Montaña*. She had always admired the house, even as it was being erected, not realizing she would spend many nights under its roof once she formed a close friendship with Serena Morris.

"Everything about *La Montaña* is still beautiful," Evelyn stated, her dark gaze sweeping around the enormous space before pausing to linger on the curving staircase.

Serena nodded in stunned silence. The warmth and slight weight of the child she cradled to her breast garnered all of her attention.

"How old is she?"

"Three months."

Serena glanced briefly at her friend before returning her attention to the baby. "Why didn't you call me to let me know that you were pregnant?"

"It was touch and go at first. I spent the first four

months of my pregnancy in bed, because of spotting. As it was, she was six weeks early."

"Come and sit down. We have so much to talk about." She led Evelyn to the area off the living room and both women sat on the love seat. Evelyn placed a large, quilted bag down on a side table.

Serena stared at the sleeping child in her arms, marveling at how much the tiny girl resembled her father. An undertone of deep rose pink shone through the delicate, pale skin covering her dewy, soft face. She removed the tiny, white cotton eyelet hat, smiling at the tufts of black curling hair covering the small, round head.

"She's just like Francisco. You'd think I had nothing to do with helping to create this baby," Evelyn said solemnly.

"She's beautiful, Evelyn." Raising her head, she stared at her friend. Evelyn was beautiful. Tall and slender, she claimed a dark brown coloring that she'd inherited from her Jamaican ancestors, while her thick, jet-black hair was styled to flatter her attractive features. Large dark eyes framed by thick lashes and a full, lush mouth arrested one's attention immediately.

"She's my life. I wanted to conceive for so long that I had just resigned myself that I would never be a mother."

"How is Francisco taking to fatherhood?"

Evelyn's smile was dazzling. "He's a little *loco* about her."

Serena shifted a delicate eyebrow. "Only a little?"

"Okay, a lot crazy. Right now he's in Panama City for the next six weeks with a group of archaeologists who are convening to discuss the artifacts uncovered during a dig along the border with Panama."

"How is he dealing with the separation?"

"Not well. He calls me every night."

Serena smiled. It appeared as if her friends were still very much in love. "Now, tell me. How did you know that I was back?"

"My cousin saw you at the *Mercado Municipal*. When did you get back?"

"Last Wednesday."

Evelyn glanced down at the highly polished parquet floor. "I heard about your brother." Her gaze swept back to meet Serena's. "I know he's innocent."

She nodded, biting down on her lower lip before she forced a smile. "Thanks for the vote of confidence. Let's hope and pray that a Florida jury will find him innocent."

"Anyone who's met Gabriel knows that he's the kindest—"

"It's all right, Evelyn. You don't have to say it." Her expression brightened. "I've been rude. Let me get you something to eat and drink." Leaning over, she handed the sleeping baby back to her mother.

"Is there some place I can lay her? I don't want to get into the habit of holding her while she sleeps. It doesn't take much to spoil her."

Serena rose to her feet and took the quilted bag. "Sure. Bring her upstairs to my bedroom."

The two women took the staircase to the second story bedroom, walking the length of a hallway they'd traversed many times in the past. Evelyn spread a lightweight cotton blanket over the crocheted coverlet on Serena's bed, then gently placed her daughter on the blanket. Placing pillows strategically around the baby to prevent her from rolling off onto the floor, they walked out of the room.

David sat on the armchair, drawing and then erasing pencilled notes as he worked feverishly on a composition for a guitar solo. He wanted to put all of the notes down before he went downstairs to play what he'd composed.

He could discern the distinctive sound of an acoustical guitar playing a classical Spanish flamenco rhythm with a pair of castanets as an accompaniment. He wanted another instrument, but he hadn't decided on which one.

What he needed was a deep, moanful sound—bass violin, organ? *"Cello,"* he whispered. He would use the cello, utilizing half the tempo of the guitar. The cello would represent the low murmur of the wind, the guitar the rustle of leaves before the storm broke, and the castanets the wild, unrestrained tapping of rain against the windows. He wanted to capture in his music the sounds of the exotic, sun-drenched world of the rain forest. And he also wanted to incorporate the peace and tranquility he'd discovered in Serena's arms.

He heard a mournful cry, recognizing it as that of a howler monkey. When he'd first heard the eerie sound he thought it was that of a baby crying.

Forcing his thoughts back to the pad on his lap, he hummed the notes resting on, above, and below the staff of music. The crying began again, this time louder than the first time. He listened intently, sure now the crying came from a human baby. But, he wondered, where was there a baby at *La Montaña?*

He put aside the pad and pencil, rose to his feet, and made his way across the bedroom. The crying grew louder as he neared the door. Moving down the hallway, he stood outside Serena's bedroom. On her bed amid a barricade of pillows lay a tiny baby whose arms and legs flailed wildly. Its face had darkened with a rush of frantic screaming.

"Whoa, Fella," he crooned, limping into the bedroom. "What can be so bad that you have to scream like this?"

He reached down and picked up the fretful infant, cradling it to his chest. The soft, clean smell associated with babies wrang a smile from him. The baby snuggled closer to his warmth and stopped crying. A pair of tiny, round, dark eyes stared up at his larger, darker pair.

"You look as if you've had a lot of experience with babies," said a familiar female voice behind him.

Turning slowly, David smiled at Serena and a woman, he assumed was the child's mother. "I have," he admitted, his gaze fused with Serena's. "I'm uncle to a hoard of nieces and nephews. He was crying, so I picked him up," he explained quickly.

"Ella," the women chorused in unison. "She."

David arched his sweeping eyebrows and flashed a sheepish, dimpled grin. "I can't tell one from the other when they're fully clothed," he explained, switching to English.

"You're welcome to change her," Evelyn suggested in Caribbean-accented English.

"No, thank you," he replied, handing the child to its mother.

Serena saw the spark of interest in Evelyn's gaze as her dark eyes swept in a leisurely way over the tall figure of the man who had just comforted her daughter. He'd changed his rain-soaked, cream-colored shirt and slacks for a pair in black linen. The overall effect was powerful, given his dark coloring.

"David Cole, Evelyn Comacho."

Evelyn shifted baby Serena to one arm and extended her free hand. "My pleasure."

He took her hand and brought it to his mouth. "The pleasure is mine," he replied in Spanish. Evelyn blushed and fluttered her lashes. "What is Mistress Comacho's first name?"

"Serena. Yes, she's named for Serena," she explained quickly.

"A beautiful name for an incredibly beautiful child," he countered in a soft voice. He spoke to all in the room, but gazed only at the woman Serena. His midnight gaze was riveted on her face, then moved slowly down her body, leaving a trail of burning longing everywhere it touched.

Serena felt the heat as if he had stoked a gently spreading fire. She forgot that they weren't alone when she permitted him to reach across the invisible space to wrap her in a cocoon of longing. His eyes widened enough for her to see his pupils dilate with the rising passion he was unable to conceal from her. His breathing deepened, his delicate nostrils flaring, while his lips parted.

Evelyn's shocked gaze flitted from her friend to the tall man with the scar running along the left side of his face. He was hypnotically attractive, the scar making his features less delicate while not detracting from what was an obviously beautiful male face. The scar, his black attire, and the small, gold earring in his left ear afforded him the appearance of a modern-day pirate. And there was no doubt that there was something going on between her friend and the man who shifted between fluent English and Spanish with equal facility.

"I'm going downstairs to change the baby," she said in a hushed tone, breaking the munificent silence filling the bedroom.

"And I'm going for a walk," David offered as an excuse to escape Serena. He had to get away from her or else embarrass the both of them in front of her friend.

Serena nodded, unable to force a word from her constricted throat. *How could he?* she raged inwardly. How could he look at her like that in front of a stranger? Only a blind person would miss the silent interchange that had passed between them. What was it about David Cole that made it possible for him to seduce her without saying a word?

She moved to the bed, picked up the baby's bag, and followed Evelyn out of the room, leaving David staring at her back. Just before she reached the top of the staircase, she glanced over her shoulder and found him standing in the hallway, staring.

David had begun what he'd promised to do: wait for her.

Twenty-two

Serena met Evelyn in the sitting area where she sat breastfeeding her baby. The two women stared at each other, smiling.

"Are you going to tell me about him, or do I have to pry?"

Serena shrugged a bare shoulder. "There's nothing to tell. He's a business associate of my father. He's staying with us because he had an accident."

"No, *Amiga*, it's not the accident I want to know about. I know what I see."

"And that is?" Serena asked, refusing to make it easy for her friend.

"The fire between you two is . . . *caliente!*"

"There's no fire, Evelyn."

"The man burns for you. Didn't you feel the heat?"

"Nope."

"Mentirosa! Don't you dare lie to me, Girlfriend," Evelyn continued, switching to English.

Serena struggled not to laugh, but couldn't keep the chuckles from escaping when she saw the indignation on Evelyn's face.

"You're right," she admitted softly. "The heat between us is incredible."

She disclosed all that had happened from the moment David Cole lay under her parents' roof, omitting the part where they'd made love. She also told Evelyn of Luz Maria's prediction.

"It's weird, Evelyn. I didn't even want to like him, but meanwhile I find myself believing that I love him."

"What's not to like or even love? The man's absolutely gorgeous."

"It's not his looks," she argued softly. "That's too superficial."

"Whatever it is, don't fight it, *Amiga.*"

They talked for another hour, catching up on what had transpired in their lives since their last meeting; she kissed her friend and tiny namesake, promising she would return the visit before Evelyn returned to San José with her daughter.

Raul Vega emerged from the sanctuary of his study at the same time Serena headed for the stairs, lines of tension ringing his mouth and crisscrossing his forehead.

"Chica."

Stopping, she glanced down at Raul. "Yes, Poppa."

"Let David know that he's expected to take his meal with us at eight."

Noting the strain of his drawn features, she offered a comforting smile. *"Sí,"* Poppa." Raul nodded, then turned and reentered his study.

She continued up the staircase, knowing the only time she would see her stepfather would be during dinner. Whenever he was troubled by something he retreated to his study, leaving it only to share the evening meal with his family. She and Gabe had learned early never to enter the room without knocking, or venturing in even when Raul was not in attendance.

She'd tried over and over during her adult years to analyze her relationship with her stepfather, failing to understand his passions. He loved her mother, his children, and his country, but that love was sometimes all-encompassing and suffocating. There were no in-betweens for Raul Cordero-Vega—it was all or nothing. He loved hard and hated even harder.

She was aware of the enmity between the two men in her life, knowing she would have to choose. But she was also confident that Raul would forgive her, because he had become her father and she his daughter.

She walked into David's room and found it empty. Making her way to the adjoining bathroom, she peered in. It was apparent that he hadn't returned from his walk. The pad she had given him lay on the seat of the armchair, and she moved over to pick it up. Half the pages in the bound pad were filled with pencilled musical notes. He'd composed solos for piano, guitar, sax, and flugelhorn. Along the margins he'd indicated the key and tempo, and a few bore titles: *Book of Secrets. Exotic Pleasures.*

Staring at his latest work-in-progress, she smiled. This composition featured a guitar and cello. A most unusual pairing, but then she had to admit that David was unusual. Instinctively she knew that beneath his tailored clothing and regal bearing was a tempered wildness he'd learned to control with maturity. The pierced ear and tattoo were overt evidence of his atypical behavior for a man born to his station. He'd admitted rebelling against his father's insistence that he join the family business on graduating from college when he pursued a career as a musician. And it was also apparent that he'd substituted Raul Cordero-Vega for his father whenever they met to discuss his family's holdings in Costa Rica. The battle lines were drawn, and neither wanted to concede.

"What do you think of it?"

Serena felt the heat flare in her face at the sound of the deep, musical voice. Turning slowly, she smiled at David. He stood in the doorway, leaning on the cane.

"I'd love to hear it," she replied, her voice lowering seductively.

He limped into the bedroom, stopping less than a foot from her. "I decided not to play what I've written until I finish."

Her gold-brown gaze moved slowly over his face, coming to rest on his mouth. "When do you think you'll finish?"

He returned her enraptured gaze, his lids lowering over his large black eyes. "When I stop hearing the music in my head."

The fire Evelyn had referred to was back—hotter than before. It scorched her face, throat, chest, and lower—to the secret, pulsing area between her thighs. The heat and the throbbing intensified until she doubted whether she could stand unaided.

"Stop that, David," she whispered.

He took a step closer, then another. "Stop what, *mi alma?*"

Her lids fluttered close. "Don't look at me like that."

A half-smile curved his mouth. "Like what?"

Serena's chest rose and fell heavily under her tank top, bringing David's burning gaze to her heaving breasts. "Like I'm—" Her words trailed off. She couldn't say it. She wasn't quite that uninhibited.

His smile widened as he shifted a sweeping, silky black eyebrow. "Like you're something I'd like to eat," he crooned quietly.

Her shuttered lids flew open and she stared at him with an expression that mirrored her shock. He'd read her mind. She nodded, numbly, unable to form the words to verify her thoughts.

Reaching out with his free hand, he took the pad from her limp fingers. "Tonight you'll find out just how much I want you."

The heat increased in her face, making it impossible for her to continue to look at him as she turned her back. Was she that open? Were all of her emotions on the surface for him to see? How was it everyone read her so well? Luz Maria, David, and Evelyn.

"I came to tell you that my father expects you to eat dinner with us."

The mention of Raul Vega broke the sensual spell. David's smile faded quickly, a frown taking its place. "At what time has he ordered that I sit at his table?"

Serena spun around, her own passion replaced by annoyance. "Stop it, David. Why must you attack him like this?"

"Because I don't like him, that's why."

"That's not a reason to be deliberately ungracious."

David wanted to shout at her that he wasn't the one who was ungracious. That it was her father who had him assaulted, threatened his life, that before he killed him he would begin a systematic mutilation until he died in agony.

"What do you want from me, Serena? Do you want me to genuflect and kiss his ring? He's set himself up as a despot. He wants absolute control of everyone and everything. I've taken insults from him that I would've never taken from another man, all in the name of maintaining a professional business decorum with an official of a foreign country. But all of that is going to end because there won't be any negotiations for the sale of the banana plantation."

A sudden chill shook her body. "What are you going to do?" Her voice was a breathless whisper.

He leaned down until his face was inches from hers. "I'm walking away from it. The employees of ColeDiz International Ltd. can take what they want, or leave the bananas to rot where they lay."

She shook her head in disbelief. "No one can touch the plantation unless the government decides to nationalize the property. And that can take months."

His expression was impassive, and that frightened her

more than if he'd affected a frown. "I really don't give a damn, because Vega will be left with nothing, and I don't believe the Costa Rican government will want to throw its money away on a worthless piece of property. Your *Poppa* wants to play dirty. What he'll get is someone who's been taught to play dirty by one of the best."

"Who?"

He straightened, recognizing the glimmer of fear in her wide-eyed gaze. "My father."

"If that's the case, then why don't you let our fathers fight this battle?"

David gritted his teeth, welcoming the pain radiating from his temple to his chin. "They are, Serena."

"What are you talking about?"

"Don't ask me. Ask your, *Poppa,*" he drawled in a nasty, sarcastic tone.

Serena brushed past him as she walked quickly to the door. "You can believe I will."

David flung the pad across the room, wishing he could bellow out his frustration. He was trapped, a prisoner in the home of a man whose daughter he coveted. He couldn't tell her about the betrayal and deadly revenge taking center stage, where a word from her stepfather would shatter their love and the hope of a future together.

His only hope was that his father could survive long enough to secure his freedom. A freedom that would give him back his son as well as claim to another daughter-in-law.

Serena sat opposite David at the dining room table, holding her breath. She'd approached her father after her hostile confrontation with David, but Raul refused to see her. She'd pounded on the locked door until her fist ached, but he hadn't opened the door.

Waiting until Luz Maria brought out all of the dishes, she glared at Raul's expressionless face. "Will you talk to me now, Poppa?"

Raul spread a snowy white napkin over his lap and glared at her. "You know the rules, *Chica*. We do not discuss business at the table."

"If you don't talk to me now, when will you? You owe me that much. Remember, I'm your daughter, not a business associate."

He inclined his gray head. "That is true. You are my daughter." He smiled, softening the hard lines in his face and making her aware of why her mother had married him. Raul Cordero-Vega was still an extremely attractive man at sixty-two.

"But I refuse to discuss business at *my* dinner table," he continued.

"Your table, your house," she ranted, refusing to back down. "When is it ever *our* table, *our* house?"

Raul's fingers tightened around the handle of his knife and fork. "Enough, *Chica.*" The two words were spoken quietly, but there was no mistaking the repressed rage in the man staring down at the contents on his plate. His head lifted as his eyes widened.

Something within Serena exploded as she stood up. "No! It is not enough!"

Raul didn't move. "Sit down." When she did not comply, he put down his silverware. The deafening silence swelled as the two men at the table stared at the petite woman who stood facing her stepfather, trembling with defiance.

"Why is it always what *you* want, Poppa?"

"Serena!" Her name exploded from the back of his throat.

David placed both hands on the table and rose to his feet. Rage he did not know he was capable of surfaced, making breathing difficult. "Don't ever raise your voice to her again." His warning, though spoken softly, denoted a threat.

Raul's head jerked around as he glared disbelievingly at the man who challenged him over and over. "You forget your place, Señor Cole. This is between me and my daughter."

"And you forget yours, Señor Vega. In case you haven't noticed, your daughter is an adult. It's time you saw her as one."

"And it is apparent that you've forgotten who you are and where you are, Señor Cole."

"I know exactly who I am. It is you who has forgotten. It is only because I *do* respect *your home* and your daughter that I don't say what I'd like to say."

Raul stood up and threw his napkin down to the table. "I will not take your insults. Not at my own table. Serena, tell Luz Maria to serve me in my study." Pushing back his chair, he stalked out of the dining room, leaving them staring at his back.

Serena hands were shaking as she covered her face and sank slowly down to her chair. "When will it end?" she whispered, her voice breaking with raw emotion.

David made his way slowly around the table. He resisted the urge to hold her and comfort her. "He's angry and frustrated." He wanted to rationalize her father's pain, but knew Vega's pain had not started with his son's arrest. It'd begun years before, with his obsession to save his country from foreigners.

Her hands came down and she stared up at David, her golden eyes awash with unshed tears. "There are times when I feel that he hates me, David. Why, I don't know."

"He doesn't hate you, *mi amor.* He's angry with himself. And it's up to Raul Cordero-Vega to solve his own problems and come to terms with himself."

"You're wrong. He's always loved my mother and brother. It seems as if he picks and chooses his time to offer me what he's always given them. We can't spend more than three days together before we're at each other's throats. I don't know what's going to happen with my brother, but I swear that when I leave Costa Rica this time only death will bring me back."

She pulled away when David reached out for her and stood up. "Excuse me. I have to tell Luz Maria to bring *my father's* dinner to his study."

David wanted to tell Serena that she did not have to say anything to Luz Maria, that if Raul wanted his dinner served in his study he could tell the cook himself. But the words were lodged in his throat. He'd come to Serena's defense without considering the consequences. It was apparent that she had quarreled with her stepfather many times in the past. She did not need him to fight her battles.

But something would not permit him to sit silent while Raul shouted at her. At that moment he'd wanted to reach across the table and strangle the man, choking off his words and his life's breath. And it was in that instant that he knew he would've willingly given up his life for Serena. He loved her that much.

He waited for her to return from the kitchen. It was only after she reclaimed her chair that he sat down. Both of them ate in complete silence, lost in their private thoughts.

David drank three glasses of a premium red wine while Serena toyed with the stem of her wineglass before she drank one. The wine helped relax him. He soon forgot Vega's virulent exchange with Serena, and he looked forward to taking her into his arms to calm and soothe her fears. He wanted her to know that she didn't have to solicit her stepfather's love, because he loved her. His love was all she would ever need from a man—any man.

Twenty-three

Serena retreated to her bedroom after eating dinner, stripped off her clothes, and spent the next hour soaking in the bathtub. The scented candles, perfumed bath oil, and the softly playing, all-music radio station worked their magic as she willed her mind and body to relax.

She forgot the confrontation at the dinner table, the fact that she could not confide in her mother, and even the knowledge that Gabe was locked away in a Florida prison.

She forgot all of the madness affecting her family as the realization that she had fallen in love transported her to a place where she languished in the comforting arms of serenity.

Picking up a bath sponge, she trickled water over her shoulders and down her breasts, her flesh shimmering from the scented oil. It was only when she stood up to step out of the tub that she saw him.

David stood in the shadows of the candle-lit bathroom, watching her. Her breath caught in her chest before it started up again in an erratic rhythm that left her feeling lightheaded.

"How long have you been here?"

Pushing off the wall, David closed the space between them. "Long enough to see everything I like." His hands circled her waist and he effortlessly lifted her from the bathtub. Holding her water-slick body aloft, her feet dangling in the air, he pressed his mouth to hers. He molded her flesh to his, fusing their naked bodies and making them one.

Serena gloried in the feel of the crisp hair on his chest grazing her sensitive nipples. She curved her arms around his neck and deepened the kiss, her tongue easing slowly, deliberately, into his mouth.

David gasped at the heated invasion of her tongue, opening his mouth wider until she branded him with her soul-searching kiss. He felt her trembling, the quickening of her respiration, and knew her passions were soaring as quickly as his own. He carried her into her own darkened bedroom and placed her on the bed, his body following.

After dinner he'd returned to his bedroom to shave and shower, then come to her, as promised. He'd turned off her bedside lamp and drawn the drapes before he walked silently into her bathroom. He'd stood in a corner, watching her as she lay in the bathtub, eyes closed, listening to the soft music coming from a radio, while ignoring the slight twinge of pain in his right foot. He saw the peace that settled into the features of the woman he'd fallen in love with. She had found solace in a tub filled with scented water, while he needed the scented softness of her body before he found his own peace.

David pulled back to catch his breath before his head dipped again. He drank from her honeyed mouth like a man dying of thirst, and she did quench his thirst, but not the gnawing hunger for the rest of her body.

Serena reveled in the scent of his smooth shaven jaw, the tip of her tongue tracing the length of the healing scar transforming his beautiful male face. Her fingers swept through the short, silken strands covering his well-shaped head before they cupped his ears, then moved still lower to cradle his face between her palms.

"*Te amo,*" she whispered reverently between nibbling kisses. And she did love him. She loved him with a reverent passion that unlocked her heart and soul to offer him all that she possessed.

· Her declaration of love battered down the last resistance he'd erected to keep women at a distance. The iron-will control he maintained when taking a woman to his bed fled, leaving him completely vulnerable for the first time in his adult life.

A violent shudder shook his large body when he buried his face in her fragrant, unbound hair. "And I love you," he confessed hoarsely. He repeated it over and over, it becoming a litany. Her slender arms tightened around his neck. Heart to heart, skin to skin, they became one.

"Love me, David." Her husky whisper broke the silence.

He wanted to do more than love her; he wanted to be inside her; he wanted to become one with her.

His lips brushed her lush, soft mouth before he moved lower to taste the silken flesh covering her throat. The soft moans coming from her parted lips impelled him to take her quickly; he ignored the twin emotions of lust and desire becoming one and the same, because he no longer feared not being in control of his passions.

His tongue continued its exploration of her moist body, sweeping over her flat belly. She arched off the mattress at the same time his hot mouth searched and claimed her moist, throbbing femininity. A strangled cry filled the darkened space when he cradled her hips in his hands and lifted her higher. He feasted, his rapacious tongue relentless. Serena could not believe that he'd awakened a dormant carnality that threatened to consume all of her.

He had taken her to such heights that she feared if she didn't jump she would die from the pleasure building in the hidden place where he'd buried his face. His hands shifted from her hips to her thighs, raising her legs until they lay over his shoulders.

Her head thrashed back and forth on the pillow and Serena lost herself in the violent explosion that shook every part of her body. The explosions persisted, one following the other. She opened her mouth to scream out the last cry of ecstasy, only to find her breath captured again by his mouth. David paused to protect her, then entered her pulsing body with a powerful thrust that rekindled her desire all over again. They rode out the violent storm of passion together, losing themselves in a love predestined from the beginning of time.

David strained valiantly to keep from exploding. He wanted the lustful delirium to continue, but knew it couldn't. He had to release his passion or his heart would explode. Quickening his powerful thrusts, he lowered his head and gave into the eruptions hurtling him toward heaven. The moment before he gave into the force sweeping him beyond himself he surrendered all that he was to the woman who lay beneath him, their hearts beating in unison.

His body shuddered once, twice, and then a third time. He collapsed heavily on Serena's slight frame, laboring to slow his runaway pulse. He did not remember rolling off her and pulling her to lie atop his chest, nor did he remember when they fell asleep.

Streaks of the rising sun had just begun to pierce the cover of the fading nighttime sky when they did wake in each other's arms. Serena felt more relaxed than she had ever been in her life. Moaning sensuously, she rubbed her nose against David's cheek, inhaling the familiar scent of his aftershave.

"Good morning, Lover."

Opening his large eyes, he smiled down at her. "Good morning, Sweetheart. Did you sleep well?"

She stretched, raising a well-shaped leg in the air. "I slept wonderfully."

"I take it you like using me as a mattress," he teased.

"You could've pushed me off if I was too heavy."

David combed his fingers through her curling hair. "You don't weigh enough to be considered too heavy."

"How much do you weigh?"

"An even two hundred," he admitted.

"You don't look as if you weigh that much."

"Muscle weighs a lot more than fat."

Turning over on her side, she faced him, trying to make out his features in the darkened bedroom. The drawn drapes filtered out most of the light from the rising sun.

"How do you keep fit?"

"Swimming."

"How often do you swim?"

"Weather permitting—every day."

"Do you have a pool at your house in Boca Raton?"

"Yes. But I haven't had the chance to swim in it."

"Why not?"

"Because it was just built and I haven't moved in. I'd planned to have my sister-in-law decorate it when I return to the States. But that's going to change now."

"Why?"

He pressed his lips against her hair. "The house will be yours, to decorate in any style you want."

"We'll decide together."

"So, you're going to be a compromising little wife."

"Only this one time, David Claridge Cole."

"What about children?"

"What about them?"

"Do you want any?"

Raising her head, she stared up at him. "I want your babies."

"How many babies do you want?"

"Three."

David laughed softly, pulling her closer to his chest. "I've heard people say baby-making love is very different from regular lovemaking."

"I've never heard that. Besides, I don't believe it."

He shifted his eyebrows. "How would you know if you haven't tried it?"

"I'm not much of a risk-taker, David. Sleeping with you without protection is not something I'm willing to try again."

"How long an engagement do you want?"

"Not long," she confessed, dropping light kisses on his shoulder.

"Good."

"David!" she gasped when his hand eased up between her thighs.

"I need some regular lovemaking, Baby," he crooned against her moist lips.

"I can make it special if you let me get on top."

"Climb on," he urged, settling her body over his. And she did make it special. She took him to heaven with a burning sweetness that shattered him into a million tiny pieces before he lay shaking, spent from the passion she'd aroused in him.

He lingered in her bed until the sun broke the horizon to signal the beginning of another day of his captivity.

Day One had come and gone, and he refused to think of the other fifty-nine that lay ahead.

Twenty-four

July 17
West Palm Beach, Florida

Martin Cole, Joshua Kirkland, and Samuel Cole left the large gathering of the Cole family in the dining room, retreating to the library. Children, in-laws, grandchildren, and great-grandchildren had come to the large West Palm Beach mansion to celebrate the seventieth birthday of the family matriarch. Marguerite Joséfina Diaz Cole's stunning beauty had not faded with age. Her silver, stylishly coiffed hair framed a smooth, tanned face that claimed a few laugh lines at the corners of her large, dark eyes. She had passed along her delicate features and dimpled smile to several of her offspring, and her superior genes were repeated in several of her grandchildren.

Joshua Kirkland waited for Martin to settle Samuel Cole on a large recliner that had been designed expressly for the elderly man, then sat down opposite his father and brother.

"Everything is set. Vega has agreed to meet with me."

Joshua's penetrating green gaze registered his father's and brother's reaction to his announcement that he was to leave for Costa Rica. Samuel nodded slowly, while Martin smiled.

"Do you think Vega will believe what you're selling?" Martin questioned.

"The man's a botanist," Joshua argued. "I'm told he has a greenhouse filled with several varieties of the tree I'm going to pitch to him. I intend to put his paranoid mind at ease when I tell him that Markham Pharmaceutical will not set up a plant in his country, that our scientists want the bark and needles from the Anneda pine tree." It had taken him a month to set up his cover as a salesman for a pharmaceutical company that was interested in a plant indigenous only to Costa Rica.

"When are you going to bring my boy back?" Samuel asked, his wavering voice breaking with emotion.

Martin reached out and covered his father's hand in a comforting gesture. "Patience, Dad. It's only been thirty days."

"That's thirty days too long," Samuel countered angrily.

Joshua rose to his feet, nodded to Martin, then walked out of the room. He would give his brother time to calm their father's fear that David Cole's life would be forfeited in an act of deadly revenge; legal attempts to solicit support of granting bail for Gabriel Vega had failed. No elected official wanted to take responsibility for securing the release of a murderer and drug trafficker.

Joshua and Samuel Cole had reconciled, both acknowledging the bond which made them father and son. But Joshua was always aware that he would never experience the affinity Martin and David shared with Samuel. However, at forty-three he was mature enough to accept what he could not control. He realized that he had to put the circumstances surrounding his illegitimacy to rest. His wife and daughter had become the most important people in his life.

"How is he taking it?" Joshua asked when Martin met him on the loggia.

Martin slipped his hands into the pockets of his slacks. "Not well. I don't know if he's going to make it."

"It's wearing on all of us. I think it's time we tell the family."

Martin's coal black eyes met his half-brother's pale gaze, a flash of fear sweeping over his deeply tanned face. "We can't."

Folding his arms over his chest, Joshua leaned against a coral column. "I told Vanessa last night. I had to," he continued when Martin stared at him as if he'd never seen him before. "How do I explain bringing her and Emily to Florida for M.J.'s birthday, and then take off for Costa Rica?"

Covering his face with his hands, Martin shook his head. "Why didn't you tell her that you were going on ColeDiz business?"

"Have you forgotten that Vanessa oversees every investment I've acquired? And nowhere in my portfolio does the name ColeDiz appear." As Samuel Cole's illegitimate son he had not been granted a share in the family business.

Martin lowered his hands. "How did she take the news?"

"Not well at first. It's hell living with a woman who won't respond when you talk to her. It was only when I began packing this morning that she realized that I was going to go through with it."

Martin muttered a savage curse under his breath. He felt so powerless. He had earned the reputation as the consummate risk taker and deal maker, responsible for a billion dollar family owned enterprise, yet he could not negotiate for his brother's life.

Combing his fingers through his gray, curly hair, he nodded. "Okay. We tell them."

Joshua smiled and let out his breath. "I'll tell Nancy and Josephine. I'll leave you to tell M.J." He knew it would be easier for him to disclose the news of David's captivity to his half-sisters than to his father's wife.

Martin returned to the dining room, winking at his wife Parris as she sat with their six-year-old daughter on her lap, offering her small portions of cake. Making his way over to her, he hunkered down beside her chair. "I need to talk to you in the library."

Parris Cole's eyes widened slightly. A hint of green sparkled in their clear-brown depths. "What's up?"

"Family business," he whispered.

"What family business, Daddy?" Arianna chimed in her clear, childlike voice.

Running a forefinger down the length of his daughter's nose, he placed a kiss on the tiny tip. She giggled as he pulled her from her mother's lap and handed her to one of his teenage nieces.

"Take care of this chatterbox for me." His sister's daughter tickled Arianna, and the child dissolved into peals of laughter.

Martin walked over to where his mother sat at the head of the table. Cupping her elbow, he helped her to stand. "I have to talk to you in the library."

Her large, dark gaze seemed to race over her son's face. "What's going on?" She arched a sweeping eyebrow when Martin did not respond. "It's about David, isn't it?"

Martin nodded once. "Yes, Mother. It concerns David." He'd told his mother that David couldn't make her birthday celebration because he hadn't concluded his sale of the banana plantation in Costa Rica.

M.J. closed her eyes and placed a slender, manicured hand over her breast. "Is he alive, Martin?"

"Yes, Mother. He's alive."

Pulling herself erect, M.J. tilted her chin and walked out of the dining room. Martin was always amazed at how his mother was able to compose herself so quickly. He had never seen her resort to hysterics during a family crisis. She'd always chosen to grieve in private.

He whispered to his sisters that Joshua wanted to talk to them on the loggia, then informed Vanessa Kirkland that she should join him in the library.

Joshua straightened from his leaning position with Nancy and Josephine's approach. He took their hands and escorted them to several white, twisted rattan chairs with plump coral and white cushions, seating them. Pulling up a chair, he sat down and stared at the expectant expressions on their faces.

Nancy Cole-Thomas, the elder sister, returned her half-brother's stare. "What's going on, Joshua?"

He decided to be direct. He would handle their reactions later. "David couldn't be here today because he's being held hostage in Costa Rica."

"What!" Nancy screamed.

Josephine's eyes widened in shock. Then she broke down, sobbing uncontrollably. Joshua stood up, pulling Josephine up with him. He held her gently while she sobbed out her grief. When her crying quieted he related the terms of David's release to his sisters.

Josephine glared at her half-brother, anger replacing her anguish. "Why have you waited so long to tell us about this?"

"We had hoped to resolve it before now."

"Resolve it how, Joshua?"

"Using legal means."

"Whose decision was it not to tell us about David?" Josephine continued with her questioning.

"We all agreed."

Josephine arched a sculpted eyebrow. "We?"

"Sammy, Martin, and I."

The women stared at each another. Their father and brothers had decided among themselves not to tell them that their youngest brother had been taken hostage by a deranged foreign official, and threatened with death if his son was not released from a Florida prison.

"How dare you! You had no right to make that decision without consulting us," Josephine said accusingly. "After all, he is our brother."

Joshua stared at her, chilling her with his icy gaze. "As he is also *my* brother."

She nodded, blinking back tears that threatened to flow again. Verbally attacking Joshua would not change things. As a family they needed to pull together, not fight one another. "I'm sorry, Joshua. Forgive me."

He inclined his head, his gaze softening. "This hasn't been easy on any of us."

Nancy wiped away her tears with her fingertips. "What are *you* going to do, Joshua?"

"I'm flying to Costa Rica in the morning."

She rose to her feet and wrapped her arms around her sister and brother. The three stood silently, feeding on each other's strength, then turned and walked back into the large house.

Martin examined the women sitting in the library. They were similar, yet very different. All were tall, slender women who affirmed their own personal strengths, but not without pain and sacrifice.

His wife Parris at forty-one had entered middle-age with a sensuality that left him gasping whenever she offered him her love. Having given him three children, her ripened body was still slim. She'd acquired an abundance of gray hairs in her dark brown, blunt-cut hair that she refused to color. She joked often that she'd earned them.

And she had. A failed first marriage, an abduction and blackmail that separated them for ten years, and subsequent murder attempts had given Parris Simmons-Cole more than her share of pain. But what Martin could not understand was that it was Parris, not he, who offered Samuel Cole forgiveness for what he had done to her and their daughter Regina. She confessed that she had prayed for strength to find the mercy to forgive her father-in-law. She forgave Samuel before he did.

His gaze moved to Vanessa Blanchard-Kirkland. His half-brother's wife was truly Joshua's soulmate. Her gentle love had helped him let go the bitterness he carried for years, and he'd become a loving husband, father, brother, and uncle.

He looked at his father. "David couldn't be here today because he couldn't get out of Costa Rica."

"What do you mean he couldn't get out?" Parris asked.

"He's being held hostage."

There was a chorus of gasps from Parris and M.J. Martin disclosed the telephone call David had made to Samuel with Cordero-Vega's demands. He left nothing out, deciding on complete honesty.

M.J. glanced from her husband to her son. "What are *we* going to do?"

"Joshua's leaving for Costa Rica in the morning," Samuel explained.

All gazes shifted to Vanessa. There was nothing in her expression to indicate the inner turmoil she felt when she realized her husband was going back into the shadowy world of intelligence he'd left behind four years before.

M.J. rose to her feet, throwing her husband an angry glare. "I don't care what you do, but I want my baby back."

Samuel lifted a hand. "M.J.—"

"Dammit! Don't M.J. me, Sammy," she ranted. "Get him back!" Turning on her heel, she stalked out of the library.

Samuel attempted to rise from his chair, but Martin moved quickly and pushed him down. "Let her go."

Shaking his head, Samuel slumped weakly back to the chair. It was all his fault. He was being paid back for his sins. *The sins of the father will fall on the sons.* The words attacked him until he sat sobbing uncontrollably.

Parris and Vanessa left together, leaving Martin to console his father.

Both of them were familiar with waiting—it had happened at another time in their lives, and it was to begin again.

Twenty-five

July 18
Puerto Limón, Costa Rica

David sat in Raul Vega's study, staring out the window. The strain of waiting had begun to fray the nerves of both men.

His call to the American embassy in San José was acknowledged, but the ambassador sent his regrets, and there was no way he could tell the ambassador that he was being held hostage with Vega listening on an extension.

Raul tapped a pencil against his forefinger, his dark gaze fixed on David Cole's cheek. His face had healed, the scar only noticeable at close range, and instead of ruining the young peacock's face the scar enhanced it. It made him look dangerously attractive.

Raul knew that the earring he wore in his left lobe was his daughter's. What he had to uncover was their relationship. Whenever he observed them together there was an obvious attraction, but it was coupled with a formality that was unnatural. They would bear watching closely.

"So, your answer is still no."

David affected an expression of indifference. "And will remain no."

"You will lose millions."

"So be it."

Raul's hand came down hard on the top of his desk. "Fool! You risk losing millions—"

"It's *my* millions," David interrupted.

Leaning back against the leather chair, Raul flashed a sinister smile. "I think I can get you to change your mind about selling the plantation."

David ran a hand through his longer wavy hair. "I doubt that."

Lacing his fingers together, the older man met David's steady gaze. "What if I shorten the time for your sentence to thirty days instead of sixty?"

He was past threats and intimidation, knowing that Vega needed him—alive. "You're a day late, because yesterday was thirty days."

"And you have only twenty-nine left before I begin taking you apart."

David stood up. "Save the threats," he sneered. Turning his back, he walked out of the room, closing the door quietly behind him.

Instead of retreating to the sanctuary of his bedroom, he decided to brave the oppressive heat. Opening the door, he stepped out into the sultry afternoon. The beauty of the land surrounding *La Montaña* was breathtaking, and he didn't think he would ever get used to the sun-drenched world where every living organism coexisted in perfect harmony.

The cloying fragrance of tropical flowers growing in wild abandon lingered in his nostrils. Putting one foot firmly in front of the other, he stared down at the flagstone path leading to the enormous greenhouse and connecting aviary. He walked past the structures toward the ocean, ignoring the heat of the sun beating down on his bare head and arms.

He had come to recognize and distinguish a macaw,

quetzal, and a three-wattled bellbird after spending hundreds of hours in the aviary. A few of the birds flew over to him whenever he walked in, looking for bits of ripe fruit he usually carried with him.

Walking past an overgrowth of tangled trees, he stepped out into a clearing, stopping short when he saw a man pointing a rifle at him.

"You must not go any farther, Señor Cole."

Nodding, he turned and retraced his steps. It was the third time someone had stopped him from leaving the boundaries of Raul Vega's property. His walks had taken him east, west, and north. The only route he hadn't tried was south. That he would leave for another time.

He returned to the house at the same time Rodrigo maneuvered the Mercedes-Benz up to the garages. The driver alighted and opened the rear door to the spacious sedan. A man's foot touched the concrete, followed by the glimpse of pale, close-cut, silver hair. Then the tall, slim figure emerged. Nothing in David's expression revealed the relief washing over him. He'd come. His brother had come for him.

Joshua's pale eyes, hidden behind the lenses of his sunglasses, missed nothing. He saw David glance at him before he disappeared into the large house situated on a rise above a deep valley. There was a time in his past when David had come to take him home as he lay close to death in a tiny Mexican town. Now he had come for his brother before a madman could follow through on his promises of mutilation and death.

His sharp gaze swept around the land surrounding *La Montaña*. Its location atop the mountain made it almost impenetrable. A sardonic smile touched his mouth. *Almost, but not impossible*, he mused, following the driver's lead into the house.

* * *

David lay across his bed, eyes closed, his chest rising and falling in an even rhythm. When he first spied Joshua he thought he had imagined him. He hadn't had any contact with his family, and suspected that their political connections had not met with success; he was fully aware that his father was not above going outside the law to secure his release. And Samuel Cole had sent the best: Retired U.S. Colonel Joshua Kirkland, former Associate Coordinating Chief of the Defense Intelligence Agency.

Seeing his half brother summoned a repressed distress that he hadn't wanted to acknowledge: his father's failing health, his mother's anxiety, and his brothers' and sisters' fear that they would lose a sibling. He had come to depend on Serena with a ferocious craving that threatened to break him emotionally. His emotions vacillated between rage and fear; a rage so violent that he considered murdering her father, and a fear that he would lose her—forever.

He shared her bed—every night, returning to his own bed with the rising of the morning sun. Their lovemaking was strong, passionate, and satisfying, but always leaving him wanting more.

He counted off the days, one merging into the other, while he spent the time exploring the property surrounding *La Montaña*, visiting the exotic birds in the aviary, and writing music. It was only at night that he truly came alive, when he lost himself in the scented embrace of the woman he loved more than his own life.

Opening his eyes, he stared up at the whitewashed ceiling. Joshua had come to take him home. He had to let his brother know that he would not leave Costa Rica alone. Serena would go back to Florida with him.

* * *

Serena replaced the telephone receiver on its cradle. Her mother's call had elicited an emotion of uncontrollable euphoria. Gabriel had granted his mother an audience.

Juanita laughed and cried at the same time, reporting that her son looked wonderful, he was treated well, he was extremely optimistic, and that he was segregated from the general prison population. She ended the conversation saying that she would remain in Florida until Gabriel's release.

Rushing out of her bedroom, she raced down the back staircase, taking the shorter route to her father's study. The door was ajar, and he stood in the middle of the room, arms folded over his chest. The smile softening his features was radiant. He lowered his arms, extending them, and he wasn't disappointed when she walked into his embrace.

"Oh, Poppa," Serena sighed, curving her arms around her father's waist.

Raul tightened his hold on her tiny body. The strain of sidestepping and tiptoeing around each other for the past month vanished like rain on a heated surface once the sun reemerged.

"It's all right, *Chica,*" he crooned over and over.

Gabriel is safe. Safe from himself and those who seek to take his life. Luz Maria's prediction calmed and soothed her as she stood in the protective arms of her father.

Raul Vega loved her. How could she have thought otherwise? And she loved him as much as she could've loved her biological father.

Pulling back, she smiled up at him. A flicker of amusement lit up his dark eyes when he returned her smile. "I love you, Poppa."

Cradling her face between his hands, he kissed both her cheeks. "Not as much as I love you, Daughter." One hand cupped the back of her head. "I need to ask a favor of you."

Vertical lines appeared between her eyes. "What?"

"Will you act as hostess for me tonight? An American businessman will be staying here for several days, and I'd like to offer him the hospitality we Ticos are known for."

"But—but you don't like foreign businessmen, Poppa."

"It will be different this time."

"Different, how?"

"His factory will remain in the States. We will export what he needs."

Serena nodded. She would agree to anything after the call from her mother. "Yes, Poppa. I will act as your hostess. How many are we serving?"

"There will be just the four of us tonight. And that includes David Cole."

She sighed in relief. Four was a small number compared to the twenty or more she'd seen her mother host in the past. Before she left to live in the United States she'd watched her mother smile, laugh, and chat with a living room filled with people. Juanita had a special gift that made everyone who met her like her on sight. Not only was she stunningly attractive, but she claimed a gentleness that put anyone in her presence immediately at ease.

"When will he arrive?"

"He's already here. Right now he's taking *siesta.*"

"Where is he from?"

"New Mexico."

She estimated the time difference between America's southwest and Costa Rica, her mind racing quickly. "I'll tell Luz Maria that we'll eat at six instead of eight. That will allow Mr.—"

"Señor Kirkland."

"Mr. Kirkland," Serena continued smoothly, "to recover from his jet-lag more quickly than if we had a late dinner."

"I'll leave everything up to you, *Chica.*"

She kissed him again, then turned and walked out of his study, encountering Rodrigo. He inclined his head, then knocked on his employer's door before walking in and closing the door behind them.

David. She wanted to share her good news with him, but they had promised each other that their only direct contact would be when they shared dinner or her bed. She would have to wait for him to come to her tonight before she told him about Gabriel.

Serena checked the dining room table for the second time, making certain all of the silver was free of tarnish, and the crystals goblets free of water spots. She adjusted the table's centerpiece—a magnificent lead crystal vase filled with a profusion of orchids, ranging in colors from the deepest purple to the palest white. The snowy white tablecloth and matching napkins complemented the translucent china ringed in silver.

"The table looks beautiful, and so do you," crooned the last voice she'd heard before she fell asleep at night.

Turning, she smiled up at David. Instead of his usual slacks and shirt, he'd opted to wear a exquisitely tailored, oatmeal-beige suit, a snow white shirt, chocolate brown silk tie, and a pair of imported, brown, slip-on loafers. His graying hair had grown out where he'd brushed it off his high forehead and over his ears. But he hadn't removed the tiny, gold hoop in his left ear.

"Lose the earring," she whispered.

His obsidian gaze raced quickly over her lightly made up face. "No. It stays."

He admired her hair, which was brushed off her face

and secured in an elaborate twist on the nape of her neck. A seductive, woodsy fragrance clung to her body under a sleeveless, silk dress in a vibrant orange. The simple, elegant garment cut on a bias skimmed like water over her firm breasts, flat belly, and hips. The hem ended inches about a pair of three-inch, black satin sling-back heels. A generous slit up the front of the dress allowed for a lush view of her strong, bare legs from ankle to knee. Her only jewelry was her single strand of pearls and a pair of matching stud earrings.

The image of her bare legs wrapped around his waist during their passionate bouts of lovemaking caused his stomach muscles to contract. Everything about her, from the orange color on her temptingly curved lips to the matching color on her toes, drew him into a surging vortex of desire that made him want to spend every hour of the day in her arms.

"It doesn't go with the suit."

"It still stays. Speaking of earrings, I owe you a pair."

She flashed him a saucy look. "I'm going to hold you to that."

Rodrigo walked into the dining room, breaking the sensual spell surrounding the secret lovers.

"Señor Cole, may I prepare a drink for you?"

The frown that had settled between David's eyes vanished quickly. "Sí, I'd like a Scotch and soda with ice." Of all of Samuel Cole's children he had been the only one who shared his father's penchant for Scotch.

Rodrigo made his way over to a bar and placed a linen napkin over the sleeve of his dark bolero jacket. "Señorita Morris. May I serve you?" he asked, filling a glass with ice from a small refrigerator concealed beneath the massive bar. Tonight his role had changed from driver to bartender.

"I'll have a glass of sherry, please."

Rodrigo quickly and expertly prepared their drinks,

and as they stood sipping them Raul Vega and his houseguest walked into the dining room.

She felt a shiver of uneasiness the instant her gaze met and fused with that of the man with the silver hair and deeply tanned face. She missed the expert cut of his dark suit, pristine white shirt, navy blue tie, and black shoes as she felt his pale green, hypnotic gaze trap her within a maelstrom of fear and danger.

Unconsciously, she moved backward, bumping into David. His free hand went to the small of her back until she regained her balance.

David successfully concealed a smile. Serena's reaction to Joshua Kirkland was similar to that of most who met him for the first time. His cold eyes made people feel as if they'd glimpsed their own death. And his brother *was* deadly when crossed.

Raul placed a hand on Joshua's shoulder, smiling. "Señor Kirkland, I would like to introduce you to my daughter and our hostess for this evening, Señorita Serena Morris. *Chica,* Señor Joshua Kirkland."

Serena extended her right hand, forcing a smile she did not quite feel. "Señor Kirkland."

Joshua took her hand and inclined his head. "My pleasure, Señorita Morris."

An eyebrow shifted at the same time she withdrew her hand from his warm grip. His Spanish was flawless, and she knew that, like David, he'd learned the language as a child.

"You may call me Serena."

Joshua smiled, the gesture transforming his stoic expression and making him an extremely attractive man. "And you may call me Joshua," he teased.

David stepped forward and extended his right hand, preempting Raul from introducing him to Joshua. "David Cole."

Joshua took the proffered hand. "Joshua Kirkland."

His smile froze, masking a cold fury that sucked the breath from his lungs. Nothing in Joshua's expression indicated the rage he felt toward Vega when he saw the scar on his brother's cheek. He wanted to repay Vega for his brutality. He longed to mangle his host's face instead of preparing to sit at his table under the pretense that he would enjoy his food and hospitality.

Raul glanced at Rodrigo, who nodded. "Joshua, may I offer you something from the bar?"

"Scotch, straight up," he replied.

Raul glanced at the bottle of aged Scotch on the highly polished surface of the bar. It appeared that these Americans liked their Scotch. He waited until Rodrigo served Joshua his drink, then took his usual tequila and lime juice.

Raising his glass, he smiled at the others in the room. "Much success for all that we want from this life."

Everyone touched glasses, murmuring their own acknowledgement, while David's gaze never left Serena's face. Joshua watched his brother's reaction to the beautiful, tiny woman in orange silk. Aside from the scar on David's left cheek, he appeared not to have suffered too much at the hands of his captor. He suspected that Raul's daughter had made David's captivity more tolerable.

Serena waited until everyone had finished their predinner drinks, then escorted them to the table. She had instructed Rodrigo to remove a leaf from the table, reducing the seating from its customary twelve. Raul seated her at one end of the table before taking his place at other end. Joshua and David sat opposite each other.

"Even though I make it a policy not to discuss business at my dinner table," Raul began, his gaze fixed on his daughter's face, "I will make an exception this evening. Joshua will only be with us for a few days, and it's going to take time for him to adjust to our weather and a different time zone."

Joshua smiled a cold smile. "I'm honored and flattered that you've decided to break a tradition." What he didn't say was that he wanted to break Vega's neck.

Raul waited for Isabel to bring out the first course—a flavorful cold fish soup—then picked up his spoon. Everyone followed suit.

"I wonder if there will time for me to take a tour of your property, Raul," Joshua stated after he'd swallowed a bite of succulent shrimp. "I didn't get to see much of its magnificence from the car coming in from the airport."

"That can be arranged." There was obvious pride in Raul's voice. "By the way, David Cole is also an American businessman."

Joshua appeared surprised by this disclosure. "How long will you be staying in Costa Rica?" he asked David.

"I can assure you that it'll be more than a few days. *Raul* and I have a few unresolved issues to work through before I go back to Florida. By the way, where are you from?"

"Santa Fe."

David flashed his dimpled smile, shaking his head. "Never been there."

"It's beautiful," Joshua confirmed.

"So is Costa Rica," Raul countered.

Joshua's left hand stilled, and the light from an overhead chandelier glinted off the gold band on his third finger. "That it is. Unpolluted air, clean water—"

"And I intend to make certain it remains that way," Raul interrupted vehemently.

"Which is why I'm here," Joshua said quietly. "As a scientist I recognize the importance of ecological balance."

Raul spooned a portion of soup into his mouth, then

touched the edge of his napkin to his lips. "Tell me what you've discovered about the Anneda pine tree."

David listened, smugly amused as Joshua outlined the healing properties found in the needles and bark of the tree. It was apparent that his brother was using the cover of a botanist. The few who knew Joshua well were always astounded by his superior I.Q. and photographic memory.

Raul, enraptured by what Joshua was telling him, said, "You're saying that the bark and needles contain a very potent bioflavonoid."

"Proanthocyanidin. It is stronger than any known citrus bioflavonoid. But when I tested it I discovered that it protected and extended the properties of Vitamin C, which is usually destroyed by oxidation in the body."

"A fascinating discovery," Raul whispered.

"That it is," Joshua agreed. "It is the most fantastic antioxidant ever found. It's fifty times more powerful than Vitamin E and twenty times stronger than Vitamin C."

"I, too, find all of this incredible," Serena stated, joining the discussion for the first time. "I'm aware that antioxidants destroy free radicals, which attack cells and destroy many of them, even altering DNA and making it impossible for cells to reproduce themselves. You claim you can get this miraculous antioxidant from the Anneda tree. Wouldn't you endanger these valuable trees by stripping their bark and needles?"

Joshua arched a pale eyebrow, turning his attention to Serena. A background check on Raul Cordero-Vega had revealed that Serena Morris wasn't his biological daughter, but she could've been, with her line of questioning. She sounded like Vega did when he ranted that he wanted to save Costa Rica for the Ticos at any cost.

"Not necessarily," he replied in a soft, quiet tone. "My research team is currently working on a renewable plant source of this proanthocyanidin, so we won't endanger the supply of trees."

Raul winked at Serena. She'd voiced his very concern. He shifted his attention to Joshua. "We will talk tomorrow about your research study. Eat, drink, then rest. I'm certain you're still fatigued from your journey."

"*¡Mil gracias!*" Joshua said, offering a smile. He had given himself three days to confirm that David was still alive, survey Vega's property, then formulate a plan to get his brother out of Costa Rica.

Twenty-six

Serena lay in the warmth of David's embrace, savoring the unyielding strength of his hard body. "Do you think my father's softening?" Her sultry voice was a whisper in the stillness of the darkened room.

"What about?"

"Americans."

David chuckled, placing his arm over her back. "I doubt that, Darling."

"You have to admit that he was rather charming tonight."

His grip tightened on her waist, shifting her body effortlessly until she lay on his chest. "You were charming, brilliant, and very, very beautiful. I can't wait for you to host our dinner parties."

Angling for a more comfortable position, she settled her legs between his and laid her cheek against his shoulder. "Neither can I."

His left hand played in the curls she'd unpinned from the elaborate chignon just before slipping into bed. "There are so many things I can't wait for: marrying you and seeing your belly swell with our unborn children. I want our home filled with love and lots of noise. The noisier the better."

"I want to be able to go to bed with you and wake

up with you by my side, David," she confessed. "I'm tired of the deception."

"It will end soon."

Nodding, she rubbed her nose against the crisp hair covering his broad chest. She prayed it would end soon, because she was unsure how long she could continue to hide her feelings for the man holding her to his heart.

Turning her head slightly, she kissed his chest, moving down his body until her hot mouth seared his flat belly and still lower. David threw a muscled arm over his head, swallowing back the groans threatening to erupt from the back of this throat.

Serena had offered her body, holding nothing back, but this time she offered more. She was selfless as she worshipped him, taking him into her mouth with a claim that made him surrender all he had, all that he was to her.

It took Herculean strength for him to sit up, reach down, and pull her up to his chest. Within the span of several seconds he reversed their positions, slipped on protection, and entered her, both of them gasping from the force of his penetration. He took her hard and fast, and when they returned from their erotic trip to heaven, both were breathing and sobbing with emotion wrung from their souls.

"This can't continue," David rasped, pulling her closer to his damp body. "Not like this."

"I know," she confirmed, willing the tears staining her cheeks to stop. But they continued until she cried herself to sleep. She never knew when David left her bed six hours before sunrise.

Opening the French doors to her bedroom, he stepped out into the heavy tropical heat, then closed the doors behind him. He stood on the veranda, staring out into pitch blackness, swearing silently that he would not sleep with her again until they were back on American soil. Their desperate game of deception had changed him, and instead of feeling joy after making love he felt guilty, guilty for sneaking into her bedroom each night, and guilty for pretending he felt nothing for her in the presence of others when all he wanted was to hold her and kiss her until she was breathless.

He walked the short distance to his own bedroom, slipped in through the partially open French doors. He hadn't taken more than two steps when light flooded the room and Raul rose from the chair where he'd sat waiting for him.

There was no mistaking his rage as a cold, loathing smile twisted his lips. "I bring you into my home and you disgrace me by using my daughter."

David's temper rose quickly, matching Vega's. "I haven't used her."

"What do you call it? You treat her like a *puta*. You have your way with her, then you leave her after you've spilled your lust. You've made her your whore!" he shouted in English.

David lunged at him at the same time Raul brought up his right hand, striking him across the left cheek with a riding crop. The blinding pain caused him to stumble backward, but he righted himself and lunged at Vega again.

This time he found his target. His long fingers curved around his nemesis's neck, tightening and cutting off precious air to his lungs and brain. "I love her!" he shouted, punctuating each word as he shook Vega, his head rolling around on his shoulders as if he were a rag doll.

Through the red haze of rage, he heard a solid click, then a familiar voice saying, "Let him go, Señor Cole."

David looked up into the large, round bores of a double-barreled shotgun. A deranged smile curled Rodrigo's lips as he wiggled his eyebrows in an unconscious, agitated gesture. Rodrigo might have just pleaded for him to release his boss, but something in the emaciated man's eyes said *don't.*

Closing his eyes briefly, David felt his anger ebbing. For a moment he'd been ready to take a life and give up his own at the same time. His hands fell away and Vega slumped to the floor, gasping and wheezing.

Rodrigo lowered his weapon. He stared down at his employer, uncertain whether Señor Vega would want him to help him. He decided against it as Raul rose to his feet on wobbly knees.

"You're a dead man, David Cole," he whispered, holding a hand to his injured throat.

"So are you," David countered. He bent over and picked up the riding crop. What he wanted to do was flail the skin off the older man, but threw it at him instead. "The next time you take a whip to me, be prepared to kill me, *Señor Vega.*"

He watched the two men leave his bedroom, then collapsed across the bed. Fire radiated along the left side of his face when he pressed the rapidly swelling flesh with his fingertips. They came away with only a trace of blood, but he knew without looking in a mirror that Vega had reinjured his cheek.

Serena slept late the following morning, and it wasn't until she heard a knock on her door that she woke up. Pulling the sheet up over her naked breasts, she pushed an abundance of unruly curls up off her forehead.

"Come in." The door opened and her father stalked in, his mouth set in a hard, tight line. She smiled at him. "Good morning, Poppa."

He did not respond as he sat on a chair in her sitting room. The silence was deafening. She stared at him while he looked out the French doors.

"You've disgraced this house," he whispered, breaking the silence.

Her eyes widened. "What are you talking about?"

"I bring *him* into my house and he takes you like a *puta* under my very roof."

Serena scrambled from the bed, tucking the sheet around her body. "How *dare* you call me a whore!"

Raul sprang to his feet. "What else are you?" He wanted to scream at her, but his injured vocal cords throbbed painfully. "How could you let him use you in such a manner?"

"He didn't use me. I love him, Poppa. And when I return to the United States I'm going to marry him."

"No, *Chica,*" he said, shaking his head. "That cannot happen, because in less than a month he will be dead. Your lover has a death sentence hanging over his head." He gave her an evil smile when her eyes filled with tears. "Did you think he was waiting for you, so the two of you could leave *La Montaña* together?" Watching the play of emotions cross her face, he knew that was what she'd thought. "I'm sorry to disappoint you, but the truth is he hasn't left *La Montaña* because he *can't.* And if he tries to escape I'll have him shot on sight."

He took a half-dozen steps, bringing them face-to-face. "Don't try to leave, *Chica*, because you'll never make it through customs. I've taken the liberty of holding on to your passport for safekeeping."

Serena clapped her free hand over her mouth to keep from slapping her stepfather's face. She turned her back instead, and waited for him to leave her bedroom. As soon as the door closed, she walked over and locked it.

What happened next was a blur, because she didn't remember taking a shower or dressing. What she did remember was flinging open her door and pounding on David's, screaming his name at the top of her lungs.

When he finally did unlock the door, she took one look at his face and crumbled to the floor in a dead faint.

David scooped her limp body up in his arms and carried her down the rear staircase to the kitchen. Her head hung loosely over his arm, eliciting a rush of fear when he could not detect her breathing.

Luz Maria rushed toward him. "Put her on the table," she ordered. He stood helplessly by, watching the cook as she placed a cool cloth on Serena's forehead. She stirred and let out an audible sigh.

Blinking furiously, she stared up at the ceiling. "What happened?"

"You fainted."

She turned her head to the right, her round eyes widening and filling with fear when she saw the angry welt running across David's left cheekbone. "David." His name came out in a weak mewling.

"I'm all right, *mi amor.*"

Reaching out, she caught his wrist. "Did he do that to you?"

"It was an accident," he lied smoothly. Curving an arm around her waist, he helped her to sit up.

"Drink this," Luz Maria suggested, handing her a cup of tea. "It should help settle your stomach."

Serena's hands shook slightly as she grasped the cup. She took several swallows, then handed the cup back to Luz Maria. "I've had enough."

Luz Maria shook her head. "You need it, and so will the baby."

"What baby?" Serena and David asked in unison.

Luz Maria stared at David, then Serena. "Why do think you fainted?"

It was Serena's turn to stare at David as she mentally calculated when she'd last had her period. "Oh, no," she whispered with the realization that she hadn't had a menstrual flow since she left the States. It had been the last week in May, and it was now the middle of July.

Her gaze was frantic. When had it happened? After the first time she and David had been very careful . . . The first time! The first time they slept together he'd gotten her pregnant.

"David . . ."

"It's okay, Darling," he crooned, rubbing her back in a comforting gesture.

She pressed her face against his arm, shaking her head. "He told me everything. He said you're a prisoner, and that he's going to kill you."

David's hand halted. "When?"

"He came to my room this morning. He—"

"Don't," he said, cutting her off. "We're going to make it through this."

"How can you say that?" She replayed Raul's threats, the fearful image of David lying shot flooding her mind.

Cradling her face his hands, David flashed his dimpled smile. "Do you trust me, Darling?" She nodded. "Then let me handle everything."

What he had to do was find Joshua. Whatever his brother planned to do, he had to do it quickly.

Things had changed: Vega was aware that they'd been sleeping together. There was the possibility that Serena was carrying his child. And there was no doubt that the stress of not getting his son back had forced Vega to panic.

David left Serena with Luz Maria as he returned to the main part of the house, hoping he would meet up with Joshua. He had to find a way to communicate the sudden change in his hostage situation.

He found Joshua and Vega in the greenhouse. They were examining the pine needles of a tree when he approached them. Joshua noticed him before Vega did. He went completely still, his eyes turning pale until they appeared virtually transparent. David shook his head, the motion barely noticeable. He folded his hands together, then opened them like a book. Just before Vega turned he put up two fingers.

"What do you want?" Vega snapped before he could catch himself. He didn't want Joshua Kirkland to suspect that things were not well between him and his fellow American.

"I'm sorry to interrupt you—"

"But you are interrupting me, Señor Cole," he said facetiously.

Joshua held up his left hand. "Raul, you and I have time. Take care of whatever you need to do with David. I'm going to take that walk I've been promising myself before it gets too hot." He gave Vega a feigned smile. "I'm overwhelmed with the magnificence of everything I've seen thus far."

David offered Joshua his right hand. "If I don't get to see you before you leave, have a safe trip back home."

Nodding, Joshua took the proffered hand. "Same with you. If you get the opportunity to come to the southwest I'd like for us to get together. I have a close friend who lives in Las Cruces. He's south of where I live, but we get together every once in a while and go hunting."

"What does he do?" David questioned, stalling for time.

"He breeds horses. The name is Sterling. He's easy to find. Ask anyone in Las Cruces where his ranch is, and they'll give you directions."

"I'll keep that in mind if I'm in the neighborhood."

"In fact, I'm supposed to meet with him next week. If you're back by that time and have nothing on your calendar, drop by."

David nodded. Joshua had given him what he needed

to know. He would return to Costa Rica in a week, and he wouldn't come alone.

Raul waited impatiently while the two Americans concluded their inane conversation. He walked back to the house, David following. He didn't why, but he felt a shiver of icy fear snake up his spine. He'd turned his back on David Cole, and only hours ago the man had his hands around his neck. If Rodrigo hadn't been there he was certain David would've strangled him. *No*, he thought. It would the last time he would ever show David his back.

The two men walked into the study, Raul closing the door. He rounded on David. "What was so important that you had to interrupt me?"

"I'm willing to negotiate the sale of the plantation."

Raul stared, complete surprise on his face. But the surprise was momentary. "Why now?"

"Why not? I want to get my affairs in order before I die."

"You won't die if my son is released on or before the designated date."

David crossed his arms over his chest in a gesture of defiance. "I'm not willing to wait that long."

"It is not possible. I have business to conclude with Mr. Kirkland."

"What you have to discuss with Mr. Kirkland is conjecture. Maybe you'll let him have your trees, or maybe you won't. The banana plantation is a reality—several million realities."

Raul's mind began working overtime. He could get two for the price of one. He would secure the plantation outright, without the government having to wait to nationalize it, and he could keep David Cole as a hostage beyond the sixty-day limit if necessary.

If he wanted to he could keep David in Puerto Limón for an eternity. David couldn't walk off the property because of the armed guards watching the perimeter, and he couldn't make any outside telephone calls without his being aware of it.

He had come to accept the younger man's quick temper and arrogance, but David had compounded it by sleeping with his daughter. That he could not and would not ever accept.

"We'll talk."

David hid a smile. "When?"

"After the *siesta*. But first I must offer my regrets to Mr. Kirkland. He and I will have to reschedule our very interesting deliberations." He massaged his tender throat. "Perhaps he will want to remain at *La Montaña* until you and I conclude our business."

I doubt that. David mused. Offering a slight bow, he turned and walked out of the room. He had redirected Raul's focus to ColeDiz. It would give Joshua the time he needed to return to the States to plan his return trip *and* rescue mission.

Twenty-seven

July 21
Las Cruces, New Mexico

Joshua sat in the pickup truck beside Matthew Sterling as Matt drove out of the parking area at the Las Cruces airport.

"When was the last time you got any sleep?" Matt asked, the slow drawl of east Texas evident in his speech.

"I don't remember," Joshua admitted. "And I don't think I'm going to get any until this madness is over."

Matt's gold-green gaze was fixed on the road ahead of him. Joshua had called him, saying that he needed his *assistance*. And he knew exactly what he meant. However, it had been four years since they both retired from the shadowy, gray world of undercover intelligence. He had been an independent operative, while Joshua was a key player in US. military intelligence.

"Are you going back in?"

"No, Matt. This is personal."

Pushing back the front of his wide-brimmed straw hat with his thumb, Matt threw Joshua a quick look. "Who?"

"My brother David."

Shifting into a higher gear, Matt increased his speed,

the pickup eating up the dusty road. "Tell me about it."

Joshua did, leaving nothing out. He related the details of the telephone call, his trip to Costa Rica, and evidence of David's injuries.

"I'm going to take perverse pleasure in gutting Vega," he stated quietly.

"Forget about gutting him. Leave the knives to me. Guns are more your specialty."

Joshua wanted to smile, but couldn't. He hadn't slept in nearly seventy-two hours. He'd left Costa Rica after a day and a half, enraged. He'd left his younger brother with a madman whose intent was to destroy David's face before he executed him.

"Why don't you catch a few winks? Whatever we need to plan can't be done with you falling on your face."

Closing his eyes, Joshua mumbled a low thanks, and willed his mind blank. He slept, but violent dreams disturbed him as he stirred restlessly. He saw Vega's face with a gaping mouth but no words coming from it. Then he heard a baby crying, but couldn't see the baby. The nightmares continued in vivid color before they finally faded, leaving him in peace.

Matt curved an arm around his wife's waist. He saw the terror in her eyes. "It's all right, *Preciosa.*"

Eve Sterling shook her head. Her dark eyes filled up with unshed tears and she bit down hard on her lower lip to keep it from trembling. "It's not all right, Mateo. I could lose you."

He knew she was frightened. Eve only called him Mateo when she was frightened or angry. He still found it hard to believe that his marriage of convenience had become a marriage for life. He'd married Eve Blackwell under the guise that he would look for her abducted son in Mexico, but during the charade he'd fallen madly in love with her. They had gotten her son back, and given three-year-old Christopher Delgado a sister a year later.

"I'll be back, Eve. I'm too ornery for anything to happen to me."

"If you're coming back, then why are you sending me and the children to Florida?"

"Joshua and I have made arrangements to fly into Florida. We'll spend a few days there before we come back. It will give you and Vanessa a chance to see each other."

"Don't try to placate me, Matthew Sterling. Vanessa and I got together last—"

Her words were cut off when he covered her mouth with his, robbing her of her breath. "They're announcing your flight. Come, I'll see you to the gate."

Matt leaned down and swung his three-year-old daughter up in his arms. Her hazel eyes were a stunning contrast in her gold-brown face framed by fat, black curls that bounced over her forehead.

"How big is Daddy's big girl?"

Sara Sterling raised her chubby arms upward. "This big, Daddy."

He waited until they reached the gate, then handed his daughter to her mother. Turning, he held out a callused hand to his stepson. "Shake or a hug?" he asked Christopher Delgado.

Christopher shrugged his narrow shoulders. "Anything."

Matt solved his indecision when he swung the seven-year-old up in his strong arms. "Let's do the guy hug."

Chris pounded his broad back, while Matt's large hand thumped his son's lightly. "Take care of your mother and sister for me."

"Sure thing, Daddy." Chris had started out calling

Matt Papa, but changed quickly once his sister started
calling him Daddy.

He lowered the boy to the floor. He gave his family
a final, lingering look before turning to walk out of the
terminal to the parking lot. Slipping into the rental car
beside Joshua, he met the pale gaze of the man sitting
behind the wheel.

Letting out his breath slowly, he said softly, "Let's
rock and roll."

Twenty-eight

July 28
Puerto Limón, Costa Rica

Luz Maria's predication that Serena would bear David Cole's child was confirmed.

Dr. Leandro Rivera displayed a tender smile. "Congratulations. You're at least six weeks along," he said, stripping off his latex gloves. "How have you been feeling?"

"Tired."

"That's natural. I'll let you get dressed, then we'll talk."

She waited for Leandro to leave before she attempted to sit up. What was there to talk about? She was pregnant and David Cole was the father of the tiny life growing in her womb.

Meanwhile her stepfather had retreated into a state of madness. She did not know who he was anymore. He locked himself in his study, refusing to come out, except to eat. He threatened to kill David immediately if she mentioned anything to her mother when she called. Serena discovered that he taped every call—incoming and outgoing—so she couldn't lie and say she hadn't said anything to Juanita even if she wanted to.

David continued to come to her room, but not to

sleep. They lay together, talking about everything except the madness tearing their world apart until she fell asleep. He left then, using the door instead of the veranda. Their love and what they'd shared was no longer a secret.

She buttoned her blouse and tucked it in the waistband of her slacks before pushing her feet into a pair of sandals. Her limbs felt leaden as she made her way slowly out of the examining room to Leandro's office.

He rose to his feet when she walked in. Taking her elbow, he escorted her to a large, comfortable chair. "Did you drive here alone?"

"No. Rodrigo brought me." Even though Raul had taken her passport, he still did not trust her to go out alone.

"Lucky for you."

She yawned, covering her mouth with her hand. "I can't keep my eyes open."

Leandro sat down behind his desk. "I suggest that you take a lot of little *siestas.*"

She yawned again. "I'll try."

"Don't try, Serena. Do it. That's an order."

Staring at the young doctor, she gave him tired smile. "Yes, Doctor."

He was Dr. Rivera when he lectured her sternly about what she could do and not do. Then he became her friend Leandro when he said that if she needed his help—for any reason—she could call on him.

She left his office with samples of vitamin supplements, and prescriptions for more. She waited in the car while Rodrigo filled the prescriptions. The wait afforded her the opportunity to sleep, and when the Mercedes sedan stopped at *La Montaña* she arrived refreshed.

David was waiting in the living room when she walked in. She saw the tension ringing his generous mouth and detected a throbbing muscle in his lean jaw. The angry welt over his cheekbone had taken a week to fade without leaving further permanent scarring to the area.

He stood up and crossed the room to meet her. "How are you?"

"Very pregnant."

Closing his eyes, he let out his breath in a slow, audible sigh. Nodding, he opened his eyes and smiled down at her. "Congratulations."

Serena placed her hand over his heart. The heat from his body was stifling. "Congratulations to you, too."

He covered her hand with his, smiling the smile she'd come to love. "Come upstairs with me. I have something to show you."

Hand in hand they climbed the staircase to the upper level. Their footsteps were muffled in the runner along the hallway. It seemed like years rather than weeks when they had walked the hallway for the first time. It was a time when David promised Serena that he would solicit his father's help for her brother's release. It was also the first day that she'd kissed him—really kissed him.

It was also the first time later that afternoon that they lay together and shared a love that had deepened despite the betrayal and deadly revenge that threatened their lives and, now, that of their unborn child.

David pulled Serena into his bedroom and closed the door. Leading her to the armchair where he'd sat waiting for his face and foot to heal, writing pages of music, and watching and waiting for the sun to rise, he eased her down to the plump cushion. Sitting down on the footstool, he pointed to an envelope on the nearby table.

"Pick it up, Darling."

Serena felt the heat of David's gaze on her face when she picked up the white, business-size envelope. Sliding her finger under the flap, she opened it and withdrew a single sheet of paper. Her head came up slowly and she stared numbly at the man sitting at her feet.

"What does this mean?"

"It means that I've sold the plantation and the proceeds will be deposited in a bank in Florida in your name."

Clamping a hand over her mouth, Serena shook her head. "No," she mumbled through her fingers.

David grasped her shoulders, holding her captive. "Yes. I have to take care of you and the baby."

"And what about you? Do you think I want to have this baby by myself?"

"If something should happen to me you'll—"

"I'll what, David!" she screamed at him. "I'll go on living and pretending that you never existed? That having more money than I could hope to spend will take the place of having a father for my child?"

"Serena," he crooned softly, hoping to calm her.

"Don't Serena me, David Cole!" She crumbled the paper and threw it at him. It hit his shoulder and fell to the floor. "How can you give up like that?"

"I'm not giving up. What I'm doing is securing your future."

"Without you, I have no future." Closing her eyes, she squeezed back angry tears.

Pulling her from the chair, David settled her over his lap. He buried his face between her neck and shoulder, inhaling her scented flesh. "And without you I'm nothing."

"We have to get away. We have to escape from this hell."

Cradling a hand under her chin, he raised her face to his. "We will, *mi amor.* Have patience."

"I'm sorry. I don't have your patience."

His mouth brushed over hers. "Yes, you do."

Serena reveled in the feel of his moist lips, caressing

and healing. She opened her mouth, allowing him free rein as he kissed her with a passion she'd almost forgotten.

His kiss deepened until she found herself writhing with a heated desire that matched the drums pounding out the sensual rhythms of ancient Africa.

David carried her to the bed, leaving her to lock the door, the French doors, and draw the drapes. Then he returned to the bed. He undressed her, then himself. His midnight gaze swept leisurely over the tiny, compact body that carried the fruit of their love before he came into her outstretched arms.

Parting her thighs with his knee, he pushed into her hot, moist, throbbing flesh, sighing as she closed around his swollen flesh, welcoming him home.

Their lovemaking was slow, gentle, and healing. It was only when he touched heaven and floated back to earth that David realized that he hadn't kept his secret promise not to make love to her again until they were on American soil.

A part of him wanted to believe he was going home, and a part said that he'd never go home. Joshua left Costa Rica a week ago, and hadn't returned. It was now the eighth day, and he did not want to believe that he had abandoned him.

Joshua thanked Rodrigo when he opened the door of the spacious sedan. He glanced up at the lines of the beautifully designed house Raul Vega called *La Montaña*, frowning. Behind its magnificent facade was a man who had lost touch with reality. A man who'd used his political office as a ploy to abuse and control. A man who was ruthless and cavalier in his disregard for other human beings. Shifting a pale eyebrow, Joshua followed the driver into the coolness of the house. The abuse and power would end in another twelve hours.

Joshua was shown to the spacious room he'd occupied during his first trip to *La Montaña*. It was on the first level at the rear of the house.

"Tell Señor Vega that I would like to take my *siesta* early. I will meet with him for the evening meal."

Rodrigo inclined his head "*Sí*, Señor Kirkland. I'll let him know your wishes."

Joshua swung his single piece of luggage to the bench at the foot of the massive four-poster bed. He had traveled light because he did not intend to spend the night.

He took off his clothes, placed them neatly on the bench, then lay on the bed and slept.

Twenty-nine

Raul's mood was ebullient when he emerged from his study to share dinner with the returning Joshua Kirkland. Things had gone quite well during the week Joshua had returned to the States. David Cole had sold his banana plantation, and now he was ready to negotiate with Markham Pharmaceutical for his prized Anneda pine trees.

He walked into the dining room, his smile widening when he spied his daughter talking to Joshua. It was the first glimpse of animation she'd exhibited in more than a week. It was unfortunate that Joshua Kirkland was a married man, because he appeared better suited to Serena than David Cole. Shaking his head, he dismissed David from his mind.

"Joshua," he exclaimed, offering his hand in greeting. "Welcome back to *La Montaña.*"

"*¡Mil gracias!* Raul," Joshua returned, giving the man a warm smile. His penetrating gaze searched for his brother. He'd thought he would be joining them for dinner.

"Something to drink?"

"I'll wait for dinner."

Raul dropped an arm over his shoulder. "How was your flight?"

"Excellent."

"I hope you'll be able to spend more time with us this trip."

Joshua stared at Raul, chilling him with his icy gaze. "I left my ticket open. I'll stay as long as it'll take me to conclude my business. Providing my visa doesn't expire."

He removed his arm. "Don't worry about your visa. I'll have someone take care of that."

"Gracias," Joshua said softly. He waited until Serena took her place at one end of the table, then sat down on the chair he'd occupied during his last visit.

Raul signaled to Isabel, and she rolled the cart in bearing the evening's first course.

Joshua stared at the empty chair opposite him. He hadn't realized how hard and fast his heart was pounding until he clenched his hands under the table. Where was his brother?

"Has David Cole returned home?"

Raul stared at Serena instead of Joshua. "Yes, he has. He left Costa Rica three days ago.

Joshua stared at his place setting rather than look at Raul Vega. *Stinking, filthy liar,* he ranted inwardly. Within seconds he'd composed himself. "I'd hoped to see him again."

"Perhaps you will if he comes to visit New Mexico."

"Yes, perhaps."

The dinner continued with little or no conversation. Serena ate as if she were in a trance, not tasting any of what she'd swallowed. It was only when Rodrigo entered the room to whisper to Raul that he had an important telephone call and he left the room did she speak.

"He's lying. David's still here," she whispered.

"Where is he?"

"Upstairs."

Raul came back into the room, a deep frown settled into his forehead. "I'm sorry, Joshua. I must offer my apologies again. I just received a call from my president. I must return to San José immediately."

Pushing back his chair, Joshua stood up. "No need to apologize."

"I'm not certain how long I'll be away. But it shouldn't be long because the government is on holiday during July and August."

Joshua stood up. "I'll wait, Raul. Remember, I need your approval for the exportation of this drug."

"*¡Mil gracias!*" He stared at Serena, then turned on his heel and rushed out of the room.

She watched Joshua staring at her stepfather's departing figure. "Sit down, Mr. Kirkland, and finish your dinner. Luz Maria has outdone herself tonight."

Joshua took his seat, his jaw tightening. He'd wanted Raul in attendance when he rescued David, but Matt disagreed, saying they were going to Costa Rica to bring his brother home, not torture his captor.

The two people ate in silence, neither wishing to intrude on the other's thoughts. Joshua finished first, refusing dessert.

"I'm going for a walk before I retire for the night," he informed Serena.

She gave him a polite smile. "Good night."

"Good night," he returned softly.

She sat at the table, watching Isabel clear the table. Then she made her way to the kitchen. She found Luz Maria sitting at the table writing furiously and pushing sheets of paper into an envelope.

"What are you writing?" she asked, sitting down beside her.

"The recipes for my teas. You will need them."

Placing an arm around the older woman's back, she laid her head on her shoulder. "It's late, Doña Maria. You've prepared a wonderful dinner, and it's time you went to bed."

"I will go to bed when I finish this last one."

"Why the rush?"

"You will need it tonight."

"Why tonight?"

Luz Maria stopped writing, her eyes filling with tears. "I will not see you after tonight. Not for a long while."

"Stop that." Serena's voice broke with emotion. "I'm going to be here for a while."

"No, *Chica.* You will leave here. You must." She scribbled another two lines, then pushed the sheet of paper into the envelope with a stack of others. "Here. I have written down everything."

Serena stared at the envelope as if it were a snake. David had given her an envelope the day before. Its contents had changed her life, and she knew the contents of Luz Maria's would also change her life.

She took it, blinking back tears. "Thank you."

Luz Maria smiled a sad smile. "Thank you for being the daughter I never had."

Serena stood up and fled the kitchen as fat, hot tears rolled down her face. She hated herself for crying, but somehow crying came so easily now that she was pregnant.

She made it to the sanctuary of her room, closed the door, and fell across the bed—fully clothed.

A large, dark shape moved silently along the veranda. The man found the room he sought, then forced the lock to the French doors. They opened easily, quietly. He spotted his target. David Cole lay on the bed, asleep. He smiled. At least he didn't have to wait for him to get dressed.

Clapping a hand over his mouth, he pulled him up as if he weighed two pounds instead of two hundred. "Don't move, David. It's me, Matt. I'm going to take my hand away slowly. What I want you to do is take only what you need and what you can carry with you. Don't bother with a passport. I have one for you. I'll give you a minute. *Comprende*, Friend?"

David nodded, trying to slow down his runaway heart. How did Matt Sterling get into the room without making a sound? Moving quickly, he headed for the door.

"Where are you going?"

Matt's voice stopped him. "I have to bring Serena."

"Serena?"

The door opened and Joshua stepped into the room. There was enough light from a half moon to make out his dark clothing. "What the hell is going on here? We have to leave—*now!*"

"Who is Serena?" Matt whispered.

"The girl." Joshua groaned.

"We can't take her. We don't have enough room in the chopper," Matt argued softly.

"You can't leave her." There was no mistaking the panic in David's voice. "She's pregnant." There was a stunned silence. "She's carrying my baby."

Joshua whispered a vulgar curse about what David had found time to do while in captivity.

"We've got less than fifteen minutes," Matt warned, glancing at the glowing numbers on his watch.

"Take the girl," Joshua ordered. "I'll come later."

"No!" David voice echoed loudly in the dark.

"Get him the hell out of here," Joshua ordered Matt. He turned and disappeared, silent as a whisper lingering on a breath of wind.

Matt grabbed David and pulled him to the veranda. He showed him a cord attached to a grappling hook. "Lower yourself to the ground and wait for me."

David obeyed, sliding down the nylon cable until his feet touched solid ground. He refused to think of how Matt Sterling had made it past the armed men guarding the property. Glancing up, he waited for Serena. His heart raced wildly when he saw Matt lead her to the area of the veranda where he'd climbed down. She couldn't climb down by herself. What if she fell?

His fears were allayed when he saw her clinging to Matt's back as he made his way down the rope with the agility of a mountain goat.

Serena clutched Luz Maria's recipes to her chest, her eyes wide with fright. She wasn't given much time to react when Matt swung her over his shoulder in a fireman's carry and raced across the lawn. David followed, listening for footsteps that would signal that one of the guards had spotted them.

Matt led them to an area that had been cleared for the planting of trees, where a helicopter sat, its blades whirring in preparation for a liftoff.

Serena was settled on one of the rear seats. Matt motioned for David to sit beside her. Then he hopped in beside the pilot moments before it rose horizontally above the ground.

David cradled Serena at his side, trying to calm her quaking. "It's okay," he crooned over and over until she stopped shaking long enough to realize what had just happened.

"David." She sighed.

"I'll explain everything later."

Serena lost track of time once they transferred from the helicopter to the sleek confines of a private jet. She slept, clutching her chest, as David held her gently.

It was over. He was free. She was free. Both were free to live and share a love that promised forever.

The ColeDiz jet touched dawn at a private airfield in West Palm Beach. The three passengers deplaned, and an hour later found themselves speeding away from the airport in a car that was parked in a lot awaiting their arrival.

David and Serena dozed while Matt sat watching the attractive couple. He nodded his approval. They would make beautiful babies.

The driver maneuvered into the curving driveway leading to a mansion overlooking a lake. A small crowd had gathered in the bright early morning sun. Matt stepped out first, a grin creasing his sun-browned face.

Eve rushed into his arms, holding tightly to his neck. "Welcome home, my love."

"Glad to be back, *Preciosa.*"

Martin walked slowly toward the car, the tiny lines at the corners of his eyes fanning out when he saw his brother. David had changed. There was a lot more gray in his longer hair. The sun glinted off the gold earring in his left ear. And in that instant he knew David the businessman was gone forever, replaced by David the musician.

Holding out his arms, he embraced his youngest brother roughly, kissing both cheeks. Pulling back, he surveyed his face, examining the scar.

"You were always a little too pretty for your own good."

David laughed, patting his older brother's back. "Jealous, brother?"

"I don't think so, brother." His obsidian gaze noted the tiny woman standing behind David. "Who have you brought home?"

David reached out and pulled Serena in front of him. "Serena Morris, my future wife and the mother of my children."

Leaning down, Martin kissed her cheek. "Welcome to the family."

She lost track of names and faces as she was kissed and hugged by people who fussed over her as if she were an ancient relic.

She noticed one woman standing off by herself, staring out at the car that had backed out of the driveway.

"Where's Joshua?" Vanessa Kirkland questioned.

David walked over to his sister-in-law and folded her to his chest. "We left him behind, Vanessa."

"No!" she screamed hysterically, pulling away from him. She continued to scream as everyone stared at her, shocked.

Three-year-old Emily Kirkland's chin quivered when she heard her mother screaming. "Mommie. I want my Mommie."

Matt Sterling swept Vanessa up in his arms before she collapsed to the ground and carried her into the house.

Martin turned to his wife. "Call a doctor. She has to be sedated before she upsets all of the children."

Serena pressed closer to David, her questioning gaze meeting his. "Who is Joshua to you?"

"He's my brother." Her round eyes widened until he could see into their clear-gold depths. "He'll be back. And when he does, then we can plan our wedding."

Everyone turned to walk into the house, their joy temporarily dampened by the knowledge that Joshua hadn't returned with the others.

David kissed Serena, then went upstairs to see his mother and father. He would reunite with them before introducing Samuel and M.J. to their latest daughter-in-law. He would wait until later to tell everyone that he was to become a father.

Epilogue

Serena stared at her reflection in the mirror. She could not believe the vision that stared back at her.

Turning, she smiled at her mother. "I think this is the happiest day of my life."

Juanita returned her smile. "Wait until you give birth. That will be the happiest day."

Cradling her slightly rounded belly, Serena closed her eyes. She was beginning the third month of her first trimester, and it was only the second day that she hadn't experienced a bout of nausea. It was as if the baby decided to cooperate for her mother's wedding.

Joshua returned from Costa Rica two days after she, David, and Matt returned. Vanessa Kirkland had alternated between fits of tears and rage when she told him that if he ever left for another mission she would divorce him.

She'd met her future mother and father-in-law as well as her brothers and sisters-in-law. She lost track of all of the names of their children and grandchildren, deciding it would be years before she would call them by their correct names.

Gabriel was released from prison in a special plea bargain. Guillermo Barranda's father offered to turn himself over to the American authorities in exchange for his son and his son's friend.

It was only after Gabriel was safely back in Costa Rica
that he told his mother that the U.S. Government had
approached him to help them force the elder Barranda
from his Colombian sanctuary. The drugs were smug-
gled onto the boat without Guillermo's knowledge, and
the death of the DEA agent was also staged. Juanita got
her son back, the U.S. imprisoned the Western Hemisphere's most powerful drug lord, and Raul Vega was
asked by his government to resign his position as Interior
Minister.

Raul had become a recluse. He sent his love and his
regrets, refusing to attend her wedding. Serena was relieved, because she knew it would take a long time, perhaps even a lifetime, for her to forgive him for the pain
he'd caused her and David.

Sara Sterling and Emily Kirkland skipped into the
room, giggling excitedly. Both girls were dressed in pale
pink with garlands of tiny pink rosebuds entwined in
their dark, curling hair.

"My princesses are here." Serena smiled at the grinning little girls.

"Are you ready to get married now?" asked Emily.

Serena noted the child's exquisite, delicate beauty.
She was her mother's child, with the exception of her
eyes. They were green—a darker green than her father's—but they had the same penetrating stare, and
that sometimes seemed too wise for a child.

Parris rushed into the room, stopping short when she
saw the bride. "You look beautiful, Serena." She wore
a simple, pale pink, silk gown with long sleeves and a
rounded neckline. She had opted for a garland of flowers in lieu of a veil.

"David says it's bad luck to see the bride before the
ceremony, so he gave me these to give to you."

Serena took the small box and opened it. A pair of
brilliant diamond studs lay on a bed of white velvet.

Parris peered at David's gift, wincing. She estimated each stone was at least two carats. "They're breathtaking."

"Help me put them in, Parris."

Juanita glanced at her watch. They were late. "It's not good to keep the groom waiting."

"He'll wait, Mother. He's confessed to being a patient man."

"I know you're not talking about David Claridge Cole," Parris sputtered. "He's the most impatient man I've ever met."

Serena shrugged. "Well, that's what he told me."

"Cole men will tell you anything until they hook you."

"But is it worth it, Girlfriend?"

"Hell, yeah."

"Oo-oo," Emily said, putting a hand over her tiny mouth. "You said a bad word, Auntie Parris."

"Let's go, ladies," Parris said, shooing the little girls from the room. "Take your places. We have a wedding to go to."

Juanita stood up and extended her hand to her daughter. "I've been waiting a long time to give you away to a man who will love you forever."

"I've been waiting, too, Mother."

Serena stood beside David in the coolness of the loggia at the West Palm Beach house where he'd grown up, exchanging vows. He'd elected not to cut his hair, replaced her gold hoop with a small diamond stud, and transferred his shares in ColeDiz International Ltd. to Joshua. He was in the preliminary stages of starting up his own recording company—Serenity Records—but most of all he looked forward to beginning his life anew with a woman who was sent from heaven to show him how to love.

They exchanged rings and kisses, then turned to receive the good wishes of everyone who'd come to celebrate another generation of Coles who dared to risk everything for love.

"Uncle David!"

He glanced up to find his niece rushing into the loggia. He'd sent Regina Cole an invitation, but she'd called to say that she hadn't completed her latest film, and that she would not be able to attend his wedding.

She had blossomed into an incredible woman, her beauty eliciting gasps when her image filled the screen. Her first role at seventeen had garnered her an Academy Award nomination, and now at nineteen she was one of the most sought after actresses in the film industry.

Holding out his arms, he folded her against his body. "I'm glad you could make it."

"You know I wouldn't have missed this for all of the money in Tinseltown. I still can't believe you married. Not Mr. Player, Player."

"Shh-hhh," he whispered, placing a finger over his mouth. The bright Florida sunlight glinted off a band of diamonds on her left hand. "What's this?" he questioned, raising her hand.

"A wedding band," she replied, flashing her trademark dimpled smile.

"I can see that. But who did you marry?"

Regina turned and pointed to an elderly man standing a few feet away. "Him."

"What!" The word exploded from David's mouth before he had a chance to censor himself. He recognized the man immediately. He was the award-winning director Oscar Spencer. He was well-known, and he was fifty years older than David's nineteen-year-old niece.

Martin Cole turned slowly, unable to believe his ears. His oldest daughter married—and to a man older than he was. "The S.O.B. is old enough to be her grandfather."

"Careful, Buddy," Joshua said, his eyes narrowing. "Let me handle this."

"No, let me," Matt Sterling interrupted. "I'm not her father or her uncle. I'll cut him up in so many little pieces that they'll have to blot him up to find his DNA."

Parris clutched her chest, hoping to slow down her heart. Quickly regaining her composure, she extended her arms to her daughter. "Darling. Why didn't you tell us you were getting married?"

"I wanted to surprise everyone. You are surprised, aren't you, Mommy?"

"Yes, I am," she replied slowly. "Very surprised." She waved to her husband. "Martin, come meet your daughter's husband."

"Careful, brother," David whispered as Martin stalked past him.

Everyone held their breath as Martin Cole extended his hand to his daughter's husband. He slapped the older man on the back, knocking the breath out of him.

"Welcome to the family."

Oscar Spencer's dark eyes brightened in the network of lines crisscrossing his face. "Thank you for accepting me."

"I told you the Coles were extraordinary," David whispered to Serena.

She nodded, touching her belly, knowing that the child she carried beneath her heart would also be extraordinary.

Rising on tiptoe, she kissed her new husband, then whispered what she wanted him to do to her later—much later.

ABOUT THE AUTHOR

Rochelle Alers is a native New Yorker who now resides in a picturesque fishing village on Long Island where she draws inspiration to write her novels and short stories. Her interests include music, art, gourmet food, mediation and traveling.

Dear Readers:

David and Serena have taken their final bows, along with all of the characters from the *HIDEAWAY* legacy. I hope you've enjoyed the Coles, Sterlings, and the Kirklands as much as I enjoyed creating them as a generation of men and women who dared to risk everything to live happily ever after.

I've been asked whether the legacy will continue with another generation of Coles . . . only time will tell.

I would like to thank you for your support and for making this series the highlight of my writing career.

I look forward to hearing from you. Please include a self-addressed stamped envelope for a reply.

Sincerely,

Rochelle Alers
Post Office Box 690
Freeport, New York 11520-0690

E-mail: Roclers@AOL.com
Web Address: http://www.infokart.com/alers
/rochelle.html

COMING IN AUGUST...

BREAK EVERY RULE, by Francis Ray   (0-7860-0544-0, $4.99/$6.50)
Dominique Falcon was known amongst the elite for her wealth and beauty. But behind the glamorous image was a lonely dreamer who had fallen for a money-grubbing charmer. She vowed that her next lover would be richer and socially her superior. But then she meets the unrefined Trent Jacob Masters, falls in love and breaks every rule.

CHARADE, by Donna Hill   (0-7860-0545-9, $4.99/$6.50
Tyler Ellington enrolled in film school and fell for filmmaker Miles Bennett. But his deceit fled her back to her hometown where handsome photographer Sterling Grey entered her life in an opportune moment. He is everything that Miles is not, and she finds herself falling in love. For career reasons, she must return to New York, where Miles awaits to shower her with apologies. Will Miles' charade blind her to the true love that awaits her with Sterling?

ONE SPECIAL MOMENT, by Brenda Jackson (0-7860-0546-7, $4.99/$6.50)
To salvage her brother's struggling cosmetics company, schoolteacher Colby Wingate seeks superstar actor Sterling Gamble to endorse her brother's new perfume. Sterling thinks she is answering his ad for a woman to bear his child. He is deeply attracted to her and is determined to convince her to agree to his proposition. He didn't expect to fall deeply in love with her. Now he must prove his love is genuine.

IT HAD TO BE YOU, by Courtni Wright   (0-7860-0547-5, $4.99/$6.50)
After many sacrifices, Jenna Cross became a successful lawyer at a prestigious law firm in Washington. Her ambition will not let her stop until she becomes a judge. When love threatens to intervene, she pushes it away. She wants nothing to divert her focus from her career—not even her gorgeous senior partner Mike Matthews. He vows to show her that love does not threaten her career and that she can have it all.

Available wherever paperbacks are sold, or order direct from the Publisher. Send cover price plus 50¢ per copy for mailing and handling to Kensington Publishing Corp., Consumer Orders, or call (toll free) 888-345-BOOK, to place your order using Mastercard or Visa. Residents of New York and Tennessee must include sales tax. DO NOT SEND CASH.